SINGLE DAD IN A KILT

A FRIENDS TO LOVERS, SINGLE DAD-NANNY, PARENT TRAP, SMALL TOWN SCOTTISH ROMANCE

KILTED HEARTS
BOOK 5

KAIT NOLAN

TAKE THE LEAP PUBLISHING

ONE

Hamish Colquhoun had known there'd be challenges when he chose to move back home to Glenlaig from Edinburgh. He'd been ready for the endless list of renovations and repairs to the two-hundred-year-old farmhouse he'd bought. He'd braced himself for the back and forth necessary to ensure that his daughter, Freya, retained some kind of relationship with her mother. He'd even known that the switch from contract law to a family law practice would lead to an entirely different sort of caseload, and he'd welcomed the change of pace.

But nothing in his varied legal career had prepared him for this.

One of the... things in the enclosed livestock

trailer screamed, and Hamish stumbled back, wondering if he'd somehow wandered onto the set of a slasher film. Maybe he was dreaming.

Stuart MacDonald grinned.

Drawing on every shred of remaining professionalism he possessed, Hamish managed to choke back the impassioned, *What the fuck?* and instead asked, "What have you got here, Stuart?"

Looking inordinately pleased with himself, Stuart rocked back on his heels and folded his arms. "Your new landscaping crew."

"I beg your pardon?"

"I remembered what you said at your office a couple months back, when we were doing the reading of Mum's will. About how you were having a hard time keeping up with the weeding and clearing of the land since you bought the place."

Hamish barely remembered the conversation. It had just been small talk to ease what had been a difficult day for the son of his late client, Catriona MacDonald. When Stuart didn't continue, Hamish arched an expectant brow. "Aye?"

"Well, these were Mum's goats. Certainly, we can't keep them at our flat in Glasgow, so they need to be re-homed. When I remembered you had this place, I thought this was the ideal solution. You've got a barn right here that's empty and ready to go."

It was empty. Hamish didn't know about ready to go. Other than making sure the place wasn't about to cave in and pose a danger to his daughter, he hadn't done a bloody thing with the barn. It hadn't even rated going *on* the priority list, and he didn't want to add it now. He couldn't handle another living thing to care for beyond himself and Freya. He'd already been fending off her daily requests for a puppy and a horse. At no point had goats ever been under consideration.

Struggling to find a more tactful response than "*Not no, but hell no*," Hamish tried to offer a friendly smile. "I appreciate the offer, but I dinna know the first thing about taking care of goats."

Stuart waved that away. "Oh, it's easy. This time of year, you'll keep them in the barn. They've got hair, no' wool like sheep, so they're no' waterproof. And you dinna want to leave them out in the wet or they'll end up with foot rot. But on the days that it's no' raining and no' completely freezing, you'll just let them out to forage, and they'll eat everything that you dinna want."

They were goats. Didn't they eat *everything*? Wasn't that a thing?

"But—"

"You've already got a fence." Stuart scanned the overgrown length of it. "You might need to patch it in a couple of places, but that willnae be a big deal. You've got plenty of time to do that before spring. In the meantime, they'll basically be barn animals. I even brought you enough hay to get you started for a couple of weeks."

A low-level panic began to bubble in Hamish's blood. He was already struggling. Being a single parent was so much harder than he'd thought it would be, even with his parents' help, and even though Freya was reasonably self-sufficient at twelve. The idea of adding something else—multiple some-things, based on the shifting and milling happening inside the trailer—was absolutely overwhelming.

Later, he'd decide it was the overwhelm that had kept him from being able to make his brain work to find a polite way to decline the lunatic offer.

"I dinna know what to say." That was the God's honest truth.

"You gave so much peace and comfort to my mother by helping sort out her will and her estate. She would want you to have them."

How the hell was he supposed to say "No" after that?

"Well, I... guess we should unload them."

Beaming, Stuart climbed into his 4x4 and backed the trailer up to the barn.

In the back of Hamish's brain, he was already plotting. Stuart didn't live in Glenlaig. His mother's estate was all sorted, other than this. The house was already under contract, so Stuart would be headed back to Glasgow soon. Hamish could take the animals for now and find someone else who'd want them. Surely there was someone at one of the crofts at Lochmara or Ardinmuir who could use some free goats?

The moment Stuart dropped the gate of the trailer and began herding its occupants out, Hamish started rethinking his plan. The lead goat screamed at him, aiming one wide, golden eye in his direction as he—she—it?—charged past.

Okay, how could anything with a horizontal pupil *not* be demon spawn?

The remaining goats—there were six in all—took a more leisurely stroll down the gate and into the open barn.

"I... uh... Do they have to be milked?" Goat milk was a thing, wasn't it?

Stuart laughed. "No, no. These are meat goats, no' dairy goats. They're the best for clearing land. None of them have had kids. You've got four females and two wethers."

"Wethers?"

"Castrated males."

"So, I dinna have to worry about any of them making more baby goats?"

"No. There are no billies in the herd. Which is just as well. They smell right manky."

Small mercies.

Stuart did most of the herding of the goats into the pens inside the barn that had been used for some sort of livestock in the past. They unloaded the four rectangular hay bales he'd brought, and Stuart made some observations about lighting and heating that had a headache clawing at the back of Hamish's skull as he added more things to his never-ending to-do list.

After shutting the barn doors, Stuart clasped his hand in a warm grip. "Thanks again for all your help with Mum. Death is never easy, but you made handling the aftermath a lot less hassle than it could've been."

At the end of the day, that was the biggest reason Hamish had decided to shift into family law instead of continuing work for his Edinburgh firm through telework. The personal aspect of having a direct impact on people's lives. "That was what your mother wanted."

As Stuart started to climb back into the driver's seat, Hamish called out. "Wait. What are they called? Their names?"

"Mum changed her mind on the regular. You can call them anything you want. Just not Billy. That old goat is my father-in-law." With one last cheeky grin, he drove away, leaving Hamish the very reluctant new owner of a half-dozen goats.

"How the hell has my life come to this?"

There was no one around to answer the question, as Freya was off with her grandparents for the afternoon while he did some solo work on the house. The rambling structure had been added on to repeatedly over the past couple of centuries, up and out on both ends, such that it looked like something that ought to house a family of Weasleys rather than a lawyer and his daughter. But that was part of what had drawn him to the house. Dayna, his ex-wife, wouldn't have even gotten out of the car, let alone come inside to see the charm and history of the place. And yeah, maybe there were a million-and-one projects that still needed to be finished. But he and his daughter had done a lot of bonding over painting and repairs and deciding what they wanted things to be. Given how Dayna seemed to have largely opted out of parenthood since the divorce, that was more important now than ever. There was still a long, long way to go to update the house, but they'd managed to pull off a lot in six months.

A sound from the barn reminded him of his new charges.

Right. He should call Malcolm. The estate manager over at Lochmara would probably have some suggestions about what he needed to do with the goats. He might even know someone who could take them off Hamish's hands immediately. That would probably be better. God forbid Freya catch sight of them. She'd never expressed an interest in goats, but she was so desperate for some sort of pet that he didn't want to see her get attached to these, only to get heartbroken when they were re-homed. And they *would* be re-homed. Hamish was determined.

Maybe Malcolm's fiancée, Charlotte, would want them. She adored the trio of Valais black nose sheep Malcolm had given her...

Before Hamish could make the call, his phone rang. His mother, according to the display. She was probably going to invite them over for dinner tonight, and he'd probably say yes, even though he knew he needed to work on being better about planning and executing meals at home.

"Hey, Mum."

"Hamish."

At the strain in her voice, he went ramrod straight, his fingers tightening on the phone. "What's wrong? Is it Freya?"

If anything had happened to his daughter—

"No. Freya's fine. It's your grandmother."

AFTON LENNOX ROLLED up to the three-story Victorian with a sense of relief. The drive into the mountains from Nashville, up to the tiny town of Eden's Ridge, had been a lot longer than what she was used to having grown up in Scotland, where one hundred miles was considered a long way. She was tired, but it felt good to be out of the city. She was a village girl at the core. The hustle and bustle would never be her natural milieu, and this little corner of Tennessee had carved out a place in her heart, because the people here had saved her life.

Or, at the very least, her sanity, which kind of amounted to the same thing.

At this time of day, the staff of The Misfit Inn would be split between the inn and the spa, depending on bookings. But she'd come to see someone else. Parking in the guest lot, Afton climbed out of her car and strolled down the familiar manicured path between the house and the converted barn that housed the spa. Though it was chilly, it wasn't nearly as cold here for the first week of December as it would be back home, so there were still pops of color from pansies and dianthus, verbena and dahlias. Something else she hadn't gotten used to.

At the back of the property sat The Misfit Kitchen, where Afton had found that second home. Part studio, part cooking school, The Misfit Kitchen was the brainchild of Athena Reynolds Maxwell, a James-Beard-award-winning, Michelin-starred chef who'd returned home to Tennessee after a scandal around her restaurant in Chicago. She'd reinvented herself, starting a web-based cooking show that had taken the internet by storm. That was the purpose of the studio. But Athena still taught the occasional small-format, in-person class, and it was through one of those that Afton had met her and found a new purpose. It had taken considerable work to convince Athena to take her on as an apprentice. But the farm-to-table cooking that Athena promoted on her show and in her cookbooks was something that appealed to Afton on a visceral level. Deep down, it was something she hoped to eventually take back to Scotland.

But that was getting way ahead of things.

Mindful of the fact that they were quite possibly taping, Afton slipped inside, carefully easing the door shut behind her. Scott, the twenty-something camera guy, was in his usual spot, rapt attention on Athena as she pulled something out of the oven that already had Afton's mouth watering.

From the side of the room, she heard a gasp and turned.

Athena's seventeen-year-old niece, Ari, straightened from the wall with a silent pantomime that almost had Afton laughing. After many months of working with her, Afton could clearly follow the wild gesticulations.

Oh, my God, you're here! Why didn't you tell us you were coming? It's so good to see you!

This last part was communicated through an enthusiastic hug that Afton returned.

From the studio kitchen, Athena smiled at the camera as she held out the plated final dish. "There now, doesn't that look delicious? It's sure to impress whatever company you're having over. Those judgey in-laws. That boss you're hoping will promote you. That special someone you want to wow. Remember, you can find the recipes from today's episode on the website. With lots of love from my kitchen to yours, I'm Athena Reynolds. Bye, y'all."

"That's a wrap!" Scott announced.

As soon as the camera shut off, Athena scooted out from behind the counter and crossed over to fold Afton into a hug herself. "Well, aren't you a sight for sore eyes?"

"Back at you."

Her friend and mentor pulled back to study

her. "So, are you finished, or are you just here for a visit?"

"I'm through with all my externship hours. I have officially been minted a gourmet chef."

Athena grinned. "I knew you could do it. Come. Sit. We'll eat some of what I just cooked, and you can tell us everything."

"Sounds perfect."

The food was divvied up among three plates and some takeout containers. The latter were pushed on Scott, who apparently hoped to impress a date. With a promise to have the next episode edited and ready to post by the end of the weekend, he darted out the door.

Then Afton, Athena, and Ari sat around one of the tables.

Athena pointed to the plate. "Analyze it. Tell me what's in here."

Well used to the exercise by now, Afton examined her plate, forking up a bite of the first side. "Wild rice with butternut squash and cranberries." She dipped into the greens beside it. "Collard greens with smoked bacon and a splash of apple cider vinegar for that tang." Cutting into the meat, she brought a bite to her mouth. "And cider-braised pork shoulder with apples and onions."

Nodding in satisfaction, Athena picked up her own fork. "Very good."

Afton basked in the glow of approval.

Ari dove into her own food. "So you're done with the externship and have all the credentials and stuff. Now what?"

"I have no idea." She turned to Athena. "But I wanted to come and thank you, because I wouldn't have gotten here without you."

"You would've. It just might've looked different. And I owe you thanks, too. I never really thought I'd like teaching to that degree. When I had Olympus, I didn't have apprentices like that. But it's been a lot more fun than I thought it would be. Teaching someone who really wants to learn and has a legitimate aptitude makes all the difference."

"You made it easy."

Her mentor laughed. "I know I didn't. I'm many things as a chef. Easy isn't one of them. Take your props, woman."

Afton laughed. "Fair enough."

"What do you want to do next?"

"Well, I need a job. That's kind of important. But the lease on my flat in Nashville is up at the end of the month, so I have to decide whether I'm going to renew it and try to find something there, or go somewhere else."

Rolling her lips between her teeth, Athena exchanged a look with Ari that made it clear the two had been discussing Afton. "What about home?"

Home was a long way off, and Afton had been putting a lot of concerted effort into not thinking about it. "I dinna know."

Athena put down her fork. "Real talk: Honey, it's time. It's been over a year and a half. You need to go home. Even if you don't stay, you need some closure on that whole situation."

How exactly did a runaway bride get closure?

"It's not that easy. I dinna know exactly what I left behind or how anybody feels. I pissed a lot of people off when I ran, and I dinna know that anyone wants to hear from me."

She'd made an art form of avoiding contact with everyone she knew. She hadn't checked email, got a new phone number. She'd walked away from her entire life to get out of an arranged marriage, gambling her whole legacy away to someone else in Vegas. Which had put a friend in the hot seat as the next intended bride for a marriage pact that should never have survived into the modern day.

Ari, ever the optimist, protested. "You don't know that. Things might be going swimmingly, for all you know."

Because she said it as if she knew something, Afton just stared at the girl.

Holding up a finger in a wait-a-minute gesture, Ari tapped something on her phone. "For example, it seems that your former intended is getting married this weekend.”

Afton blinked. “Connor? Connor MacKean is getting married?”

“Mmmhmm.”

“Where are you seeing this?”

“The Glenlaig village Facebook page. It’s a whole thing.”

“Let me see that.”

Ari smirked with satisfaction as she handed over her phone.

Afton scanned the announcement. Connor was marrying Sophie Cameron at the village kirk on Saturday, with a reception to be held afterward at Ardinmuir Castle.

So they didn’t lose the estate.

One of the knots she’d carried since she left finally loosened. That meant things had worked out, at least on a couple of fronts. Right?

The post was accompanied by an engagement photo of her friends. They looked well together, with Connor’s blue-eyed blond good looks, and the flawless brown skin and heavy mass of satiny black hair Sophie got from her Indian mother. The stress and strain Afton remembered was nowhere to be found in her pretty grey eyes. And Connor... Connor looked at her as if she’d hung the moon.

He’d never once looked at Afton like that.

As the silence spun out, Ari asked softly, "Does this upset you? I didn't mean to step in it."

Shaking off the brief pall of melancholy, Afton handed back the phone. "The whole reason I left was because I wasn't in love with Connor. That would've been like marrying my brother. No, this is exactly as it should be. I always suspected he had feelings for her, and with me out of the way, he could finally act on them."

When they both continued to stare at her in expectation, she fought to keep from hunching her shoulders. "What?"

"Don't you want to be there for your friend? To see him be happy?" Ari asked.

"Of course, I do."

But Connor's wasn't the only life she'd upended.

There was Raleigh Beaumont, the Texas cowboy who'd "won" the estate in Vegas after she'd deliberately tanked multiple hands of poker. He wouldn't have known an arranged marriage was part of the package until he arrived to claim Lochmara. Then there was Kyla MacKean, Connor's sister, who had been left to fulfill the pact in Afton's stead, given the new owner was male. And Malcolm Niall, the estate manager who'd been something of a surrogate father to Afton after the death of her own, whom she hadn't done more than leave a note for when she ran.

Then there was Hamish Colquhoun. The man who'd given her the answer to her freedom. The man who'd kissed her before she left, as if she were everything that had been missing in his life.

She couldn't think about Hamish. He was off limits. Always had been.

But now that Ari had put the bug in her ear, Afton couldn't *not* think about the prospect of going home. She'd love to see Connor and Sophie get married. Love to see the proof that things were working out, despite—or maybe because of—the desperate choice she'd made. And if it wasn't? Well, maybe she'd spent long enough hiding from her mistakes.

"I suppose you're right. I should go home, at least to wrap things up. And after that, we'll see."

"Book the ticket now," Athena urged.

"Now?"

"Now. Before you talk yourself out of it. I know you. You'll overthink it, same as you did that béchamel when I first taught you how to make it."

"Fine." Knowing her friend would never let it drop, Afton pulled out her own phone and searched for airfare. If she wanted to make it back in time for the wedding, she had to fly out tomorrow.

The cost of the last-minute fare made her wince, but she bought it anyway.

"Okay, it's booked. Are you both happy now?"

"Yes," they chorused.

Afton couldn't help but laugh. "Well, in that case, there are some more goodbyes I need to see to before I leave."

They all pushed back from the table.

"Fair enough." Athena pulled her in for a hug. "You keep in touch now, you hear?"

Afton squeezed her tight, wondering when they'd see each other again. "Yes, Chef."

TWO

"The doctors say it's a broken hip. Not good, but she's stable."

As Hamish's mother, Niamh, tossed more clothes into a suitcase, he tunneled a hand through his hair. "Do I need to be clearing my schedule? Making arrangements to help?"

"No, your da and I are going to go. She's scheduled for surgery in the morning."

"Poor Gran." His grandmother wasn't one to rest on her laurels. A hip replacement was a big bloody deal, and she was likely to be an absolute thrawn patient. "What can I do? How can I help?"

Niamh paused to lay a hand against his cheek. "Nothing, just now. It'll be a long recovery. Your father and I will likely be in Glasgow for quite a while. I'm sorry we have to leave you with everything here."

It finally penetrated Hamish's brain what she meant. 'Everything' meaning Freya. They'd been doing a lot of the picking up and dropping off and providing meals, so he could handle all the things that needed handling. And he'd barely been making it. With both of them gone, how was he going to manage?

Because his mother looked so apologetic, he forced a smile. "It's fine. We'll be fine. I've been meaning to hire a nanny, anyway." It was something he should've done well before now. His parents weren't retired, and they were both juggling their own jobs. It really wasn't fair to expect them to pick up the slack where he'd been failing.

Niamh zipped her bag and called down the hall. "Graham! Is the car unlocked?"

"Aye." Hamish's father stepped into the room and eyed her suitcase. "Are you expecting to be there halfway into next year?"

"Well, I dinna ken, now do I? Better to be prepared."

"Fair enough." He hefted the bag and carted it down the hall.

Freya emerged from the kitchen, biting her lip. Worry lit up the blue eyes she'd inherited from him. "Is Great Gran going to be okay?"

Hamish wrapped an arm around her shoulder. "She's exactly where she needs to be. The doctors know what they're doing."

"I made a card for her." She held up a construction paper creation with lots of glitter and stars.

"Aren't you the sweetest? She'll love it." Niamh pressed a kiss to her brow. "We'll call as soon as we have more news. Please send our regrets to Connor and Sophie. There's no way we'll be back for the rehearsal dinner tomorrow night."

Seeing his father hovering in the doorway, Hamish began herding his mum out of the house. "Think nothing of it. They'd want you to be with Gran."

Outside, they all exchanged another flurry of hugs. Then his parents loaded into their car and pulled away.

For a long minute, Hamish and his daughter stood staring after them. Knowing she'd be looking to him for cues on how to handle this whole situation, he locked away his own anxiety and squeezed her shoulder. "Well, that's a lot of excitement. It'll probably be tomorrow before we hear anything. I'm guessing you didn't get a chance to eat dinner?"

Freya shook her head.

"The pub?" he suggested. They'd already eaten there twice this week, but there weren't a lot of options in Glenlaig, and at least The Stag's Head had menu options that weren't fried. That put it slightly ahead of The Village Chippy on nutrition, right?

His daughter offered an apathetic jerk of her thin shoulders. "Sure."

Father of the year, right here.

He was going to figure out this cooking thing. After his best friend's wedding this weekend, when he had a little more bandwidth. It wasn't so much the cooking as the planning he was falling down on. He could put meals together when he had the time. Maybe he could look into one of those meal kit delivery services where they provided the recipes and all the ingredients. Surely, he could manage that?

The pub was already half-full when they arrived. Laura Craig, one of the owners of the place, shot them a smile. "Back again? Your table's free."

They had their own table now? Damn it. He was really falling into that bachelor stereotype. Holding in his wince, he nudged Freya forward. "Last-minute change of plans. My grandmother broke her hip, so my parents are on their way to Glasgow."

Laura lost the smile. "Oh, no! Is she alright?"

Hamish gave her the update, knowing that would effectively spread the news across the village and save him time. "They'll likely be staying for a while, so I'm looking for a part-time nanny to help out. Do you know of anyone looking for extra work? Maybe one of the servers?"

The older woman wagged a finger. "Dinna you be tryin' to steal my waitstaff, Hamish Colquhoun." A wink took any sting out of her protest. "I'll certainly put the word out, and we'll see what happens."

"That'd be great. Thank you."

Freya waited until they'd sat down before pinning him with a look. "Why do I need a nanny? I'm twelve, Da."

This was going to be a sensitive topic. "It's not because you need a babysitter. A nanny would be someone to help, ferrying you to and from school, maybe making some meals, since that's obviously not my strong suit. There's just a lot going on right now, with work and renovations on the house. It's hard to get everything done."

"What about Uncle Connor and Aunt Sophie? Aunt Kyla and Uncle Raleigh? Charlotte and Malcolm?"

As she listed off his friends, he worked not to cringe. He knew they'd help. Hell, they *had* helped. All of them. They'd made offers repeatedly to do more. He just... didn't want to take advantage. Or maybe he didn't want to admit he needed as much help as he did. He'd always been the guy other people came to for assistance. He'd never really had to ask for any, and he didn't like the change that had come about because of his divorce.

"You know they all adore you. But for the immediate future, Connor and Sophie will be leaving this weekend for their honeymoon. And Kyla and Raleigh are tied up with the baby." And Charlotte and Malcolm had their foster son, Gavin, who was fourteen and currently the object of a not insignificant crush. Hamish didn't want to do anything that encouraged *that*.

His daughter's shoulders curled in, and her gaze dropped. "I dinna want to be a burden to anyone."

The instant burst of temper at his ex-wife, at himself, left Hamish momentarily speechless. There were always casualties in divorce, and he was doing everything he could to make up for Dayna's apathy. The last thing he wanted was to make Freya feel as if he was pawning her off on someone else.

He struggled to find the right words. "Look at me." When she didn't, he injected a note of dad-authority into his tone. "Freya." She lifted her gaze. "You are not a burden. You are my joy. My looking for a nanny isn't a reflection on you. It's all about me. I'm having a hard time juggling everything by myself." And if admitting that out loud was like swallowing razor blades, so be it. "If I have somebody who can help with the driving around and food and a few other things, then I'll be able to manage my workload more effectively during regular work hours, so I dinna have to bring it home. Which means I'll have more quality time to spend with you."

Freya looked dubious about the whole thing. "Okay. But I reserve veto rights."

His lips twitched because she was so obviously his child. "Fair enough. You may have veto rights. Shake on it?"

She took his extended hand and pumped it once, with a firm grip and decisive nod.

"So, we're settled, then?" he prompted.

"We're settled."

Feeling better about the situation, he picked up a menu.

"Oi, Hamish." Across the pub, Hugh McGowan lifted his pint in acknowledgment. "I hear Stuart MacDonald gifted you with his mother's goats on his way out of town."

Freya went brows up. "We have goats?"

Hamish just closed his eyes. *Well, fuck.*

AFTON FOLLOWED the road that wrapped along the edge of Stockton Quarry Lake, feeling a mix of grief and joy. Would this be the last time she came here? Surely not. Rebecca and Grey would never allow her to disappear from their lives. Not after everything they'd been through together.

She hadn't known, when she approached the American couple on their honeymoon in Scotland and asked to join them for their ride to the airport, that she'd be making more than a temporary connection. If they hadn't said yes, hadn't taken one look at her on that desperate day and known she was in trouble, she didn't know what would've happened. Oh, she'd have found some other way to escape, but she probably wouldn't have been able to disappear as entirely and effectively as she had. She wouldn't have been able to so fully change her life for the better. For that, they'd earned her undying gratitude.

They'd done so much more than give her a ride. They'd invited her to visit them here in Eden's Ridge. They'd given her a place to stay until she could get back on her feet and find a new direction. More, they'd become another set of parents. After losing her own in a plane crash twelve years ago, that was something she'd desperately craved. Having someone to ask for guidance, for support, someone she knew accepted her exactly as she was... It was a gift without price. She loved them both. So while going back to Scotland felt necessary and timely, she didn't want to abandon what she'd found here.

Their house perched on a hill overlooking the lake. An expansive two stories of wood and stone, it seemed to have grown out of the mountain itself. Porches on both levels overlooked the water. Just now, the railings of both were draped in fresh evergreen garland and fairy lights. Rebecca loved Christmas and had cheerfully browbeaten everyone in the family to help decorate the day after Thanksgiving. The massive twelve-foot Frasier fir sat in a place of honor, framed by the picture window. Its white lights twinkled, inviting her in.

It was a hell of a house, far too big for just Grey and Rebecca, but they'd built it for the massive extended family that included their son, Jonah; his wife, Rachel; Rebecca's daughter, Samantha; her husband, Griff; Jonah's business partners and their wives, and all the grandbabies, of which there were currently six, though Afton wouldn't at all be surprised if Jonah and Rachel were thinking about another.

Theirs was a house filled with love, and it was so very different from the empty, echoing halls of Afton's ancestral home, Lochmara.

Not my home any longer.

If her heart twisted with a pang at that, it was a price she'd learned to endure. Her freedom was worth more than memories and legacy.

Shaking off the blanket of melancholy, she gathered up the bags of groceries and headed for the front door. Though she knew she was welcome, she rang the bell. Rebecca and Grey were, in a sense, still newlyweds, having found each other again after decades apart. She didn't want to risk interrupting anything.

The door opened a few moments later, and Afton found herself wrapped in a swaying mom-hug from Rebecca. Hands full, Afton could only tuck her head against the other woman's shoulder and soak in the love.

"Oh, honey, it's so good to see you! Why didn't you tell us you were coming?"

"It was a surprise." When Rebecca released her, she held up the bags. "I brought supplies to make dinner."

"Wonderful! We're not gonna say no. Come in, come in. Grey! Afton's here!"

Rebecca's husband, retired Naval Captain Mitchell Greyson, emerged from the kitchen. A smile curved his lips as he, too, wrapped an arm around her shoulders and squeezed. "Hey, sugar. Here, let me take those."

Because she knew he wouldn't take no for an answer, Afton allowed him to relieve her of the grocery bags as they all wandered back to the kitchen.

"To what do we owe the pleasure of your delightful company?" he asked.

"I wanted to see you both. I need to talk to you about something."

"Oh?" Rebecca's tone held that faux casual note that didn't fool Afton for a moment.

"Let me get dinner started, and I'll tell you."

"Sure. What's on the menu?" Grey asked. "Can I open a bottle of wine to go with it?"

"We're having a warm roasted beet salad with goat cheese and walnuts; pan roasted chicken with lemon-garlic Brussels sprouts, and sweet potato mash; and an apple pear crisp for dessert."

He looked to Rebecca. "Remind me why we haven't kidnapped her to be our permanent culinary slave?"

"Labor laws." She nodded very seriously.

Afton snickered as she began unloading the bags onto the wide soapstone counters.

"And we love her too much to put her in another cage."

Well, didn't that just choke her right up? Swallowing past the lump in her throat, she addressed Grey. "If you've got a Voignier or Chardonnay, those would pair well. Or even a light Pinot Noir."

"Coming right up."

They let her take over the kitchen, leaving her be as she set the oven to heat and began to prep the ingredients. For a little while, she lost herself in the simple pleasure of the food, of preparing a meal for people she cared about, in a kitchen that was familiar. She'd cooked for them so many times during her apprenticeship with Athena. She'd missed it during the six months of her externship, working in a commercial kitchen in Nashville. Missed the easy conversation and the unquestionable feeling of belonging that was so much a part of who the Greysons were, the vibe they extended to everyone around them.

"So, first off, my externship is officially finished. I've got my chef credentials."

Rebecca's eyes brightened. "That's wonderful! Oh, honey, I'm so proud of you."

"Thank you. That means a lot." Afton slid the tray of foil-wrapped beets into the oven. "And... I'm flying back to Scotland tomorrow."

When neither of them spoke, she turned to find them exchanging one of those married-people looks. Anxiety curled in her gut.

With an expression of speculation, Grey set a wineglass in front of her. "Why now?"

Needing something to do with her hands, she picked up the glass and sipped. Chardonnay. An unoaked one, if her palate didn't lie.

"Well, Connor is getting married, as he absolutely should, to the one-hundred percent right person, and I want to be there."

"That's both admirable and wonderful," Rebecca declared. "How are you feeling about all that?"

Afton huffed a humorless laugh. "Frankly, I'm kind of scared shiteless. I left a lot of things up in the air, and my actions impacted a lot of people. I have no idea what happened. I've done everything I can to avoid finding out because I've been afraid of the answer."

"You could look," Grey suggested. "There's a lot of information out there on the internet. And it happens you know people who can find things out."

Jonah and his business partners, Holt and Brax, had all been in various branches of the military before they'd retired and opened a bakery together. Holt's brother-in-law was former Army Intelligence and had a reputation for being able to find out anything about anybody.

"I'm not calling in Cash to fill in the gaps." That was like using a shovel when a teaspoon would do. "The wedding announcement on the village Facebook page says Connor and Sophie's reception is at Ardinmuir. I have to believe that means they didn't lose the estate. Honestly, that's the only reason I can go back. If he and Kyla had lost everything because I ran, I'd never be able to forgive myself."

Rebecca scowled. "You were in an untenable situation."

"Aye, I was. But so were they, and Connor was

still prepared to do his duty. Anyway, I guess now that the bubble of curiosity has been burst on one piece, I want to know everything. And I want to find out in person. I need to do that for myself. I just have to hope that they'll all forgive me." Which was a very tall order.

Grey accepted the announcement with a little more ease than his wife. "What time are you leaving?"

"I fly out of Nashville tomorrow afternoon."

"I'll drive you."

"That's not necessary." The protest came automatically.

"Come on now. Then you can leave your car here instead of in long-term parking. Since you don't know how long you'll be, this will save you the expense. And then we'll know you got off okay."

It had been so damned long since she'd had anyone worry about her, she couldn't say no. "I appreciate that. Thank you."

"Do you want to talk about the whole thing before you go?" Rebecca asked.

"No, I dinna think I do. I might talk myself out of it."

"I think this trip will be good for you. No matter how it turns out, you need the closure."

There was that word again. But none of her Tennessee family was wrong. She did need closure.

Her life in Scotland had been a big, open question for more than a year and a half. Before she could move on with her life, whatever that looked like, she needed to resolve this.

"That's certainly the hope. But tonight, I really just want to cook for you and hang out. I don't know how long it'll be before we can do this again."

Rebecca hustled around the counter to squeeze her again. "We're really gonna miss you."

This time, Afton had her hands free to squeeze back. "I'm going to miss both of you, too. It's meant so much that you made me a part of your family. And who knows? Depending on how everything goes, I may turn right around and come back to Tennessee."

Keeping her arm around Afton's waist, Rebecca snagged her wine. "Well, if you do, of course we'd love to have you. You know you'll always have a place here."

Grey lifted his glass. "To the family we make."

Throat burning, Afton clinked her glass to theirs. "I'll drink to that."

THREE

"Well, don't you look all grown up?" Sophie crooned. "That dress is absolutely lovely, Freya. It really brings out your eyes."

Hamish watched pleased color streak across his daughter's cheeks and wished he could be pleased as well. But he didn't like all the signs that his baby was growing up. She'd already added two inches since the summer. His mum had taken her shopping for the navy dress she wore. Made of some stretchy fabric, it clung to her frame in a way that made it obvious she was getting the first hints of curves. Seeing her in a dress and heels—even low ones—made it ever so clear that Freya was on the cusp of womanhood.

Past the cusp, actually. They'd survived *that*

talk a few months ago, and he'd successfully navigated the purchase of feminine hygiene products before Kyla had kindly introduced them both to period underpants, which had been a less traumatic option all around.

Shaking off his thoughts, Hamish pulled Connor in for a hug. "Mum and Dad send their regrets that they couldn't make it for the dinner."

His best and oldest friend thumped him on the back. "Think nothing of it. What's the news on your gran?"

"She came through surgery just fine. The doctor says it will be a few weeks, at the very least, before she regains sufficient mobility to function at home, so Mum and Dad are both taking leave and staying for the first couple of weeks. Then they'll be telecommuting from there as work allows. The longer-term recovery is more like three to six months."

Connor whistled.

Kyla strode up, her six-month-old daughter, Lily, perched on one hip. "Are we going to make bets on how long it takes her to browbeat her physiotherapist into letting her go early?"

"I take it your grandmama is stubborn?" Raleigh slid an arm around his wife's waist and pressed an absent but adoring kiss to Lily's strawberry-blonde fuzz, prompting the baby to coo and flail one little fist to catch her father's finger, which she promptly pulled into her mouth.

Hamish ached at the sight, remembering Freya at that age. Not that he hadn't loved every stage after that—with the possible exception of the terrible twos. But he just... wished he could still hold her. Still press his lips to the baby down of her hair and soak in the smell of baby shampoo. He was deathly afraid of what was coming. That she would hit teenager and suddenly decide she hated him and wanted to live with her mother back in Edinburgh. Not that he thought Dayna would go for that. Which opened the door to the potential for all sorts of other rebellion he simply wasn't prepared to cope with.

"Hamish?" Sophie prompted.

Shaking himself, he traced the conversation back to Raleigh's question. His gran being stubborn. Right. "That's putting it mildly. She was still pretty out of it when I spoke to Mum earlier, but I expect she'll be back to her usual self as soon as the painkillers are out of her system."

"We'll send her some flowers to brighten up her room," Sophie promised.

"Mum has sworn to stream the wedding for her tomorrow, so I hope the AV is all sorted."

"On it!" This announcement came from Ciara McBride, Connor and Kyla's younger cousin, who worked part-time for the event planning company that Kyla and Sophie ran out of Ardinmuir. Her other job was waiting tables at The Stag's Head, as her brother, Ewan, was the other owner. Hamish knew she was rapidly headed toward full-time for Ardinmuir Event Planning, but he wondered if she had any hours she could put toward nannying in the meantime. He still hadn't found anyone.

Swayze Parish, the Georgia-born social media influencer who'd helped put Ardinmuir Event Planning on the map and had been instrumental in Connor and Sophie getting together in the first place, waved her phone. "Not to interrupt this reunion, but I just got a text from Charlotte wanting to know our ETA so she can let the caterers know. We should probably get this show on the road."

In her cheerful Southern-belle way, she herded them all into the sanctuary where the rest of their motley crew was waiting with Father Grant. Raleigh took Lily from Kyla, and Freya joined them in the front row. Everyone else gathered around the altar and listened patiently to Father Grant's instructions. Then the women and Connor and Kyla's great uncle Angus peeled off, taking their position in the narthex. Hamish, Connor, and Ewan moved out to the hall just to the right of the sanctuary, awaiting the signal to come inside. Ewan's girlfriend, Isobel, AKA, world-famous violinist Elizabeth Duncan, who'd just finished her latest tour, picked up her instrument and began to play the chosen processional.

As best man, Hamish followed Connor to the front, trailed by Ewan. The doors at the back of the sanctuary opened, and the ladies began their walk down the aisle. Swayze came first. Then Kyla as matron of honor. It was a small and intimate wedding party, as Hamish's own wedding to Dayna had been. But that was where the similarities ended. Where theirs had been a small but exclusive affair at a posh Edinburgh hotel, Connor and Sophie had invited the entire village. Tomorrow, this room would be bursting with friends and neighbors come to share in the joy. Their ceremony was bursting with tradition in a way his had not, and Hamish found himself envious.

Then the music shifted, and Angus appeared, Ciara on his arm. She was playing the role of stand-in bride for the rehearsal, with Sophie trailing behind to get a sense of the pacing. She made it to the front and took Connor's arm. They beamed at each other, love bright enough to light the entire parish.

As Father Grant went over the order of the rest of the ceremony, Hamish struggled to pay attention. His mind was far away and long ago. He realized he'd done a magnificent job fooling himself into believing that what he'd had with Dayna was real.

That it was good. That it was the same as what his friends had been blessed enough to find. But the truth was, he'd pulled the wool deliberately over his own eyes because he couldn't have who he'd really wanted, and he'd thought he could will himself into loving Dayna as deeply as she deserved.

In the end, it hadn't worked. And in an act just as reckless as Afton's, Dayna had chosen her way out of the marriage through an affair that gave him unarguable grounds for a near immediate divorce.

Now he was free and full of regrets and realizations. He'd failed in his marriage, as he was failing in so many other areas. How could he have spent so much of his life feeling as if he was in control and on top of his game, only to end up here, surrounded by reminders of exactly how wrong he'd gotten it?

Except, he'd gotten Freya out of the deal. And he could never regret his daughter. Maybe he wasn't meant for the whole love thing. But that didn't mean he couldn't be the best possible father for her. No matter how tough it got.

Father Grant clapped his hands. "Okay, I think everyone's got it. See you all here tomorrow afternoon!"

With quick thanks to Father Grant, everyone started toward the door.

Hamish started to fall into step behind them, but Connor caught his eye, holding him back.

He put full focus on his friend, hoping he hadn't missed something. "Everything okay?"

"Yeah, everything's brilliant." Connor clamped a hand on his shoulder. "I just wanted to say thank you. I wouldnae be here, wouldnae be marrying the love of my life, if not for you. Hell, none of us would be where we are, with the people we love, if you hadn't set everything in motion."

Guilt slithered through Hamish's chest. In the strictest sense, it was true. He'd been the one who'd discovered that Afton's estate could be gambled away. It had been the only loophole he'd found after years and years of digging. But all he'd done was deliver the message. Afton was the one who'd had the courage to run. To break free of the cage she should never have been bound to. She'd been the one to gamble the estate to Raleigh, bringing him to Scotland for Kyla. And Charlotte had come after the son of her heart, which was how she'd met Malcolm.

Hamish had nothing to do with any of it. Because he hadn't been able to find another answer. One that didn't involve someone he cared about having to give up her legacy, her family, her home. And that was just another failure on a list that was piling up.

Afton hadn't come back. Hamish had given considerable thought to why. No doubt she was afraid to face everyone. He knew her well enough to understand that the choice she'd made hadn't been one she'd taken lightly. Her actions had had very real consequences, and he didn't know if she was aware of how the chips had fallen. Beyond that, he was afraid she'd built an entirely new life for herself wherever she'd landed. That made him a complete jackass because, while he wanted her happy, he didn't want her happy somewhere else. He wanted her happy here. Happy with him.

Which was beyond absurd. So far as he knew, she had no idea he was divorced. She had only the memory of that one desperate kiss from a married man who should never have touched her. A kiss he was perilously afraid had been the final catalyst that had made her run.

A kiss he hadn't been able to forget.

Connor's hand weighed heavy on his shoulder, and his gaze was full of expectation, so Hamish forced a smile. "You're welcome, brother. It means a lot to me to know you're marrying tomorrow for love instead of duty."

His friend grinned. "Then let's go get this party started."

As Hamish followed him out of the sanctuary, he shoved the memory of that kiss back in its mental box and locked it in a closet. He didn't have the bandwidth to think about it, and there was absolutely no point in wasting energy obsessing over a woman who was no longer part of his life.

AFTON WAS LATE.

The Universe was conspiring against her. The certainty of it had sunk into her bones while her second flight sat on the tarmac for a full four hours, waiting to have a tire changed. She'd spent the whole time questioning her decision to come back for Connor and Sophie's wedding before the powers that be finally hustled everyone off and onto a replacement plane.

They'd made up some time in the air, but instead of having plenty of time for the drive up from Glasgow and to find somewhere to stay and freshen up, she'd arrived in the village at the top of the hour, right when the ceremony was meant to start. The roads were all but gridlocked with parked cars. Everyone who was anyone was at this wedding. Finding somewhere legal to park was a no-go, so she finally wedged her rental onto a kerb and prayed that the local police would also be in attendance and thus unable to hand out citations.

Thanking God that she'd changed into her dress at the airport, she dug her heels out of her carry-on and slipped them on, hurrying as fast as she dared through the freshly falling snow toward the village kirk. It loomed up, a bastion of gray stone against the pewter sky. Greenery and vibrant red and blue ribbons added pops of color against the otherwise dreary day.

At the door, she hesitated for a moment, pausing to get her breath under control because her chest was feeling tight. The last time she'd been here was the third time the banns had been read for her and Connor. The day she'd felt as if her life was over. The day she'd run.

Was being here the right thing? No matter that Connor and Sophie were together, she'd hurt a lot of people with her actions. Should she have stayed away?

Huffing out a breath, Afton squared her shoulders. "You've come too far to back out now, lass. Chin up."

She tugged open the door. The narthex was empty, but she could hear the drone of Father Grant's voice from inside the sanctuary. They'd already processed in, then. Damn it. She'd just slip in the back and hope no one noticed.

Taking a firm grip on the sanctuary door, she pulled it open and stepped inside.

"—any lawful impediment to the marriage of Sophie and Connor, speak now or forever hold your peace."

She tried to catch the door and shut it softly, but an unholy squeak sounded from the hinges on the backswing. Every pair of eyes in the room turned her way.

Mortified, she froze, half in, half out of the doorway. Oh, God. She'd *interrupted* their wedding!

With a growing sense of dread and horror, her gaze slid to the front of the church, where she spotted Hamish, his hand on Connor's shoulder, as they both stared at her. Even from dozens of feet away, she felt the punch of Hamish's gaze. At that visceral connection, her blood heated, her skin prickling with the remembered feel of his hands on her in a way that not a single date she'd had since had managed.

So that reaction hadn't faded one iota. Good to know.

Tearing her eyes from his, she looked at Connor, his familiar face a mask of shock and bafflement. Then she spotted Sophie, whose lovely eyes were full of worry.

Oh, God.

Father Grant cleared his throat. "Do you have an objection to lodge regarding this marriage?"

Appalled, she lifted her gloved hands. "No! No, no. Please, carry on. I'm just..." Desperate, she glanced at the back pews, which were packed. On the left, Flora McGowan, one of the crofters from

Lochmara, scooted over to make room. Relieved, Afton took a couple of steps forward, pointing at the narrow seat. "I'm just going to—"

She slid into the seat.

There was a collective groan of wood as the entire congregation shifted around in their seats to face the front again. Father Grant resumed the ceremony.

Beside Afton, Flora patted her knee and whispered, "Welcome home, lass."

Afton tried to give her a grateful smile, but she was too busy heaping recriminations on herself.

I should never have come. This was a terrible idea. I can't believe I interrupted their wedding, and they thought I was here to stop it.

Instinctively, she curled in on herself, doing anything she could to make herself invisible. She'd always wanted to be invisible growing up here in the public eye. Perhaps no one outside the area knew her name or gave a damn about her, but the people of Glenlaig had known her as the heiress of Lochmara, and they'd all had expectations of her. They'd had more than two decades to pile them on. Her duty had always been to marry the son of Ardinmuir. Locals had looked forward to that wedding with almost as much fervor as that of one of the royal family. Afton had hated it, wanting only to disappear into the background.

And then she'd deprived them of the event entirely.

It seemed Connor and Sophie were making up for it. Sophie was absolutely stunning in a blue sari that paired perfectly with the MacKean tartan of Connor's kilt. Her bridesmaids—Kyla and another woman Afton didn't know—wore a vibrant red and carried profusions of blooms. Leaning a little further into the aisle, she tried to get a better look at the front.

A man with wavy blond hair sat in the front row. Raleigh, she was pretty sure. He shifted, and she spotted a small bundle in his arms. Holy shite. Was that a *baby*? Did he and Kyla have a child together? When she'd chosen Raleigh in Vegas, she'd hoped the two of them would get along well enough to manage a marriage of business. Kyla didn't have the same objections to divorce that her brother had. But she'd never imagined they'd marry and truly *work*. Not that a child was proof of that necessarily, but it was a definite surprise.

Further back, she spotted the broad shoulders and salt-and-pepper hair of Malcolm Niall, Lochmara's estate manager. He sat with a petite woman and a gangly boy. She didn't have a good enough view of either one to say whether she recognized them, but in all the years she'd known him, she'd never known Malcolm to be with anyone. If he'd somehow found happiness since she'd left, she couldn't be more pleased for him.

Now that she was relaxing a little, she noted the flowers and the ribbons and the candles. All the little embellishments that elevated the event. The decorations and the ceremony were a blend of cultures, reflecting both the groom's heritage and the bride's. The whole thing was absolutely lovely. Afton wondered if Kyla and Sophie had pulled off the event planning business. They'd intended to use her wedding to Connor as a launching point, with an eye toward saving the financially floundering estate.

Then the vows began, and Afton put her focus back on the reason she'd come. They looked so happy together, content and comfortable in a way she and Connor had never been. There was love here. True and abiding. The thing she'd wanted so much for herself that she hadn't been willing to settle. Not that she was any closer to it now, but at least she wasn't trapped in a loveless marriage.

"I now pronounce you husband and wife. You may kiss the bride."

Connor took Sophie's mouth, bending her back in a dip that had the entire congregation bursting into applause and cheers.

He'd done it. He'd married for love. Afton had to believe that meant there was hope for her yet.

Unbidden, her gaze searched out Hamish. But she couldn't really see him with the crowd, and the new Mr. and Mrs. MacKean were recessing down the aisle to the sound of a soaring violin. Ewan came next, with the unknown brunette on his arm. Then Hamish and Kyla. She got long looks from them both as they passed and had to fight not to fold in on herself.

Amends to make. This whole trip was about amends. She'd take whatever she had to take from everyone in order to close this chapter in her life.

The crowd stood around her and began to make their way toward the exit. Amid the rising chaos, Connor's Uncle Angus appeared, a kind smile on his weathered face as he offered his arm.

"I think we'd best have a chat before the reception, hmm?"

Knowing he meant with more than himself, and that she couldn't put this off any longer, she slid her hand into the crook of his elbow. "Let's go."

BY THE END of the ceremony, Hamish was fairly vibrating with tension. He'd been so acutely aware of Afton sitting in the back row, he'd barely been able to focus on the vows. After all this time, she was *right there.* And why now? He'd literally just made peace last night with the idea that she was no longer a part of his life. That he should move on and stop wasting energy he didn't have thinking about her.

Now she was back.

Well, she was *here.* That didn't mean she was back to stay. She could have simply come for the wedding and intended to be gone again tomorrow.

Would she say goodbye this time?

And why do you care? It's not like you have the bandwidth to even think about a relationship with someone. Let alone someone you have such a complicated history with. Someone who very well could have moved on since she left here.

The idea of that soured his gut, and he hoped like hell no one was looking at his face. Thank God Freya was helping watch the little ones in the church nursery.

He'd convinced himself that whatever he'd felt for Afton had been passing. Something that was a direct counterpoint to the disaster of his marriage with Dayna. A fantasy attached to some dream version of them that could never be. Except his was the first gaze she'd met when she walked into the sanctuary, and he'd felt the sonic boom of that link all the way to his marrow as all the feelings he'd been repressing since she'd left and his world had fallen apart burst out of the box he'd shoved them into and left him reeling.

So when Angus's husband, Munro, caught him in the narthex after the recessional and began herding him and the others toward a room in the back of the church, he didn't fight it. He definitely needed to get his head on straight before he interacted with anybody at the reception.

Before he saw Afton again.

Would he see Afton again?

Christ, Colquhoun, you're a mess.

Raleigh was the first to break the silent tension as the door shut behind them. "Well, that just got even more excitin'."

"That's one word for it," Sophie murmured, tucking closer to Connor's side. "What do you suppose she's doing here?"

Kyla moved to her husband, shifting a sleepy Lily into her arms, clearly more to soothe her own disquiet than the baby's. "Surely, she's not here to reclaim Lochmara?"

Hamish roused himself from his own mental turmoil enough to set that fear to rest. "No, that's done. Raleigh is the owner. There's no contesting that. And I dinna think she'd contest it to begin with." He'd made the consequences of gambling the estate clear before she'd run. But he still couldn't figure out why she was here, after more than a year and a half without a word.

In the corner, Charlotte turned to Malcolm. "You okay?"

He grunted in his usual taciturn manner. Of all of them, the estate manager had probably been the closest to Afton, having stepped up when her parents were killed in a plane crash years before. She hadn't said goodbye to him either, other than a note, and she hadn't been in contact since.

The door opened again, and Angus stepped in, Afton on his arm.

Unable to help himself, Hamish drank in the sight of her. Her figure was a little fuller than it had been, and the extra curves looked good on her. Her long, pale blonde hair was loose over the shoulders of her navy wool coat. His hands remembered the silky feel of it sliding through his fingers as he took her mouth...

But she didn't look at him. Her gaze went straight to Connor and Sophie, color staining those fair cheeks, big brown eyes full of worry, though not in the way he'd been accustomed to seeing before. Uncertainty and a measure of awkwardness draped over her like a cloak as she knit her hands and squared her shoulders. Hands that bore no ring.

It doesn't mean anything.

"First off, I want to sincerely apologize. I'm so

sorry I crashed your wedding. I was late. My plane had a delay and—" She cut herself off with a quick shake of her head. "It doesn't matter. It's just... I found out you were getting married, and I wanted to be here to see it. We were never right, you and I, and I needed to see you happy." Her throat worked, and she offered a smile that strained with hope around the edges. "I'm so glad that you are."

Emotion flickered over Connor's face before he crossed the room and pulled her into a tight hug. "Thank you for doing what I couldn't."

Her arms came around him, and she lingered. Here was the friendship they'd always had. The friendship that hadn't been enough for a marriage. And with it, Connor's clear, uncomplicated forgiveness.

Afton looked a little lighter as she stepped back. "I'm sorry for how I went about it. I unquestionably could have handled the whole thing better."

She took a quick survey of the room, nodding to everyone. Hamish wanted to believe her gaze clung to his for a beat longer than the rest, but that was probably a delusion. He wished they weren't in the middle of a roomful of their closest friends. That he was free to say... what?

I missed you? I was worried about you? By the way, I'm divorced now, and pretty sure I'm in love with you?

How would he even begin to bridge the gap of time since last he'd seen her? Would they be able to find that easy companionship they'd once shared? Or had he blown that all to hell when he'd kissed her as a married man?

When no one spoke, she began twisting her hands again. Hamish wanted to cover them with his own. To lace those slim fingers with his and offer comfort. Support. Something.

"I want you all to know that I have no expectation of some prodigal's welcome. I didn't come back here believing I could just slide back into your lives after how I left. All I'd ask of you is the chance to speak to each of you about it, because I absolutely owe you an explanation and apologies. But now isn't the time. I've already caused enough of a stir. It can wait."

Connor automatically wrapped an arm around his wife. "Sophie and I leave for our honeymoon in the morning. We'll be gone for a little over a week. Will you be here when we get back?"

Hamish tried not to look over-eager for her response, but his mind was spinning with questions. Had she just come for the wedding? For apologies? Was she staying? Was she going? A part of him was afraid of her answer, no matter which way it fell.

She stopped twisting her hands and shoved

them into her coat pockets. "Aye. I expect to still be here at that point."

"Good." Connor smiled. "You should come to the reception. Celebrate with us."

Hamish watched her retreat into herself, but not before a faint trace of panic lit her eyes. "Absolutely not. My coming back is going to be the biggest gossip to hit the village in... well, probably since I left. So no, I'm not going to do anything else to detract from your day. I just wanted to say a very heartfelt congratulations and apologize again for making a scene in the middle of the ceremony. That was never my intention."

"We appreciate that," Sophie offered. "And we are glad you were here. It was the closing of a circle, in a way."

Afton's mouth curved in a tentative smile. It turned more uncertain as she shifted toward Malcolm. "I'd really like to speak with you tomorrow, if you have the chance. I can come out to your place at the estate. Whenever's convenient."

Malcolm nodded, his expression unreadable. "Aye, that's fine. Although, we've moved."

Her head jerked back, this evidently surprising her more than anything else. Those dark eyes flickered to Charlotte before coming back to Malcolm. "Where?"

"Remember where your da fell over that time

he was teaching you how to fly fish and got soaked from top to tail?"

"Aye. Of course."

"We renovated the crofter's cottage just past there."

Afton's gaze slid to Charlotte again, who was uncharacteristically blank-faced. But she didn't voice any of the thousand questions clearly swirling in her mind. "I know the spot. Just let me know what time."

"Any time after two."

She nodded again, and Hamish felt the moment she hit her wall with how much she could handle of this reunion even before she announced, "Okay, I'm not going to take up any more of anybody's time. Please, go have fun. Celebrate. I'll see you tomorrow."

Without giving anyone time to respond, she turned toward the door.

Hamish took a step toward her. He didn't know what he was doing. Didn't have any idea what he was going to say. But his instinct was to stop her.

Finally, those eyes met his again, close enough he could see the band of dark gray around the edges of her irises, and everything fell away but her. Questions and apologies clogged in his throat so that nothing at all came out when he opened his mouth.

"Hamish." That was it. That was all she said in that quiet voice before she walked away from him.

Again.

It was so silent after she left they could hear the click of her heels on the stone floor.

He thought about going after her. But he didn't know what to say, and he had duties here to his friend. He was the best man, after all. There were speeches to give and a little hell to raise.

He cleared his throat. "We should get to the reception. Guests will be waiting."

"You know, I spent a lot of time angry with her for leaving how she did," Kyla murmured. "But I dinna think any amount of our recriminations will be half as much as what she's heaped on herself."

Raleigh wrapped his arms around her. "Hard to stay mad when everything worked out so well for us in the end."

"It might be as she'll need to be told that whenever she does come to talk to all of you," Angus suggested.

"It's a fair point," Connor agreed. "In the meantime, I want to go dance with my wife."

Sophie giggled as he caught her up for another kiss, then everyone began filing out, making their way to vehicles.

As they strode down the hall, Connor dropped

back, draping an arm across Hamish's shoulders. "So, what are you going to do about that?"

"What am I going to do about what?"

His best friend just arched a brow in a you-know-what sort of way. Being that Connor was the only person Hamish had confessed his feelings for Afton to, he was the only one who could give him shite about it. But Hamish didn't have the bandwidth to even think about it tonight. He didn't know what Afton was really doing here, or what her plans were, or what any of it even meant.

So he just rolled his eyes. "Let's just get to your party, mate."

FOUR

The drive out to Lochmara took Afton longer than she liked. Last night, she'd ended up booking a room at a little inn the next village over. After coming face to face with all the people she'd run from, she'd needed some distance to regain her equilibrium. Plus, she hadn't at all been sure there'd be open lodging in Glenlaig, given the crush of people who'd come for Connor and Sophie's wedding. The whole thing hadn't gone badly, per se—minus her mortifyingly public arrival in the middle of the ceremony. Then again, no one had expected her to show. Maybe they'd be more vocal with their disapproval once the shock wore off.

At least Connor had forgiven her. That was one weight off her shoulders. Given he'd only been free to marry for love because she'd stepped aside, that made him the one least likely to carry a grudge. But Kyla, as the one who'd been forced to marry a stranger in Afton's stead, had the most reason to hate her. Afton didn't know any way around that. She'd known the choice she'd made was selfish. Doubly so, because at least she'd *known* Connor, and, unlike Kyla, Afton hadn't been involved with someone else.

Afton had no idea what had happened to Kyla's long-term, long-distance boyfriend, David Murray. Given that Kyla and Raleigh seemed to have a daughter, presumably David was out of the picture. Afton had never gotten the impression that he was the love of Kyla's life. Maybe she'd have chosen differently if he was. But she'd always privately thought they were ill-suited. He'd never supported her affection for and allegiance to Ardinmuir. That kind of legacy was something Raleigh understood, and Afton had hoped—prayed—that the commonality would be at least a decent foundation for a marriage.

She owed them an apology and a chance to say whatever needed saying about how poorly she'd handled things. But she wasn't quite up to that yet. Malcolm needed to come first. Both because she thought that conversation would be a little easier, and because, as the man who'd stood in for her father for more than a decade, she owed him that. And, after yesterday, she desperately wanted to know who the woman he'd been with actually was. The gorgeous Latina hadn't spoken, but there'd been an unquestionable air of possessiveness about her. In all the years Afton had known Malcolm, she'd never been aware of a woman in his life. That aloneness had been part of what they'd bonded over. It was just another of the changes she was being forced to confront.

It had been foolish to think anything would be the same. Perhaps change had historically come slowly to the estate, to the village. But she'd effectively set off a bomb when she'd left. The aftershocks of that action would have affected everything. She could only hope that most of them had been good.

As she turned onto the estate for the first time in the better part of two years, she stopped the car, absorbing the punch of seeing it again. The rolling hills stretched out before her, familiar in their winter quietude. God, she'd missed it more than she'd admitted to herself. This had been her home all her life. This was her heritage. And it wasn't hers anymore. The stab of that all but took her breath away.

She'd left on an impulse, in a fit of utter desperation, seeing no other way out of a life and a duty she'd been locked into since birth. There'd been relief in passing the estate and everything that went with it on to Raleigh, because he truly wanted the responsibility that had felt like such a noose around her neck. There was still relief that she wasn't responsible for all the tenants and employees who called Lochmara home. But it didn't change the fact that it hurt coming back, knowing it was no longer her home. That it never would be again. She'd ripped up all her roots and hadn't found anywhere to plant them again. Not really.

On the long flight over, she'd let herself dream. Imagining a scenario where she'd return to the village, make her apologies, and create a new life for herself here. She'd let herself fantasize about what it would be like to finally come home. But she didn't know if she could really do it. Didn't know if she could face the everyday reality that her home would be forever out of reach.

This trip might end up just being about making amends before turning around and going back to Tennessee. Which wouldn't be terrible. She loved the friends and family she'd found there, loved a lot of pieces of that life. But being back home meant a lot more to her than she'd realized it would.

"One day at a time."

With that reminder, she wound her way through roads she knew as well as the face she saw in the mirror. When she crested the final rise and spotted the house, she stopped again, this time in pure shock. This definitely wasn't the place she remembered. The house itself had been renovated, with an addition off to the back. But that wasn't what struck her. It was the Christmas decorations *everywhere*. Wreaths with bright, cheerful bows hung on the door and on every window across the front. Two miniature evergreens in pots flanking the front door were decorated as Christmas trees. Garland was draped along the split-rail fence, and a trio of Valais black-nosed sheep pranced around a paddock. There was even a set of fake antlers and a red nose on Malcolm's 4x4.

Malcolm Niall didn't decorate for Christmas. He'd always preferred to pretend the holiday wasn't happening. Something she'd related to after her parents' deaths.

I have entered the Twilight Zone. Maybe I have the wrong house?

But it was the woman who'd been with Malcolm at the church yesterday who answered the door with a broad smile.

"Afton! Welcome. I'm Charlotte Vasquez. It's so nice to finally meet you." The slow molasses drawl of her Southern accent rolled over Afton. "Come on in. Malcolm's just in the back."

Stepping inside, she stared with fresh curiosity

at the other woman. "You're Southern. Connected to Raleigh, somehow, I'm guessing."

There went the smile again. "I am. He's my godson. I followed him over and ended up sticking around to help run the vacation rental business."

"The what?"

Charlotte led her through the house. "Oh, that was something we've done across both estates. Took all the empty crofter's cabins and renovated them to put up on Airbnb and VRBO."

"That's brilliant." The entire crofter way of life had become almost financially obsolete. It had been one of the estate's struggles she hadn't known how to combat.

"Raleigh's idea." Charlotte beamed, obviously proud of him. "It's been very successful."

The sound of a teenage boy crowing preceded their entry into the family lounge. "Victory is mine! No mucking of the triplets' pen for me this week."

Malcolm harrumphed, but Afton didn't miss the quirk at the corner of his mouth. "Dinna get used to it, lad. You were lucky this time."

The boy grinned with the insouciance of youth. "You're just jealous I've learned your tactics, auld man."

Afton watched in fascination as Malcolm snagged him in an affectionate headlock and tickled his ribs. "We'll see who's an auld man." Then he caught sight of her. "Afton." He brightened, looking... happy to see her.

"Malcolm. I didn't mean to interrupt."

"You're no' interrupting anything but this one's false victory."

"False! I beat you fair and square. A straight flush."

"Temporary state of affairs, I assure you." He released the boy and crossed over to her, pulling her in for a tight hug. "It's good to see you."

Not expecting the blatant display of affection, Afton held stiff for a few moments before relaxing into the embrace and soaking up a comfort she didn't really think she deserved. "Likewise. You didn't used to be a hugger."

"A lot's changed around here." The rumble of his voice against her chest was soothing.

"So I see. Can I get some proper introductions?"

Squeezing her tight for a few more seconds, Malcolm stepped back and held out a hand for Charlotte. She flowed into him in a smooth motion that showed intimacy and affection.

"This is my fiancée, Charlotte. And this upstart is our foster son, Gavin."

The teenager waggled his fingers.

Charlotte ruffled Gavin's mop of dark hair.

"You may be out of one of your chores, but you definitely still have homework, young man."

That announcement elicited a groan. "But we're almost to end of term."

"All the more reason to finish strong. You've worked too hard making up for last year to blow it now. Go on," she urged. "If you get started now, you'll be done by supper."

"Yes, ma'am." His gaze slid to Malcolm. "I'll beat you again. This wasnae a one-off."

"You keep telling yourself that, lad."

"Scoot," Charlotte ordered.

They made a family. An odd one Afton was sure had a story behind it. But they so clearly clicked as a unit. It was both wonderful and weird, and made her feel, again, like an outsider.

"How about I go make some tea?" Charlotte suggested.

"That'd be great. Thanks, love." Malcolm dropped an easy kiss on her mouth and a playful swat to her butt that had Charlotte shooting him a half-perturbed, half-heated look before she left the room.

Malcolm crossed over to the table and began picking up the remains of the poker game.

Afton spotted the royal flush as he gathered his own hand. "You let him win."

One big shoulder lifted. "He needed a confidence boost, and as hard as he's been working in school, he deserves a little break this week from some of his chores. This way he thinks he earned it, so he'll accept it without argument." With a glance at her, he smiled again. "He's a decent study, but no' so quick as you were. You're much better at bluffing."

"What was it the lads used to call me? The Silent Shark?"

He huffed a laugh. "Sore losers, the lot of them."

She'd been so good, they'd banned her from coming to their monthly poker game because they'd been tired of losing. Those skills had stood her in good stead in Vegas, both enabling her to willingly choose who'd get the estate, and allowing her to take what money she'd had when she ran and turn it into enough to keep her afloat until she figured out what the hell she was doing with her life.

Malcolm finished putting the cards away, then they sat, him on the big, overstuffed sofa, her in one of the big comfortable chairs. Not that Afton could bring herself to relax into it. She perched on the edge, hands clasped together to keep from wringing them. Best to get out everything she needed to say.

"First off, I want to apologize for how I left. You deserved so much more than a hastily scribbled note."

He eased back in his seat, stretching one arm along the back of the couch. "I dinna blame you for leaving."

It was the last thing she'd expected him to say.

"You don't? But I left everything in your hands. I gambled the entire estate away."

"Aye. You did. To someone you knew would care and do right by the place and by me. You think I dinna realize you lost to him on purpose? It takes skill to be *that* spectacularly bad at poker."

Afton opened her mouth, then closed it again when she didn't know how to reply.

"It was an impossible situation. And it brought me Charlotte. But I was worried. You should have let me know you were okay."

Her shoulders rounded because she knew he spoke no more than the truth. "I... was afraid of talking to anybody from home. Afraid of letting anyone know where I was. And also afraid to find out what the fallout was in case things didn't work out like I hoped."

"Well, at least on that front, I can put you at ease. I wasnae sure about Raleigh to begin with, but he's a good man. Good at what he does. The crofters love him. He's invested in the land and the people in a way that makes him seem born to the role."

Another knot inside her loosened. "Good. That

was why I chose him. And he and Kyla?" Perhaps it wasn't fair to ask him, but she wanted at least a little insight before she confronted that particular personal demon.

"They work. They're happy."

"Truly?"

"Disgustingly so, a lot of the time." But his grimace held affection.

"And the baby?"

"Planned and wanted, no' an accident. Lily's a bonnie wee thing. We're all a little in love with her."

Afton exhaled, soaking in the weight of relief. This was a far better outcome than she'd imagined. It didn't automatically mean she'd be forgiven, but at least her own conscience would be clearer.

"I still need to talk to Raleigh. And especially to Kyla. I suppose Hamish will have to wait. He'll have gone back to Edinburgh already for work." And maybe that was for the best. Seeing him again hadn't been easy.

"No, he lives here now."

She blinked. "What?"

"You dinna know."

That ease evaporated. "Dinna know what?"

Malcolm leaned forward, bracing his forearms on his knees. "Hamish is divorced. He has primary custody of Freya. They moved back here in the summer."

"Oh." It was all she could manage because this was basically an atomic bomb. Hamish Colquhoun—the very off-limits Hamish Colquhoun—whom she'd been in love with for most of her life, was now single. And he was here in Glenlaig. She had no idea what to think or how to feel about that. But if he was no longer married…

Her mind took her back to the stone dance on the hill behind the village, where she'd fallen apart on him that last day, declaring that she had no one back at the engagement party she'd escaped from. She'd felt that loneliness down to her bones. And he'd told her it wasn't true. That he was there for her. Then he'd kissed her and lit up every nerve, every sensation she hadn't felt for Connor—had never felt for anyone—proving she wasn't broken.

They'd both known it was a mistake, though neither of them had said it out loud. He'd given her the knowledge she'd needed to get out, and she'd run rather than give either of them a chance to compound their sins.

And now he's free.

There was no guarantee. She knew nothing of the circumstances of his divorce. Had no idea if it was anything to do with her. He might feel nothing for her but the pity of that moment, and she might have been carrying this torch for no reason.

Charlotte came back with a tea tray, setting it

on the coffee table and passing out mugs. Afton was pitifully grateful to have something to do with her hands.

Malcolm settled back on the couch, Charlotte tucking in beside him. "What are your plans, lass?"

"Honestly, I dinna know. I had half a crazy idea when I got on the plane. Something I'd like to do here to stay. But it's a long shot."

"And what is that?"

Grateful to switch the topic off of Hamish, she wrapped her hands around the heat of the mug. "Well, I spent the last year and a half training as a chef."

Malcolm's eyes widened. "Really?"

"Aye. What I'd really like to do is open a farm-to-table restaurant. But that might be a pipe dream."

"Why would it be?"

"Well, apart from the expense, which isn't insignificant, after the way I left, I dinna know if the crofters would work with me on sourcing ingredients. I dinna even know how many of them are left. There's just a lot still hanging up in the air."

And now there was Hamish to think of. That half-cocked idea seemed at once more appealing and less, because she didn't know if she could be around him. She could hardly look at him yesterday without feeling things. Could she live in the same village as him and endure everything he brought up inside her? When she'd come up with the idea, it was with the notion that he wouldn't be here very often, and she wouldn't have to confront those feelings.

"Stop, lass." Malcolm's voice was matter-of-fact.

"Stop what?"

"Whatever's going through your head right now. The woman who left here wasnae a coward. Dinna start now."

That suggested he knew more or had been aware of more than she'd suspected. She hadn't thought anyone was aware of her feelings for Hamish. The idea that Malcolm had seen had heat rushing into her cheeks. She ducked her head and sipped at the tea, not knowing what to say.

"Well, regardless of your other plans, Charlotte and I are getting married in February. Will you still be here for that?"

Her gaze snapped up. "No matter what, I'll make certain I'm here for that. I'm so glad to see you happy."

"Excellent." Charlotte grinned. "I'll be sure to add you to the guest list."

Satisfied, Malcolm nodded. "The next order of business is to sort out what you want to do with your car."

Not following, Afton only stared at him. "My car?" Had she parked in the wrong place?

"You're driving a rental, I assume?"

"Aye."

"I've maintained your Volvo, for when you came back. It's no' an estate asset, so it disnae belong to Raleigh. Inspection's current and insurance is paid up. It's ready for you to take it back whenever."

"You... You maintained it all this time? Even after not hearing from me?"

"I had faith you'd be back."

The idea of that meant more to Afton than she could say. Not the car, although having at least one piece of returning home not be complicated was worth a lot. But simply that someone believed she'd *be* back. That she should come back. That he believed this could still be home for her.

"Thank you. That's..." She swallowed. "Just... thank you."

"We'll sort the details of getting your rental returned so you're not having to pay extra for it."

Charlotte patted his leg and rose. "Glad that's sorted. Afton, of course you'll stay for dinner."

Afton considered making excuses, but ultimately didn't bother. She understood that no matter her personal preferences—which were evenly split between staying and going—Charlotte belonged to the same school of Southern steamrollers as Rebecca Greyson. So she dug up her manners and put on a smile. "I'd be delighted to stay. Thank you for the invitation. Can I help?"

"I certainly won't say no to having an actual chef help out in my kitchen. Come on, sugar. Let's get to know each other." She disappeared in a swish of hips and a moment later, faint strains of salsa music spilled out from the kitchen.

Afton stared after where she disappeared through a doorway. "She's... a force to be reckoned with. In the best way."

Malcolm flashed a startling grin. "Aye. She is. I adore her."

"The feeling is mutual!" Charlotte hollered. "C'mon, sous chef. Time's a wastin'!"

Feeling a smile tug at the corners of her own lips, Afton rose. "Yes, Chef."

HAMISH EYED the energetic sixty-something woman across from him with what he hoped was a neutral expression, instead of the desperate hope bouncing in his chest. Aggie MacDougal was perfect as a nanny. She was a retired grandmother of three, who'd raised two kids by herself, had worked thirty years as a nurse, and enjoyed hill-walking and knitting. She had her own vehicle and a clean driving record. If she'd agree to preparing a few meals along the way, he was ready to call his search done.

"You've certainly got a lot of qualifications I appreciate. One other thing I'm looking for is someone who's willing to do some light cooking. It needn't be every day. But maybe dinner three days a week, with enough leftovers that we can just heat them up in the microwave on the off days. Do you cook?"

Aggie looked startled and instantly began shaking her head, silver curls bouncing with aggravation. "Oh, no. I'd never play fast and loose with the space-time continuum like that."

Hamish blinked. Surely he'd heard her wrong? "I beg your pardon?"

"By using the microwave." She pronounced it MEEK-roh-WAH-vay. Hadn't Nigella Lawson caught grief about that once?

"Uh—"

"And I wouldnae be consenting to be around the wiffy."

Hamish's beleaguered brain couldn't make sense of that one, so he cautiously asked, "You wouldn't?"

Her emphatic nod had the curls trembling with what seemed like righteous indignation. "A government conspiracy, it is. All those signals bouncing around, tryin' to get into our heads."

Wi-Fi. She means Wi-Fi.

He mentally crossed her off his list and resisted the urge to bang his own head against his desk. "I see. Well, I appreciate you coming in. But I have to be honest—I dinna think this is going to be a good fit."

"Oh, but I—"

He rose and circled around the desk, one hand extended to urge her up and herd her out of his office. "Thank you so much for your interest."

"Your Freya sounds like a darlin' girl."

"Oh, she is." As he stepped out of the office and continued to usher his latest failed nanny candidate toward the front door, his administrative assistant, Marsaili Fraser, glanced up. "Thanks so much for stopping by. Have a good week, Mrs. MacDougal."

The woman looked more confused than insulted, which he considered a win. She lived in the village, so the last thing he wanted to do was cause offense. But he wasn't putting his child in the care of a conspiracy theorist.

Once the door had shut behind her, Hamish simply dropped his head against the wood and sighed.

"That bad, aye?"

"I really thought she'd be the one."

"Isnae that the fourth or fifth one you've rejected?"

"Aye." Because a headache was brewing behind his eyes, he closed them. "I thought finding a nanny would be a lot easier than it is."

There'd been the germaphobe who wanted to require them both to wear masks at all times, even at home. Then the woman who'd proposed bubble-wrapping the corners of all the furniture, as if Freya were still a toddler. The one before Aggie apparently did taxidermy as a hobby and had brought a red squirrel dressed in a salsa outfit to the interview as an example, with an enthusiastic proposal that she could teach Freya all about it.

"It'll just take time, is all," Marsaili said.

Time was a commodity he didn't have.

"How long until my next appointment?"

"About half an hour."

"Okay. Hold my calls unless it's an emergency with Freya or news about my Gran. I'm going to eat some lunch in my office while I review the file."

"Right-o."

Bless Marsaili. She, at least, had been a jewel of a find. A recent empty-nester, she'd been desperate to get out of the house and do something now that her four boys were off to uni. Turned out, she was magnificent at organization. She was the only reason he wasn't horrendously behind professionally. He probably ought to turn the nanny search over to her, but that felt like another parental failure, and Hamish couldn't take any more.

He settled at his desk and pulled out the pathetic haul that constituted his midday meal. A tin of tuna, a slightly withered apple, and a protein bar. Freya had gotten the last proper sandwich in her lunch today. Knowing they were getting down to the dregs, he took the time to put together an online grocery order with the local market. He'd grab it on the way home, so they'd at least have something and wouldn't have to hit up the pub for another night.

By the time he was done with the order and the food, he still hadn't managed to cobble together any attention to review his client file. It was a property dispute between some cousins over the ownership of their grandfather's prize ram. He wasn't being asked to mediate, but he wanted to convince his client that taking this matter to court would be a waste of a judge's time. He also wondered if he could talk Duncan into taking on the goats. That would require more delicacy than he felt capable of at this moment.

He was tired and distracted. More, he was thinking of Afton.

He hadn't seen her. Not since the wedding. But he'd heard plenty. As she'd predicted, the reception had been rife with talk and speculation, because her return absolutely was the biggest gossip to hit town since Connor and Sophie's engagement broke. The fake one that had led to the real one a few months later. Not that the general public was aware of the fake one to begin with. Everyone wanted to know why she was back. Where she'd been. What she'd been doing.

No one had answers, least of all him. Monday she'd taken a room at one of the local B and B's for the week. Everyone was buzzing, and he'd tried not to pay much attention. Or, at least, tried not to *look* like he was paying attention. But he was desperate for news of her.

Would she come see him? Did he want her to?

Of course he did. He cared about her. They'd been friends once. Not that he could call what he felt for her friendly these days. Which mattered not one whit. His life was a mess, and the last thing she needed was to get dragged into the middle of it because he had some fantasy about who they could be together, without all the other life complications in the way.

The marriage pact had been resolved, and he was divorced, but there were still a million things standing between him and her and even the hint of something more. If she was even interested. Yes, she'd kissed him back. But maybe that heat had been the desperation of the moment. He hadn't been able to shake the idea that he owed her an apology, because he felt as if that kiss had been what pushed her over the edge into running.

It had certainly been what pushed him to take a hard look at his marriage, even before Dayna's affair had surfaced.

He probably owed her a thank you for that.

But that was it. He just needed to see her to assure himself she was okay. That she was happy and healthy. He'd give his apology. Get some closure. They'd both move on with their lives.

But before he could think about even that, he had to find a bloody nanny. Sooner rather than later. He'd spoken to his parents. They'd be gone for the long haul. At least a couple of months. Maybe longer. He absolutely had to have some help, much as it galled him to admit it.

At the knock on the door, he glanced at the clock. His appointment was early. "Yes?"

Marsaili stuck her head inside. "You have a visitor."

But it wasn't Duncan McTavish. It was the very object of his thoughts.

"Afton. Come in."

When she'd stepped into the office, his assistant shut the door. "Hi."

"Hello." Hamish drank her in. She wore the same navy coat she'd had on at the wedding this weekend. Her cheeks were flushed with cold, and that corn-silk hair was pulled back into a thick braid. She looked a bit more relaxed than she had at the wedding. And God, he hoped she knew she could be herself with him.

Her hands twisted the leather strap of her purse. "I know you have work just now. Mrs. Fraser said you've only got five minutes. I wanted to set up a time to come talk to you."

He swallowed and hoped it wasn't too obvious. "For personal or professional reasons?"

"Personal."

Well, didn't his brain go down a rabbit hole of possibilities with that answer?

"I've got time after work, if you want to come by the house."

"I heard you'd bought a place here. I was sorry to hear about your divorce."

Was she really? He didn't know what to think about this careful neutrality. Maybe she was worried about being overheard. Not an unreasonable fear, though Marsaili was considerably more discrete about gossip than many others in the village.

"Come on by after five. We'll have time to talk before Freya gets dropped off at six."

He gave her the address, and she nodded, backing toward the door. Already retreating on every level. Every cell in his body urged him to stop her. To push for that personal conversation right now. To pull her into his arms and never let go. His hands flexed with the need to touch her, but he stayed right where he was.

Then she paused, one hand on the knob, and looked back.

His heart gave a hard knock against his breastbone as she met his gaze. "It's good to see you, Hamish."

Did that mean what he wanted it to mean? That she remembered that kiss every bit as vividly as he did? That she wanted more?

Before he could follow up, she'd opened the door, and he could already hear the booming voice of Duncan McTavish in the waiting room, so he had to lock it all away and get back to the job at hand.

But he'd see her tonight and maybe... just maybe, he'd get some of the answers he craved.

FIVE

Nerves danced in Afton's belly as she pulled up to Hamish's house. That was nothing new. She'd been one big ball of anxiety since she'd gotten on the plane, worried about facing everyone again. Things with Connor and Malcolm had worked out, but she still hadn't gotten up the courage to speak to Kyla or Raleigh. She'd told herself she was saving the worst for last, in case it went terribly, so she could get out of town in a hurry.

But facing Hamish wasn't going to be easier.

Oh, she wasn't worried so much about him being angry that she'd left. He was the one who'd told her about the loophole, after all. He had to have known there was a strong possibility she'd take it. She'd even considered that he might've been relieved she wouldn't be around to remind him of their... indiscretion—AKA the kiss that had been on replay in her brain for the past twenty months. He hadn't called it a mistake outright in the moment, but she'd seen it in his face. As a man of honor, she knew the slip had plagued him.

It had plagued her, too, for entirely different reasons.

Once she'd left Vegas, no longer the Baroness of Lochmara, she'd been free to pursue anyone she wanted. To date. To fall in love for real. And, in the end, she hadn't been able to do it. There'd been a few guys. A few dinners and movies. A handful of kisses that had left her feeling... nothing, except that something was missing. Once it became clear she wasn't emotionally available, the follow-up dates hadn't happened. Eventually, she'd stopped saying yes because none of them were Hamish. What had likely been a spur-of-the-moment urge for him had burrowed under her skin, into her brain, her heart, to combine with the white knight syndrome she'd been nursing for him for years. There'd been no moving on from it. From him.

So she'd made a decision on the flight. While here to make amends to everyone else, she'd come back to confess her feelings for Hamish. Not with any expectation that they'd be reciprocated, but she thought acknowledging them might take their power over her away. That she might finally get closure. To get on with her life, whatever that looked like.

And then Malcolm had dropped the bomb that Hamish was divorced.

For the first time in her life, they were both single, and now she needed to know if that kiss had been a mere impulse or if there really was something between them. Something that could be pursued.

Afton hadn't let herself go too far down that path. She knew the danger of hope, the pain of the fall when things didn't work out. There was no realistic scenario where she walked into this house and Hamish took her into his arms to pick up where they'd left off at the stone dance all those months ago. Her life had effectively murdered whatever latent romanticism she possessed, and she just wasn't that kind of lucky. More than likely, this whole conversation would be awkward as hell, and she'd be left with plenty more fodder for therapy when she settled somewhere long enough to get back into it.

Blowing out a long breath, she approached what she thought was the front door and knocked. The house itself was something of a hodgepodge. She couldn't tell much about it in the dark, but it was obvious it was old and had been added onto several times, without a lot of thought given to the overall architectural cohesion. Under other circumstances, she'd be dying for a better look around. Having grown up on an estate that was several hundred years old, she appreciated the character and quirks of old houses.

Hamish pulled open the door. The light spilling out behind him limned his thick, dark brown hair in a halo, but she didn't have a clear view of his face. He'd shed the suit jacket and tie he'd worn in his office earlier and loosened the collar of his button-down shirt. "You're here."

"I am."

He stepped back to let her inside. She couldn't stop herself from looking around, noting the various stages of renovation happening. Lumber, paint, and other supplies were neatly stacked along one wall. Strips of a truly heinous red-orange patterned wallpaper clung to multiple places in the entryway.

"Have you tried a spray of fabric softener on the wallpaper?"

"I feel like I've tried everything short of a blowtorch. I think they must've used industrial cement to attach it. C'mon."

Afton followed him back to the kitchen. This room was more complete, with old cabinets painted a crisp white, updated hardware, and butcher block countertops. The walls were a misty blue gray that reminded her of early morning fog over the loch for which her ancestral estate had been named. A table with room for six sat in front of the darkened windows of a sunroom that spanned the back of the house.

"Want a drink?" Hamish asked.

"Sure."

Instead of moving to put on the kettle as she'd expected, he crossed to a cabinet, opening the doors to reveal a small bar. He tipped the whisky into a pair of low-ball glasses.

Well, she wouldn't say no to that. Maybe it would help settle her nerves. She slipped off her coat and draped it over the back of one of the kitchen chairs.

As he handed her the glass, she noted the fresh lines around his bright blue eyes and the scruff of five o'clock shadow along his jaw. He looked exhausted, a kind of soul-weary she understood. She wanted to ease the strain.

Instead, she sipped, arching a brow as the familiar sweet, smoky taste hit her tongue. "Laphroaig. My favorite."

"I know."

Did it mean something that he had it on hand? Perhaps just that he enjoyed good whisky as much as she did.

When he didn't invite her to sit, only watched

her with that assessing gaze, she elected to dive right in. "I want to apologize for how I left." That wasn't precisely it, but it was how she'd started with everyone else.

Hamish shook his head. "Not necessary. Better than anyone else, I understand why you left, and even why you left the way you did, without saying goodbye. But staying gone this long? Not saying a word? Not letting anybody know where you were?" Again with the head shake. "You basically dropped off the face of the earth, and we were worried. The only reason we knew you weren't dead in a ditch somewhere is because Raleigh showed up, and he'd seen you, healthy and whole."

Embarrassed again, she dropped her gaze to her drink. "I didn't know how to face anybody. I made the selfish choice to run, knowing I'd be upending everybody's life. Honestly, I was afraid of the conse-quences. You told me what might happen, and I was terrified of the worst. That Lochmara and Ardinmuir would both be lost. I didn't think anyone would want to hear from me after all that. Honestly, the only reason I felt I could come back now was because I saw the announcement about Connor and Sophie's wedding on the village Facebook page and that the reception was at Ardinmuir. That felt like proof that at least the absolute worst hadn't come to pass. And I thought, maybe, enough time had passed that people would listen, if not welcome me back."

Some of the tension bled out of his face, and those eyes softened. "You were missed, Afton. If it looks like everyone moved on without you, it's only because you didn't leave us any choice. But for what it's worth, I'm glad to see you. You look good. Happy."

That wrung a little smile from her. "I've spent a lot of time figuring my life out since I left. Thinking about what I wanted, without the lens of duty." She hesitated, knowing she needed to begin steering the conversation. "I was sorry to hear about you and Dayna."

Whatever softness she'd seen in his expression evaporated. "I'm not."

That immediate declaration gave her a dangerous hope. This was not a man still grieving the loss of his marriage. "You're not?"

His shoulders twitched. "Dayna and I weren't right for each other. We'd been having problems for a while. She just chose the nuclear option."

"The divorce was her idea?"

"No. The affair was her idea. The divorce was mine."

An affair. Then the divorce hadn't somehow been because of her. Because of that kiss. "She cheated on you?"

"Aye. With David."

Afton sputtered. "David Murray? Kyla's David?"

"Well, he wasn't Kyla's David by then, but aye."

The idea of it had her rocking back on her heels in shock. Never in a hundred years would she have imagined that scenario. "I am so sorry. That's... just... wow."

"Aye. So Freya and I came back here, which is where I've wanted to be all along."

"How's Freya doing with all of this? It has to be a huge change for her."

Hamish sipped at his own whisky. "As well as can be expected. Her mother has elected to opt out of motherhood. She didn't fight at all for custody and has been... apathetic on their visits since."

Temper sparked. "What the bloody hell is wrong with her? Freya's a wonderful kid. She deserves better."

Something shifted in his face. "She does. I'm working on it."

Wanting to navigate him away from this landmine, she leaned back against the counter. "So you've opened a law office in the village? No more corporate law?"

"I've still got my hand in. My old firm in Edinburgh asks for consults from time to time. But family law is the way of things here. It's a different kind of challenge. One I'm sure I'll appreciate once everything else settles down. But it's been a struggle to get that sorted on top of renovating the house and figuring out the single-parent thing."

"If anyone can do it, you can." Hamish Colquhoun was the poster boy for competence in all things.

"I'm glad one of us has some faith in that."

It was odd seeing a chink in his armor. He'd always been so very capable. Afton had a feeling he'd let very few people see that he was struggling, and she wondered what that said about his opinion of her.

Quit dawdling and get to the point of why you came.

He drained the last of his whisky and set the glass down. "Listen, you aren't the only one who wants to make an apology."

Her fingers tightened on her own glass. "Oh?"

With uncharacteristic agitation, he ran both hands through his hair. "I feel like I was probably a significant contributing factor to your decision to run. Not just in telling you about the loophole, but because of that kiss."

Afton's pulse began to drum. Now or never. "Yes. And no."

Her answer gave him pause. "Explain."

She tipped back the last swallow of Laphroaig

and prepared to bare her soul. "Connor's response to being caught in an arranged marriage all those years was to sow his oats far and wide while he could. Mine was to do the opposite. I didn't see the sense in getting involved with someone I couldn't be with long term. And because I also had feelings for someone that I could never act on, even if I wasn't bound by the marriage pact."

Needing something to do with her hands, she rolled the empty glass between her fingers, staring at a spot of what she thought was paint on the flagstone floor. "As mortifying as it is for me to admit this, I left after the kiss because I couldn't stay here, knowing what that was like and knowing that I could never be with you. For better or worse, it's always been you for me." At his silence, she raised her gaze to check his face, unable to read the careful neutrality there. The lack of reaction made her feel vaguely ill, but she'd say all of it. "That's not why I came back. I had no idea you were divorced. But as you are, I need to know if that's something that could ever be a possibility. Because, if not, I need to move on with my world."

Hamish did not suddenly become the hero of a romance, sweeping her into his arms and proving that her memory of his kiss was dim compared to the real thing. In fact, he looked pained by her admission.

This was a terrible, terrible idea.

When he took too long to answer, she began backpedaling to save whatever face she could. "I'm not asking for anything here. You clearly have a lot on your plate. I just needed to tell you, for my own peace of mind and closure." Now she'd done that, and it was time to make her escape before she died of complete humiliation. She set her glass on the table and reached for her coat.

"Afton." Her name on his lips sounded like a plea or an apology. That one word was enough to make her want to turn tail and run. But he closed the distance between them, finally touching her. His fingers against her cheek were feather soft, and she thought he might give in and kiss her. God, she wanted him to. Wanted more than this bare caress. But his eyes... His eyes were devastated.

"It's not that I dinna have feelings for you, because I always have. That was a big part of the problem in my marriage. But my life is a train wreck right now. I'm barely scraping by, and everything I have has to go to Freya. I have to focus on her because she has no one else. I mean, she has my parents and friends, but she doesn't have her mother." His fingers flexed against her cheek, and she leaned reflexively into the touch, soaking up the traces of his heat as his gaze bored into hers. "You deserve someone who will put you first, for once. You've always deserved that. I canna be that guy. No matter how much I wish I could."

Oh God. This was worse than an outright rejection. Because he'd just admitted he reciprocated her feelings for him. He just couldn't follow up. The double-edged blade of hope dug into her chest, carving out a hole where her heart used to be. But she didn't weep. She'd given him her tears once. She wouldn't do it again.

"Okay." She swallowed hard, lest she give in to the urge to beg him to change his mind. "That's fair."

His eyes searched her face. "I'm sorry." It helped, a little, that he looked miserable.

"No. Freya is a wonderful kid. And she's lucky to have you as a father." It took everything she had to step back, away from his touch. "I should go."

Hamish dropped his hand, something like panic flickering over his features. "Where?" Then that damnable neutrality was back. "What's next for you?"

Afton scooped up her coat. "Well, I have to find a job. I had thought originally to do that here. Under the circumstances, it might be better if I go further afield." She wouldn't stick around pining for something that could never be.

A door banged shut somewhere.

"Da! Are you home?"

Without taking his eyes off her, he called back to his daughter. "In the kitchen."

Freya came clattering into the room, dumping her backpack in a corner. "Whose car is out front? Oh, hi, Afton."

"Hello."

If the girl registered the tension lingering in the room, she didn't show it. "Da, I'm supposed to bring a dish for the class party tomorrow."

Hamish's gaze snapped to her. "You what?"

"I signed up weeks ago and forgot about it. Sorry."

They all glanced at the clock. It was after six. The market was closed.

Hamish shut his eyes and swore under his breath. "Bollocks. I forgot to pick up the grocery order."

Afton could see the fresh weight that had just landed on his shoulders. She understood it wasn't about the food or the party. This was just one more thing on top of a mountain of others he was carrying on his own, and he was right at the edge of losing it.

Though she wanted to run and lick her wounds in peace, she set her coat back down. "I can help."

He sighed. "This is not your problem."

She laid a hand on his arm, hoping to communicate her sincerity. "Hamish, you're my friend. Let me help with this."

"I dinna even know what we have in the house."

She jerked her shoulders in a shrug. "I'm a chef. I'll figure it out."

His head snapped toward her. "You're a chef?"

"Aye. That's what I've been training to do since I left." And in a kitchen she could find some of the control that had slipped through her fingers.

"FREYA, wash your hands. You're going to be my sous chef." Afton began rolling up her sleeves.

"What's a sous chef?"

"It's like an assistant chef. Do you like to cook?"

"I dinna really know how. Not beyond, like, scrambled eggs or toast."

"Then you'll learn something. Let's see what we've got to work with." Afton opened the fridge door and peered inside.

Freya dutifully went to the sink.

Hamish stood where he was, reeling.

All this time, Afton had carried some sort of torch for him, as he had for her. God, what would he have done with that information if he'd had it sooner? Before his life had gone entirely off the rails? Probably nothing. Or, perhaps he'd have pursued divorce himself sooner, which would've put him squarely back where he was now. Wanting her and knowing she deserved a thousand times better.

Across the room, she was opening his freezer and pantry and pulling out ingredients he didn't even remember buying, casually chatting with his daughter as if he hadn't just shot down the prospect of there being a them in no uncertain terms and for her own good.

He felt like the world's biggest bawbag.

How could she be this good? That she'd stick around to help him with this thing that had nothing to do with her when certainly she'd rather run. He knew her well enough to recognize the look. He'd hurt her. He knew it. Hell, he'd hurt himself in the process. But he'd meant what he'd told her. Everything he had needed to go to Freya. There just wasn't enough of him to go around anymore, and after everything she'd been through, she was entitled to so much more than the leftover scraps.

"Have you eaten?" Afton's soft voice pulled his attention back to the action on the other side of the room.

"No." Freya shot him a cautious look. "Are we going to the pub again?"

"Unless your father has objections, I think we can take care of that as well."

"He doesn't object," Freya said quickly.

They both glanced his way, and he managed a

go-ahead wave. There wasn't a chance in hell he was up to being in public tonight. Not with everything Afton had said roiling around in his head.

"Are there any limitations on what you're to bring to school?"

"No. I didn't sign up for any particular kind of food. Desserts are always popular."

"Then I think we'll go for some jam bars."

"We don't have any jam."

"Ah, but you do have frozen blueberries. So we can make jam."

"We can *make* jam?"

Afton laughed. "Of course. What did you think the stuff in jars was made of?"

She switched on the oven, setting it to heat, before tasking Freya to dig out some mixing bowls and some pots. At the island, she began organizing ingredients into two piles, one for the dessert and one, presumably, for whatever she'd decided to make for dinner.

"Why are you getting everything out at once?"

"So we know that we have all the ingredients. You lay them out like this, in the order you need them for your recipe. It's called *mis en place.* That's French for 'everything in its place.' That way, you'll find out if something's missing before you're in the middle of things."

Freya frowned. "But we dinna have a recipe."

"We do. It's just up here." With a smile, Afton tapped her temple. "Now, I want you to add those blueberries into that saucepan. Just pour until I say when."

Hamish watched, fascinated, as she waded in, not only coming up with some sort of recipe out of the dregs of his cupboards, but patiently instructing his daughter in a way that Freya was clearly enjoying. She didn't get enough positive adult female attention and adored any time she got to spend with Kyla, Sophie, or Charlotte. It was obvious by the delighted grin she was soaking up every moment of this interaction. For her part, Afton had taken complete control. That competence, when he'd felt so out of his depth, was damned sexy. But so was this caretaking side.

She didn't have to do this. But here she was, saving his arse. He couldn't have been more grateful in that moment.

Rousing himself from his shocked stupor, Hamish crossed to the island. "What can I do?"

"Do you have a stand mixer?"

"Um. No. There's a hand mixer, I think." He hunted around until he found where his mum had stuck the thing. "Will this do?"

"Aye, we'll make it work." She split her attention between giving them both instructions for the jam bars, while she diced bacon for something else.

For the next twenty minutes, the three of them danced around each other, each preparing a component according to Afton's instructions. By the time the jam bars went into the oven, the kitchen looked a little as if a bomb had gone off. He was reasonably sure they'd managed to use seventy-five percent of the kitchen gear he owned. But somehow, it didn't feel like chaos. Not with his daughter grinning and Afton already making order of things in that quiet way she had.

God, how had he forgotten how soothing he found her presence? She'd always been a quiet lake to his wife's tempestuous waves. Once, he'd mistaken the latter for passion, but he'd had enough of the contention that went along with it.

Afton nudged Freya. "Pop all those into the sink and start the washing up while I finish dinner. It'll just be another few minutes."

When his daughter went without moaning and complaining, he was half tempted to check whether she'd been body snatched. He began clearing dishes himself as Afton moved with calm efficiency at the stove, doing something with pasta.

"You wash, I'll dry?" he suggested.

Freya dove her hands into the soapy water and began to scrub.

They'd made it about half through the pile when Afton began plating the meal, artfully twisting spaghetti on a plate and adding the rendered bacon for garnish before hitting everything with grated Parmesan cheese.

Hamish stared. "You made carbonara. From scratch."

"It's a very simple dish."

"It's one of my favorites."

Her gaze caught his and snagged. "I know." She lifted all three plates, balancing them with a skill he hadn't expected, and carried them to the table.

He and Freya exchanged wide-eyed looks. She grabbed forks from a drawer, and he snagged napkins. They settled in. Freya rubbed both hands together, staring at the pasta with an avaricious gleam in her eyes that he could find no fault with.

"This looks absolutely brilliant."

"Seconded," he added.

Afton just smiled and twirled pasta on her fork.

Freya stabbed hers with great enthusiasm, lifting a massive bite and shoving it into her mouth so that the ends trailed down her chin. Before he could remind her of her manners, she groaned in ecstasy, slurping the noodles up with a noise that would absolutely have gotten her grounded by Dayna.

"This is the best thing I have ever eaten."

"Thank you. You've got a little... on your chin." Afton gestured toward her face.

Freya's tongue darted out to lick the sauce.

Hamish winced a little. "Freya, love. Table manners, please."

"Right. Right. Try it, Da."

He did as she encouraged, closing his eyes as the rich, creamy sauce melted on his tongue. Oh God. This was... perfection. It took all his remaining control not to let out a moan of satisfaction.

"That's it," Freya announced. "You should totally be the nanny."

Hamish's eyes popped open.

Afton just cocked her head. "The what now?"

"No, love, that's not what Afton's here for."

"But it makes so much sense," Freya insisted. "She needs a job, right? At least until she finds work as a chef. And it's just a temporary gig until Nan and Grandda get back."

"Get back from where? Is something going on with your parents?"

"With them, no. My gran broke a hip. She's all right, but they're both in Glasgow, helping with her recovery, which means they aren't here and able to help out with things. So I've been looking for a nanny."

"You'd be perfect," Freya continued. "We like each other. You cook like an angel. It makes so much sense."

Before Hamish could find a way to curb his

daughter's enthusiasm, Afton admitted, "I dinna actually have plans right now. I promised Malcolm and Charlotte that I'd be here for the wedding, and it'll take some time to find a position in my field. At the very least, I can help you out while you look for someone else."

The refusal was automatic. "That's not necessary."

"But Da, we need the help"

Afton just pinned him with that quiet gaze.

This was an absolutely terrible idea. Continuing to be around her when he'd outright declared that they couldn't be together? He had no idea how he was going to endure that.

"You're absurdly overqualified. This isnae what you want to do."

"I've done a lot of things in my life that I haven't specifically been trained for. I can easily help run her to and fro. Prepare meals. Whatever's needed. It'll take a little bit off your shoulders, so you can finish some of the things that need finishing, because there aren't enough hours in the day. It could take months for me to find a chef position. I'd like to be able to spend some time here at home in Glenlaig before I do that. And the opportunity to earn a little bit in the meantime, whatever it is, wouldn't be the worst thing in the world."

It might be for him. To be faced with the temptation of her on a near daily basis.

Freya folded her hands in prayer position and gave him the patented begging face he'd struggled to harden himself against over her lifetime. "Please, please, please, Da?"

Like the Grinch's plot against the Whos in Freya's favorite Christmas movie, this was a wonderful, awful idea. But what was the alternative? Continue to muck about with no help and lose his mind? And Afton had already more or less said that she'd be leaving Glenlaig. Maybe for good this time. The truth was, even if he couldn't have her, he wasn't ready to watch her walk away again. And clearly his kid liked her, and she liked his kid.

"Well, I guess I can draw up a contract for a month or two. And we can revisit that as needed." Perhaps the idea of a contract between friends sounded extreme, but if he formalized the arrangement where she was the nanny and he was her boss, that would make her inherently hands off. He'd need all the help he could get to maintain his boundaries.

"Fair enough," Afton agreed. "If that's what you need to do."

"And I completely understand that you'll continue looking for work in your field. If you find something else before the end of the contract, I completely understand."

"Okay. I'm happy to start tomorrow. Just tell me where I need to be and when."

Freya did a fist pump, then offered her hand for a high-five, which Afton returned with a grin.

With an air of surreality, Hamish arranged for her to start the next afternoon. "I'll bring the contract home."

"Okay."

The oven timer buzzed, and she rose to pull the blueberry jam bars out. Freya leapt up and bent over the pan, inhaling and groaning with pleasure. "Those smell wonderful."

"And they're molten just now. They'll need to cool quite some time before they can be cut. But once they're cool, they can be sliced into as many pieces as needed and loaded into a container for travel. Just put a piece of parchment paper or a paper towel between each layer."

She moved toward the remaining dishes in the sink.

"We'll get those," Hamish said. "You've definitely done enough for tonight. Thank you."

This time, when she picked up her coat, he didn't stop her.

"See you tomorrow, Afton!" Freya chirped.

"See you tomorrow."

Hamish walked her to the door. "Are you really okay with this? If you're not, I can make Freya understand."

Annoyance flickered over her face. "I'm not going to do a damned thing to disappoint that child."

"That's not what I meant. It's just... After the conversation we had earlier, I thought it might be too hard on you to be here."

She shrugged into her coat and huffed a breath as she tugged all that silky hair out of the collar. "Hamish, how long have we known each other?"

"Something like twenty-five years."

"Right. I know you." She laid a hand on his arm, and he felt it down to his marrow. "You dinna want anybody to know, but you're drowning right now. I know something about that. When it was me, you're the one who threw me a life preserver. Let me return the favor for a little while. It's the least I can do."

He had no idea what to say to that.

With a little squeeze of his arm, she stepped back. "I'll see you tomorrow."

Hamish watched her go, understanding that, for better or worse, she was going to be a regular part of his life for the foreseeable future.

He just had to find a way to survive it.

SIX

There was no more putting it off. With this short-term gig of being Freya's nanny, Afton had to sort things out with Kyla and Raleigh. She'd given herself the night to process everything that had happened with Hamish. Or hadn't happened. And maybe she'd considered, too, how hard this whole setup would be. Seeing him every day, knowing he felt something for her, that apparently he always had, and he just didn't feel as if he could act on it.

In the dark of her bed last night, she'd considered trying to talk him around, convincing him that scraps from him were better than everything from anyone else. But she hated how desperate that made her sound. And he was probably right. In the long-term, she wouldn't be satisfied with so little. So she'd do this thing. Help him out. And if a part of her was going into the arrangement hoping that she could alleviate some of the stress in his life so he might reevaluate his stance? Well, she was only human. If he didn't, at least she'd have made a hard transition for Hamish and his daughter a little bit easier.

Afton hesitated at the kitchen door of the manor house at Lochmara. It felt beyond strange to be knocking on her own door. Perhaps she should've used the front and made this completely formal. But that seemed the wrong tone to take with someone who'd once been a good friend. Given what she'd done to Kyla, coming to the friends and family entrance of the house might be a mistake, too. But she was here now. Best to get this over with.

Bracing herself, she knocked and waited, arms wrapped around herself against the cold. The sun would set soon, and the lowering gray sky suggested more snow was on the way.

The door swung open, and Kyla stood there, dressed in yoga pants, with a cardigan belted at her waist, red hair bundled into a messy tail trailing over one shoulder. "Afton."

"Are you busy? May I come in?"

"I can certainly take the time for a cuppa."

Afton stepped into her old house for the first

time and looked around. The kitchen was so much the same, though there was evidence of Lily's presence in the highchair at the end of the table and the array of other baby paraphernalia scattered about.

Kyla crossed to the counter and filled the electric kettle. "Your timing is good. Lily's down for a nap."

Thank God she hadn't elected to ring the bell. "I wasn't sure if you'd be here. What your work schedule would be."

"Since the baby came, I've been spending a fair amount of time working from my home office."

Afton absorbed the stab of that. Home. This house was a home again. But not hers. Because she'd given it all up in exchange for her freedom.

Breathing through the hurt, she slowly unbuttoned her coat. "You and Sophie were able to make a go of the event planning business?"

"We have. It was touch and go there for a while, but we finally hit our stride. Ciara—you remember our cousin?—joined us as an intern when she finished uni, and we're going to be able to take her to full-time at the first of the year."

"That's wonderful." Unsure what else to say, Afton curled her hands around the back of a chair and prayed for strength.

Kyla let the silence ride. Afton couldn't read her mood and was sure that was deliberate. There'd been a reserve when she'd seen Kyla after the wedding. It was no less than she'd expected.

"Where's Raleigh?"

"Oh, out and about somewhere on the estate. Feeding stock this time of day." Kyla brought two mugs to the table and pulled out a chair. "Sit and tell me what brings you by."

Afton took the seat across from her and gratefully wrapped her hands around the warm mug. *The only way out is through.* "I'm sure you know I'm here to apologize. I admit I saved you for last because I figured this was going to be the hardest, because you were the one I hurt the most. That was never my intention. I just... I felt so trapped, and I couldn't go through with it. I know that my selfishness completely changed the course of your life. I know exactly what that feels like, and I wouldn't have wished that on my worst enemy. Certainly not on someone who used to be a dear friend. And I know that there is no amount of I'm sorry I can say that will make up for that. But I have to say it, anyway. I am truly sorry for all the grief and pain I caused you."

Kyla settled back with her mug, fingers tapping against the ceramic. "When I found out what you'd done—that you left—I was livid. Absolutely furious and ready to send out the authorities to have you brought back in handcuffs just to make sure that you walked down that aisle rather than risk losing my home. Then Hamish showed up to tell us you'd gambled the estate away. That the new owner was male. And suddenly I was the one on the chopping block." She shook her head. "I have never been more terrified in my entire life. You and Connor were being forced into something that you didn't want. But at least you knew each other. You were friends. I was being expected to marry a complete stranger. Someone who himself did not know about what he was getting into. And I had no way of knowing whether he'd be willing to even entertain the idea or not."

Afton winced. She'd considered all of this since she left. And it had been a big part of why she'd stayed away.

"So yes, I was angry. But I also understood, in a way I never had before, exactly what it was you and my brother were being asked to do. What everyone —including me—expected of you. And it wasn't fair of any of us. Oh, we all gave lip service to the idea that it was awful, and obviously we tried to find a way out of it. But none of us got it. Not really. I was so myopically focused on saving Ardinmuir, no matter the cost, that I really never gave thought to what it meant. And I owe *you* an apology for that."

It was a concession Afton hadn't expected, and it meant more than she could say. Swallowing through the thickness in her throat, she tried to smile. "Thank you for that. I dinna think anyone but Hamish has ever truly acknowledged what it meant to be caught up in this antiquated betrothal."

Kyla's blue eyes widened slightly. "Hamish?"

Projecting a more casual air than she felt, Afton shrugged and lifted her mug. "We talked about it a lot over the years."

"That's why he told you about the loophole."

"He told you?"

"Not at first. There was a hospital bed confession."

Alarm shot through Afton. How much *had* she missed? "Hospital bed? Whose?"

"Mine. I was in a car crash. Hurt my shoulder. It was a thing, and he was feeling guilty. I'm fine now."

Before she could think of a response to that, a disembodied cry sounded from a nearby baby monitor.

"Herself has awakened. Be right back."

Alone for a few moments, Afton gripped the mug. This was all going so much better than she'd imagined. She couldn't help but continue to brace herself, waiting for the other shoe to drop.

A few minutes later, Kyla returned, the baby tucked in her arms. There was a softness in her expression as she settled back in her chair with her daughter in her lap. Lily fastened a wide-eyed, golden-brown gaze on Afton and burbled.

"She has Raleigh's eyes." They were unmistakable, though the peaches and cream complexion and strawberry blonde hair were all her mother.

With a smile in her voice, Kyla agreed. "She does. This is our Lily. Say hello, love."

Lily waved both chubby fists.

"She always wakes up hungry. Do you mind if I feed her?"

"Of course not."

Kyla shifted aside her shirt and sweater so the baby could nurse.

Afton tried not to stare, not because she had any issue with breastfeeding, but because seeing her friend as a new mother was absolutely jarring. "I confess, I didn't expect to come back to find this. At best, I thought you'd be freshly divorced, as you didn't have the objections to that concept that your brother does."

"That was the original plan. Raleigh and I were meant to have a marriage of convenience, just long enough to satisfy the pact. And then... well, Raleigh is Raleigh. He's one of the best men I know. We became very good friends. And then we became more. He saved me from making a terrible mistake with David. And we decided we wanted to make a real go of things. He's the absolute love of my life. So how can I stay angry with you for taking such a reckless path when it brought me my heart?"

Afton's throat tightened again. "He was lucky number seven."

"What?"

She swallowed more tea to ease the constriction. "He was the seventh I approached. I didn't just gamble the estate away with no thought to who would take it over. It's not a fluke that he's the one who's here. Admittedly, I chose him more for Lochmara than you, but I also hoped he would be someone who you'd at least to be able to be friends with until you sorted out a divorce. I spent days evaluating people, trying to find someone I thought was going to do their best by the estate and the people I was leaving behind. When I found out how he'd been screwed out of his family heritage, heard him talk about his respect for legacy and duty, it reminded me so much of you, and I knew he was the right person to send. So I deliberately lost to him."

"I wondered about that, after."

Afton twisted in her chair to find the man himself strolling through another door. Ambling over, he kissed his wife and ran a soft knuckle against his daughter's downy head. His look of love was so bright, Afton nearly had to look away.

"I owe you an apology, too, for not telling you what you were getting into."

He straightened. "A marriage with the love of my life? I wouldn't have believed you. Sure, I was mad in the moment. But everything worked out. None of us are still upset with you. Put yourself at ease and enjoy coming home."

She couldn't stop herself from closing her eyes as the blade struck again.

Kyla's voice was soft. "This has to be really weird for you."

"Honestly? Yes. I didn't know how I would ultimately feel about giving all of it up. And it's weird being back here, knowing it's not mine. But it's in the right hands." She shifted her focus back to Raleigh. "I meant what I said to you in Vegas. I never wanted all the pressure of duty. It's clear that everything is thriving under your leadership. So I'm glad it's yours. And I cannot begin to say how thrilled I am that this actually worked out for everyone. It's not what would have happened if I'd married Connor."

He snagged a beer from the fridge and sat down beside his wife. "It seems everything worked out for the best for everybody here. But what about you? Are you just passin' through, or are you really comin' home?"

"I'm... testing the waters, I suppose."

"What do you want to do?" Kyla asked.

"I spent my time away training as a chef. What I'd really like to do is open a farm-to-table restaurant here in Glenlaig."

Raleigh flashed a blinding grin. "I love that."

"So do I, but I'm not at all sure that the crofters here would be willing to work with me for sourcing ingredients. I dinna even know whether there's somewhere in the village that would suit for location, if the costs would work out. But none of the rest of it is worth researching if I canna get the crofters on board."

"I can help with that," Raleigh insisted. "Smooth the way."

"You'd do that for me?"

"Sure. And it wouldn't just be for you. It would be an investment in the people here. In the village. A solid play, all around."

"I'd certainly appreciate it. There are a million details that would have to be considered before I know whether the idea is feasible. But in the meantime, I need to find some temporary lodgings. I'm going to be around for a least a couple of months, working as Freya's nanny while Hamish's parents are helping with his Gran."

"You're gonna be Hamish's nanny?" Raleigh asked. "How'd *that* come about?"

"Freya's idea. It seemed to work out for everyone. It'll give me a little income while I'm sorting the restaurant and otherwise interviewing for chef's positions elsewhere. And it'll ensure that I'm definitely here for Malcolm and Charlotte's wedding. I just need to figure out where I can stay."

"Well, Malcolm's place is empty since he and Charlotte moved out to the house," Raleigh started.

Afton held up a hand. "Thank you for the offer. Truly. But I don't think I can live here. It just feels too... weird." Her heart was definitely too raw to live anywhere on the estate.

"Fair enough. There's also Sophie's house."

"Sophie's? What about Lorraine?" When Afton had left, Sophie's stepmother had been ruling the roost.

"Oh, Lorraine has been gone for a few months," Kyla explained. "There's absolutely a story there that she'll have to tell you when she gets back. Anyway, the house is Sophie's now. She turned the bottom floor into her flower shop, but the upstairs was converted into a flat to let. She and Connor have been trying to find a tenant, but haven't had a lot of luck. I'm sure they'd be happy to work with you on a short-term basis."

"That does sound ideal. I'll speak with them when they get back from their honeymoon at the end of the week." She checked her watch. "In the meantime, I need to get going. I'm meeting Hamish at the house in a bit for my first day on the job."

"Sounds like a plan. And just so you know, we still consider a lot of what's here to be yours," Raleigh said. "So when it comes time to furnish your place, it won't be a problem."

It was a considerate gesture, and far more than Afton had expected. "Thank you. That was something I hadn't thought of yet, but it'll certainly make things easier." Anything she didn't have to purchase out of pocket would help.

They rose when she did, and Kyla passed the baby off to Raleigh so she could wrap Afton in a hug. "I'm glad we cleared the air. And I'm glad you're home."

Afton lingered in her embrace, letting the balm of forgiveness soak in and soothe the ragged spots of her soul. "It's good to be back."

IN THE IMMORTAL words of Freya's favorite childhood storybook, Hamish was having a terrible, horrible, no good, very bad day.

That it started with the goats was no surprise. He was so close to calling someone to haul them to the nearest abattoir and offering the resulting meat up to be turned into curry. Two of them had escaped out into the yard when he'd been trying to feed them, and he hadn't had time to round them back up before leaving to take Freya to school. So, despite the forecast for additional snow, he'd left them out to graze on whatever they could find and hoped they'd have the good sense to go back into the barn if they got too cold.

He and Freya had barely gotten to campus before the bell rang, and he was pretty sure she'd be racking up a tardy, despite his efforts at intervention in the office. But at least he'd managed to get Afton added to the list of approved adults who could pick her up or be called in case of an emergency. That was the last thing that went right for the day.

He'd gotten a puncture leaving the school, which resulted in him being late to court and covered in a fair degree of mud when he arrived, because there'd been no time to call some sort of roadside assistance, and no time to change. He'd figured late and muddy would be better than even later.

Judge Sullivan hadn't been impressed.

The rest of the day spun out from there, with him being late for every client meeting and spending the bulk of his afternoon making apologies. Which meant he hadn't made it back to the house at lunch as intended to make sure the goats got put away.

So they weren't put away when he got home.

They also weren't inside the fence.

His headlights swept over the shaggy brown and white form grazing at the side of the driveway. "Oh, God. Oh, no. No, no, no, no, no."

As he parked the car, he spotted two others huddled in the lea of the house, somewhat out of the wind. The other three were clustered by the barn door, which had evidently blown closed at some point during the day.

"Just fucking perfect."

Afton hadn't yet arrived, but she was due any minute. He'd wanted a few minutes to pull himself together, and instead he was going to have to wrangle the bloody goats.

Parking his car, he got out, heading for the one at the far end of the drive. Maybe he could herd it back inside the fence. The goat didn't even look up as he approached, just continued nibbling on vegetation. Thinking of how he'd seen Raleigh interact with livestock, Hamish pitched his voice low and hoped it sounded soothing.

"I've just had a real pisser of a day, so I'm going to need you to cooperate, aye?"

The goat's ears twitched, and it stepped further away.

"Why dinna you just head back toward the

barn and join your mates? It's cold and there's some nice hay in there."

Hamish would've sworn the goat shot him a "Bitch, please" look before deliberately taking another bite of whatever it was eating.

He circled around, putting himself between the animal and the drive and raising his arms to wave it back toward the barn. Making yourself appear bigger and more threatening worked on bears, right? Why not goats? "Go on. Go inside."

The goat bleated and leapt away, not back toward the barn but to the left, bouncing up the hill.

"Shite."

Headlights made him turn. Afton pulling into the drive.

She stopped beside him, rolling down the window. "When did you get goats? Why do you have goats? Never mind. You can tell me that part later."

She parked her car up by the house and immediately jogged down to him. "Your fence isn't high enough to keep them in."

Hamish's shoulders hunched, though he knew she probably didn't mean it as the criticism it felt like. "Stuart said it was!"

"Stuart—whoever he is—was mistaken. At least for motivated goats. Go let the others into the barn. I'll go after this one."

He didn't have the energy to preserve his

pride, and she was the one who'd grown up around a multitude of livestock, so he didn't bother to argue. The trio huddled by the barn door gave a plaintive sort of whines as he approached. Reproach for their poor treatment, no doubt.

"I know. I know. I'm sorry."

They milled around him as he shouldered the door open and bolted inside as soon as the gap was wide enough. Thank God. He needed a win for the day. Turning to look for the one that had been up by the house, he felt his foot do a little slide and shimmy. He didn't even need to look to know he'd just stepped in goat shite in his dress shoes. Because that was just the poetic icing on this shit sundae of a day.

From somewhere below, Afton clapped. "Come on. Let's go home."

And damn if she wasn't walking up the drive with the escape artist, leading it along by—was that a leash? The two by the house, evidently sensing someone who knew what they were doing, trotted over to join them.

Hamish stared as they moved by him into the barn.

"Pull the door shut, will you? And turn on the light." Afton called.

He did as she asked, marveling as the goats immediately bedded down in their pens. "Are you a bloody goat whisperer, then?"

"Just someone who knows something about herd animals." She opened her coat and re-threaded her belt through the loops in her jeans. Evidently, that's what she'd used as a leash. "What are their names?"

"Paul, Prue, Mary, Mel, Sue, and Noel."

Her lips twitched. "You named them after the hosts of *The Great British Bake Off*?"

"It was Freya's idea."

"Of course it was. How exactly did you end up with them?"

"I got railroaded into it by the son of a late client. They were her goats, and he convinced me his mum would've wanted me to have them. He said they'd solve my gardening problem by eating everything that needed clearing."

"Well, he's not wrong. He's just got the wrong time of year. Come spring, they'll likely do a good job clearing up all the brambles and weeds."

"They have to survive that long."

"I'll teach you what to do. More, I'll teach Freya. That'll be a good responsibility for her."

"Good luck with that. As they aren't the puppy or the horse she's been begging for, she doesn't want to go near them. Right now, she's afraid of them.

Paul Hollywood is an asshole and head-butted her. Knocked her right down."

Hamish couldn't see her clearly in the dim light of the barn, but he had the clear sense she was struggling to hold back a laugh. "They're very smart. And they can absolutely be trained like dogs. You'll both see. Come on. Let's get inside. You clearly need to change clothes. I'll get started on dinner."

He took two steps before stopping again and closing his eyes. "Oh, fuck me. I forgot the groceries again."

"I didn't. I picked up your order from yesterday and added to it. Where's Freya?"

"Charlotte's been picking her up from school since Mum and Dad left last week. Either she or Malcolm will be dropping her off soon."

"Then we've got a few minutes to discuss the particulars of this arrangement before she gets home."

Because he was pitifully grateful to have someone else make some decisions, he let her nudge him along. Abandoning the befouled shoes by the door to deal with later, he headed straight upstairs to change clothes. By the time he came downstairs again, she was unloading supplies from a multitude of bags on the counter.

She nodded toward a glass on the end with a

couple of fingers' worth of golden liquid. "Because you look like you need it."

"Christ, do I." He picked up the drink and sipped, already feeling some of the knots of the day unravel. "Can I help?"

"Unless you have objections, I thought since I'm going to be doing the bulk of the cooking, I could arrange things to my preference."

"That's fine."

"Then you can leave me to this and tell me what went so wrong with your day."

"I thought we were going over the contract?" He'd brought it down with him.

"We will. But I think you need to take five minutes to vent and process before your daughter gets home."

"Fair point." He didn't want this awful mood to spill over on Freya, so he gave Afton the rundown, appreciating the sympathetic adult ear.

"Poor Hamish. That *is* a magnificently bad day."

He tensed, analyzing her words, but he detected none of the sarcasm that would've underpinned them if they'd come from Dayna. Afton seemed to legitimately sympathize.

"Well, as I said, I'll take over with the goats and teach Freya to take that off your plate. We've already discussed my making meals and doing the driving to get her to and from school and such. I'll do whatever I can to help with homework, and I dinna mind running errands, so you dinna have to take time out of your workday to tend to them."

"That would be... amazing." And weirdly like a domestic partnership. But he'd be paying her for the services. "Shall we go over the contract?"

"Sure." She shut the fridge door and joined him at the kitchen table.

Nothing about the document was complicated. He reviewed the basic duties and rate of pay. He'd nearly put in a no fraternization clause but had ultimately left it off. Such a restriction would've been for him, not her, and he hadn't wanted to risk insulting her after she'd made this generous offer.

"I thought we'd start with a month to see how it went for both of us. There's an exit clause here, if you find another position in the meantime. Do you have any questions? Concerns? Changes?"

"No. It's fine. I trust you." Snatching up the pen, she signed it where he indicated, then returned to organizing supplies.

Hamish signed himself just as the door banged open, and Freya came barreling down the hall.

"Hi, Da! Hi, Afton!" She fairly bubbled with positive energy, proving that at least one of them had had a better day.

Hamish absorbed her quick hug before she

dumped her backpack and went instantly over to Afton to investigate.

"What're we having for dinner tonight?"

"You're having cottage pie. It's an easy one to double, so I can make two and put one in the freezer. What's your position on leftovers?"

"I don't mind them so long as I like whatever it is. What are you having?"

Afton shot her a cheerful smile. "No idea. I'll figure that out when I get done with work."

Freya's bubbly expression fell. "You're not going to eat with us?"

"My job is to make the dinner, not to eat it. Besides, I'm a chef. I make lots of food I dinna eat myself."

His daughter turned pleading eyes on him. "But she hasn't even moved into her own place yet. You canna just leave her to fend for herself. It doesn't make sense."

It definitely didn't. "She has a point, Afton. It makes no sense for you not to eat with us, at least until you have access to your own kitchen." And it would extend her time here, giving him a longer hit of that calming energy.

Afton studied him for a long moment. "Well, that's very kind of you. Thank you."

Freya clapped. "Yay! I'll scrub up so I can play sous chef."

"Have you finished your homework?"

"Not quite."

"Then you should work on that while I work on dinner. Do you need quiet to work, or do you want to set up at the kitchen table while I'm cooking?"

"Table's good."

As his daughter pulled out her books, Afton casually asked about her day and listened, a tiny smile curving her lips as Freya chattered on about the inconsequential things that felt enormous to a pre-teen girl. Hamish just sipped at his drink and watched in fascination. Freya didn't talk to her mother like this. Not that Dayna ever asked or showed this much interest.

Afton's gaze met his, full of amusement, and she smiled. Hamish found himself smiling back, enjoying this feeling of shared delight over his kid. It had been a long, long time since he'd had that with Dayna. He hadn't realized how much he'd missed seeing that reflected enjoyment.

Afton's knife moved rhythmically as she chopped an onion. "I've got this handled, if you need to go take care of anything. You've got about an hour and fifteen."

Right. There were things he could deal with if he wasn't having to police homework or see that they didn't starve.

"Thanks."

Far steadier than he had been when he got home, he snagged the contract and retreated to his home office to make a copy for her and file it. But as he slid the original into the cabinet, he worried that this single sheet of paper and his own good intentions wouldn't be enough to keep him from reaching for exactly what he wanted.

SEVEN

Afton pulled up to Freya's school, scanning the kids spilling out of the building like ants, their winter gear adding pops of color to the monochrome landscape. Being in the pickup line felt surreal, because the last thing she felt like was a parent. And she wasn't. For now, she was the nanny. Not that she had the first idea what she was doing beyond ferrying Freya to and fro and seeing that she and Hamish were properly fed. But she'd figure it out. How hard could it be to relate to a tween girl? She'd been one herself. All she'd wanted at that age was to be treated like an adult. Talked to. Her own parents had been great at that. She figured that was as good a plan as any for how to deal with Freya.

They weren't strangers, exactly. She'd known

the girl all her life. Freya had been the only child in their group of friends. But they'd never really spent one-on-one time together. When Hamish and Dayna had come to Glenlaig, she'd usually been with her grandparents so the adults could hang out and have grown-up conversation. But Afton had seen enough to know that the girl had been quiet. Not shy, but more inclined to sit back and take everything in. Much like her father. Much like Afton herself. This older version of her was more talkative, as all girls that age seemed to be. Still, she was a thoughtful kid, one who was clearly yearning for meaningful adult connections, given how she'd glommed onto cooking with Afton the past two nights. So Afton would continue to roll with that.

She spotted the bright turquoise ski jacket Freya had been wearing that morning and waved. Freya said something to the two other girls she walked with, then made a run for the car, yanking open the door and chucking her backpack to the floor as she threw herself into the seat with all the dramatics a tween girl could manage.

Afton arched a brow. "And how was your day? Is that a thing we're going to talk about?"

Freya tugged the seatbelt in place and grinned. "Everyone is still talking about those jam bars. They want to know if I can bring more for exams."

Up ahead, the teacher directing traffic waved

her on, so Afton edged into the flow to exit. "I certainly dinna mind making more. Is that allowed? I dinna remember doing that kind of thing when I was in school here."

"You went to school here?"

"Of course, I did. Why wouldn't I? How else do you think I knew your da and Connor, Kyla, and Sophie?"

"I dunno. You were a baroness. I guess I thought you went to some fancy boarding school or something."

Afton chuckled. "Well, at that stage of my life, my mother was the baroness. Not that it mattered. My parents were very down-to-earth sort of people. Even if we'd had the money for private schools, I dinna think they'd have sent me. I certainly wouldn't have wanted to go. I love it here."

"I dinna think I'd like private school, either. I like the village school. It's a lot smaller than my school in Edinburgh. I like that I know everybody."

"That's good. Were those your friends I saw you talking to?"

"Aileen Chapman and Esme Byrne. They're in my class. We hang out some. Message a lot."

Afton considered. "Byrne. Is Esme related to Toby Byrne? The village mechanic?"

"That's her uncle."

"Ah. That would make Michael her father. He was one of your da's classmates."

"Not one of yours?"

"No, Michael was a few years ahead of me. Toby was in my class. I was the youngest in our group growing up. I dinna know that I'd have hung out with the MacKeans or your da as much as I did if not for the fact that our parents encouraged it, since everyone expected me to marry Connor."

"That must've been weird."

"Aye, it was. I love Connor, but not like that."

"It really sucks that all your parents were pushing you into that. Nobody should have to marry someone they dinna want to."

As much time as Hamish had spent researching the marriage pact over the years, it was inevitable that this would come up. Afton glanced at her charge in the passenger seat. "True enough. What did your da tell you about all that?"

"That it used to be that arranged marriages and marriages for political alliances were the norm, but that you and Connor were stuck in one because of a bunch of circumstances outside your control. He was trying to find a way out for you both."

"That sums it up, more or less. It wasn't our parents' fault. And neither of us blamed them for not wanting to lose our homes or family legacies. We understood from the time we were small how and why that rested on us. It wasn't just us. It was everyone who lives and works on both estates. We had a lot of responsibility resting on our shoulders."

"But in the end, you ran."

Leave it to the kid to drill down to the heart of the matter. When she didn't answer immediately, Freya turned her head away.

"You dinna have to talk about it if you dinna want to."

Afton could have let it go, but she didn't get the sense the girl was asking out of idle curiosity. "No, it's okay. You're right. I did run. I was desperate and unhappy, and I just hit a point where I couldn't think of a good reason why I should continue to let my life be dictated by a law that was written three hundred years ago. My only option was to give everything up. In the moment, that didn't feel as awful as continuing on the path I'd been on. It wasn't a *good* option, but it was the only one I felt like I had. So I found the best person I thought would take care of the estate. Thankfully, that's exactly what Raleigh's done."

"Was there somebody else you wanted to marry instead?"

It might've been an innocent question. It was the logical direction for the conversation to turn, and if the answer hadn't been Freya's father, maybe Afton would have answered honestly. Instead, she concentrated very hard on navigating the winter roads out of the village. "I never opened myself to the possibility." That was true enough. And look what opening herself to the possibility had gotten her. A temporary place in his life as the help, instead of as a partner.

Not that it had been Hamish's idea, and not that she believed for a second he didn't appreciate the help she was offering. But that didn't change the ache of knowing he felt something and wasn't willing to act on it. A part of her wanted to tell him to shove all those noble reasons he'd given and take a chance on them. But that wasn't how Hamish Colquhoun was wired. He had to consider every angle, all the implications. It was what made him a good lawyer. Afton had to admit she'd prefer to keep him as her friend than lose him as everything, because she wasn't satisfied with however little he could give her.

Freya hummed a noncommittal note that sounded exactly like her father. "Was it worth it? Giving up everything?"

Wasn't that the sixty-four thousand pound question? As she turned onto the road that led out to the farmhouse, Afton sighed. "I think so. To be free to live my life as I want. No one should ever make you feel obligated to do anything that doesn't feel like you. Because, at the end of the day, it's your life."

Freya hummed in agreement. "I like that." After a moment, she added, "Da was really sad after you left."

Hamish would have taken her defection as a personal failure. He'd always taken too much on himself.

Not knowing exactly what to say to that announcement, and wanting to lighten the mood, Afton parked the car in front of the house and shot her a grin. "I feel compelled to mention, for the sake of your father, that the *not doing anything that doesn't feel like you* does not apply to eating your vegetables and doing chores."

The girl rolled her eyes, but smiled. "Noted."

They climbed out of the car. "Go change. I want to give you a lesson in how to properly interact with the goats so you dinna get head butted. Then you can get started on homework while I figure out dinner."

"Can I help you cook? I like being your sous chef."

Afton tweaked the end of Freya's braid with affection. "Homework first, then we'll see where we are."

"Yes, Chef."

LATE IN THE AFTERNOON, Hamish stretched at his desk. It had been a long but productive day, as he'd been able to legitimately detach from his phone. If anything came up with Freya, Afton would handle it. If anything went wrong with Gran, his mum and da would know to call the office if they didn't reach him by mobile. The ability to truly focus on his work was a luxury Hamish wouldn't take for granted again.

Only one client remained on the schedule: Lewis Anderson, a stonemason from Braemore, the next village over. With a few minutes remaining until the appointment, Hamish pulled out his phone to check messages. He found a text from his daughter and opened it. A picture filled the screen —a selfie of Freya and Afton in the barn with the goats. Freya's blue eyes were scrunched almost shut as one of the creatures licked her face like a dog. Behind her, Afton was clearly cracking up with laughter.

Hamish stared at her face. God, when was the last time he'd seen Afton laugh like that? Maybe years. Everyone else believed it to be the lingering effects of grief from having lost both her parents at such a pivotal time. And maybe that was part of it. But Hamish knew a bigger part had been the weight of the duty that had fallen on her shoulders. Without that pressure hanging over her, he could see a joy in her that hadn't been truly present since they were children. He wished he were with them to hear it. To see it.

Maybe that mirth would still linger by the time he got home. By Freya's request, Afton would stay for dinner. So he'd get to see her. Speak with her. It surprised him how much he wanted that. It was the sort of domestic end to the day he'd once shared with his wife. Before he'd tired of all the discussions of how to make social connections that would benefit them both. Hamish didn't operate that way. And, despite having been raised in a titled family all her life, neither did Afton. Maybe that was part of the appeal. Knowing he could finally just... talk to her. About everyday things. About Freya. About the people they knew, sharing village gossip. Little as it was, he knew he'd soak up that time with her like a man parched.

The phone on his desk buzzed.

"Yes?"

"Mr. Anderson is here."

"I'll be right out."

Hearting the image, Hamish put the phone away and combed his hands through his hair before straightening his tie. He was more than ready to strip the thing off, but he wanted to make a good impression.

The man waiting by Marsaili's desk looked rough. Not because of the sturdy work pants or the heavy jacket he wore. Not because of the thick beard that no doubt helped keep his face warm during the winter months he worked outside. It was his eyes. Deep lines of worry carved into the skin around them, adding a shadow that aged him at least a decade. Those eyes were a little sunken, as if he hadn't been sleeping. His mouth pressed into a thin line, and his broad shoulders bowed, as if life were weighing him down. Hamish pegged the man as around his age, but he looked considerably older.

He offered his hand. "Mr. Anderson. I'm Hamish Colquhoun."

"Lewis Anderson. Thank you for meeting with me."

"Of course."

Marsaili offered a maternal smile. "Would you like a cuppa for your meeting?"

Lewis clutched a cap in one meaty fist. "I wouldnae say no. If it's no trouble."

"No trouble at all. I'll bring it along shortly. Mr. Colquhoun, you?"

"Yes, thank you, Marsaili."

He escorted his client back to his office, gesturing him to a chair across from the desk. Then he took his own seat and leaned back. "So, how can I help you?"

"My wife is divorcing me."

The punch of sympathy was instant and visceral. "I'm sorry. That's hard. How long have you been married?"

"Twelve years."

Just a little less than he and Dayna had been.

Lewis continued twisting the cap in his hands. "I'm no' worried about losing her. We havenae gotten along for a while. But I'm worried about losing my boys."

"How old are they?"

"Nine and eleven."

Hamish offered a smile. "I have a daughter. She's twelve."

"Then you ken what it's like to be a parent."

"Aye." More than Lewis could probably imagine.

Lewis glanced at the framed photo of him and Freya on the desk. "That her?"

"It is."

"Pretty thing."

"And smart as a whip." Wanting to steer them back toward the business at hand, Hamish grabbed a pen. "Are you looking for mediation, or do you expect to go to court?"

"Court, probably. I'm no' opposed to mediation,

but my wife—soon to be ex-wife—isnae really open to discussion. She's got a new job in Glasgow and intends to take the boys with her when she goes. I dinna want to just see them every other weekend and on holidays. I want primary custody."

Pain at the prospective loss vibrated in the other man's voice, and Hamish felt it down to his marrow. This was a man who loved his children. He thought briefly about what it would've been like if Dayna had felt this passionately about keeping Freya. As angry as he was that she hadn't fought him, maybe it was better for their daughter that she hadn't.

"Tell me a bit more about the situation. What are the grounds for the divorce? Was there infidelity? Any sort of abuse?"

"No. None of that. We just... stopped working. Wanted different things. We tried to make it work, but..." Lewis shook his head. "We've been keeping separate bedrooms for months."

Ignoring how his own memories were battering at his brain, Hamish made a note of that. "Tell me more about your wife. Is there any concern about the boys' wellbeing in her care? Any signs of abuse?"

"Nothing like that. She's no' a bad mother. But she'll be moving to a council flat in Glasgow. How are they better off there than here, where they have their own bedrooms and a garden and access to outdoors? Their friends are here. Their dog. She'll be working all the time to cover expenses. What kind of life is that for two growing boys?"

What kind of life, indeed?

"What about you? Do you have other family nearby who would be able to help? Because, speaking from my own experience, being a single parent is incredibly hard. You'll need a support system."

"Aye, I've got my parents. My sister and her family."

"Good. That's good." He made more notes.

"I know it'll be hard. And I dinna want to keep the boys from her. But I canna just let them go. They're my heart."

At the ring of pure emotion in his tone, Hamish met his gaze. "I understand completely."

Marsaili knocked on the door and stepped into the office with a tea tray. She fussed just a little, to make sure Mr. Anderson had everything he needed, then stepped back out. Hamish's tea was already made exactly as he liked it.

He brought the mug to his lips. "I'm certainly happy to take on the case and do everything that I can. We should definitely attempt mediation first, as it'll be more cost-effective than going to court. It'll be easier on the boys to not see the two of you fighting, and perhaps your wife will surprise you."

Lewis's mouth pressed back into the grim line. "I doubt that. She'll fight for them. And I truly dinna know what a fair arrangement would be. They'll have to stay in one place or the other because of school, so one of us is going to get the short end of the stick."

"True enough. Divorce is hard on everyone involved. If you both want what's best for your children, that'll make this go better because it means you agree about something. That's a starting point."

Mug clasped between his big hands, Lewis leaned forward. "Do you think I have a shot?"

Hamish weighed his words, not wanting to make unrealistic promises. "Truthfully, I dinna ken." He felt his tongue lapse back into the broader Scots he'd trained himself out of in law school. "If we go to court, it could go either way. Historically, judges are more likely to grant primary custody to the mother. But that's gradually been changing. What I can promise you is that I'll do my level best."

"That's all I can ask."

"Okay." Hamish turned to a fresh page on his legal pad and prepared to get to the real work.

EIGHT

"I canna believe your stepmother got arrested." Afton really *had* missed a lot.

Sophie had told her the tale of Lorraine's benefits fraud as they took a tour of the apartment.

"Couldnae have happened to a more miserable woman," Connor declared with a grin.

"Did she go to prison?" Afton asked.

Sophie shook her head. "No. And that was thanks to Hamish. Not out of the goodness of his heart, but he used that as leverage to get her to give up the house without a fuss. Which worked out, as I'd been given the heave-ho from the space I was leasing for Village Blume."

"John Milligan always was an arsehole." Not

that Afton had done business with the man, but his reputation had been well earned.

"Karma took its toll there, too." Connor's self-satisfied smirk and Sophie's affectionate eye roll made Afton suspect he'd had a role in delivering that karma. There was a clear intimacy and comfort between them that Afton and Connor had never had, despite the years of their friendship.

"Anyway," Sophie drawled, "will the flat work for you?"

Afton turned a circle, taking in the empty rooms and wondering what the hell she was going to fill them with. Ignoring the fresh ache at that sense of rootlessness that had been plaguing her since she came back, she fixed a smile on her face. "Absolutely. I'm grateful that you're willing to do this week-to-week lease for me since I dinna know how long I'll be in town. And I know you need to find a long-term tenant, so if someone materializes, I completely understand. I'll get my things packed up and find somewhere else." She only had the bag she'd brought from the States, so it wouldn't take long.

Connor shrugged. "Well, it's been months, and we havenae had any bites, so we're no' overly concerned about it. And it's nice to ken that someone we know will be in the space."

Sophie bit her lip. "Are you sure it's not a

problem that the kitchen is downstairs? I think that's part of our issue with letting the place. The layout is odd since we carved up a proper house and made the entire rest of the bottom floor the shop. We thought to make a separate entrance for that, but..."

"I promise it won't bother me a bit. It's no different from being in a city and living above a business." And crap, that reminded her she hadn't yet given her landlord in Nashville an answer. It wasn't as if she were likely to be back in Tennessee before the end of the month. She filed that away on her mental to do list.

"So we're agreed?" Sophie asked.

"We are."

They shook on it, and Sophie handed over the keys. "I'm sorry there's not really any furniture. After Lorraine left, I got rid of most everything. The things I really cared about from my family, I'd already moved to Ardinmuir. I didn't really want to keep anything that was hers."

"No, no. It's fine." It wasn't exactly fine. Afton didn't want to spend all her money furnishing things, and she absolutely had to figure out some basics. Like a bed and kitchen gear. But that was her problem. Still, it was incredibly surreal to have so little after she'd grown up with so much.

From downstairs, someone knocked on the door, then opened it.

A familiar Southern voice drawled, "Y'all ready for us?"

Connor yelled down the stairs, "Come on up, Raleigh!"

More than one set of footsteps tromped up the stairs. Raleigh appeared first, a small table in his hands that she recognized.

"That's from my mother's sitting room." The words were out before she could think better of them.

"Yep. We've got a whole bunch of stuff we've held onto for you."

"You... what?"

"Well, we used it for a while, until we figured out what we wanted to buy for ourselves. But we figured now's a good time for you to reclaim what's yours. Because it's one thing for you to hand off the deed to the property and everything else that went with it, but the stuff that's in the house—most of it's really yours. Your family history. Your furniture. Your belongings. And it's time you had it back. You've gotta have furniture, right?"

As he talked, Malcolm came into the room, followed by Ewan. Between the two of them, they carried the headboard from her old bedroom.

Raleigh had said they'd held onto some things

for her when she'd gone out to make amends to him and Kyla, but she hadn't imagined it would be that much. "You're... furnishing my flat?"

"I mean, technically, you're furnishing your flat," Raleigh said. "We're just the moving crew. Hamish would've been here to help, too, but he's stuck in court today."

A petite blonde carrying a duffel bag came next. She looked vaguely familiar.

She offered a smile. "Hi. We haven't met yet. I'm Isobel, Ewan's girlfriend."

"I love how you're still leading with that," Ciara snarked, barging up behind her with two more duffel bags.

"I love him, so why shouldn't that be what I lead with?"

"I love that you're in love, but do you have to be so disgusting about it? That's my brother."

"You're just jealous," Isobel sang.

"Nauseous. You mean nauseous."

"What is all this?" Afton eyed the bags they were piling up in a corner.

Kyla emerged from the stairwell, with the baby strapped to her chest. "Your clothes. And the rest of the contents of your closet. I know minimalism is all the rage, but I expect you'll be glad to have it all back. Which room are you taking for your bedroom?"

Throat too tight to speak, Afton just shook her head.

"Okay, I'm making the executive decision to put you in Sophie's old room. Girls, bring the bags."

As she disappeared down the hall, Afton gave brief consideration to running. Not because she was upset but because her heart was so very full she didn't know how to contain it, and she didn't want to cry in front of all these very kind people. Because after everything she'd done, they were giving her back something of those roots she'd so ruthlessly ripped up.

An arm slid around her shoulders, and Connor pulled her into a hug. He kept his voice low. "We wanted to clarify, in case you were still worried, that we're glad to have you home, aye? Some of us didnae do a good enough job of that while you were here before." An apology shone in his bright blue eyes as he looked down at her.

Afton squeezed him tight, swallowing down the lump in her throat. "Thank you. You're a really good brother, you know that?"

He laughed. "Thank God I finally get the luxury to be that. C'mon. Let's go get the rest."

It took a couple of hours and more than one trip from Lochmara for them to get everything and haul it inside. It took an hour beyond that for the women to browbeat the men into rearranging the furniture in some semblance of functionality. There were still dozens of boxes to unpack, but where there'd been only empty rooms before, now memories of home surrounded her.

Kyla, who'd appointed herself organizer general, given she couldn't be too much physical help because of Lily, looked around the room designated as the lounge and nodded in satisfaction. "I think that'll do. If there's any particular piece we didn't grab, let us know. Quite a few things got repurposed to help furnish the guest cottages, but we can swap things out, no problem."

"And if you want something moved around after you've settled in, just let us know," Connor added.

More footsteps sounded, and Charlotte emerged. "My goodness. Y'all certainly got a lot done." She turned a broad smile on Afton. "I've been down in the kitchen. I know you're perfectly capable of cooking for yourself, but you've got a lot of unpacking to do, so I figured the least I could do was keep you fed for a few days. There are casseroles in the fridge and freezer, and I already hit up the market for some basics."

Okay, seriously, Afton needed to have a good cry to let all this emotion out. Which meant they all needed to go.

"Thank you, all of you, for... all of it. I wasn't expecting any of this."

Charlotte patted her cheek. "Maybe that's part of your problem, sugar. Not expecting good things for yourself. Now, I know you want to get settled in, and you won't have all that long before Freya's done with school. I'm gonna get her today, and I'll bring her by in time for supper at her house, if that suits you."

"That's... Yes, that'd be great."

"Okay then. Everybody, move out! Let's give this woman some privacy."

With all the efficiency Afton imagined Raleigh used to wrangle cattle, Charlotte had everyone up and out in minutes. Then she was alone in her new place, surrounded by memories.

Overwhelmed, Afton sank down onto the sofa that had once been in her parents' room. She ran her fingers over the worn Harris tweed and remembered curling up right here and watching her mother dress for date night out with her father, a twice monthly ritual she'd credited for the success of their marriage. The visceral ache of missing them bloomed sharp in her chest, so she let the tears come, spilling out all the pain and gratitude and relief, until she felt purged.

Cried out, she washed her face in the bathroom and went down to the kitchen for a glass of water.

This was the one area it seemed Sophie hadn't completely purged the house. Probably because she'd still been using it as a break room for the shop. The kitchen table and chairs remained, and there were basic dishes and cutlery. Cookery essentials, though Afton would want to update those for her own purposes. She'd brought only her knives from the US. Gulping down two glasses of water, she felt refreshed.

She'd need to go by the B and B to pack her things. But it was already well past checkout time, so it could wait a bit. What she really wanted right now was to talk to Rebecca. Checking the time difference, she went back upstairs and found her phone.

"Afton! Hey, honey."

"Hi. Is this a good time? I can call back later."

"No, it's just fine. You caught me between clients. Jolene Lowrey called to push her appointment back by half an hour. Oh my God, it's so good to hear your voice. How are things?"

Pressing her lips together, Afton waited for a moment to see if she'd finally run out of words. "Things are... good."

"Why does that make me think they're not?"

"No, it's not that. I... Nothing has gone how I expected."

On the other end of the line, she could hear Rebecca getting comfy in one of the spinning chairs in her salon. "Tell me everything."

So Afton did. Starting with the delayed flight that led to the wedding interruption, going through all the apologies, the confession of her feelings to Hamish, his rejection, the nanny job, and all of today's surprises. When she'd finished, there was a weighted silence on the other end.

"Well, you've certainly had an eventful week and change."

"You could say that."

"There are about two dozen questions I want to ask, but time's runnin' short, so I'll stick to the biggest one. Do you think this arrangement with Hamish is a good idea? I mean, I'm not trying to mom you here—"

"Yes, you are, and I love you for it. You're worried about me. I appreciate that. As to the question... I dinna know."

"It's got to be hard to be around him."

"Mostly no. He wasn't ever an option for me, so I'm used to that as the status quo."

"But unavailable because he's with someone else is very different from the current situation. That has to sting."

"It does, aye. And, honestly, if it wasn't for Freya, then I'd probably try to find a job elsewhere and go. But he's drowning, Rebecca. I've known this man all my life, and I've never seen him anything but completely competent and capable. I gather his divorce was hell, and he's so terrified of Freya being a casualty. She's a great kid, and I feel like I owe him something for saving my life. So as hard as it is to be around him and know that being *with* him isn't a possibility, if I can help him out through this transition so he can get his feet under him again before I go, then I think that's well worth the twinge every time I see him."

Rebecca was quiet for a few moments. "Except, will you leave? Because it sounds like maybe everybody wants you to stay. And maybe like you want to stay, too."

She did have a way of cutting right to the heart of the matter. "Well, that'll depend." Briefly, she sketched out her idea for the restaurant. "Raleigh's already taken me around to speak to several of the crofters. Everyone's been incredibly kind, and they're very enthusiastic about the prospect, if a little skeptical. And they've a right to be. There are a thousand details that would have to come together for it to all work. But I have at least a couple of months to figure out whether it's a legitimate possibility. So...yes, I guess the answer is—for now—I'm staying."

HAMISH ATTACKED the wallpaper in the entryway with renewed vigor. It wasn't tearing-out-a-wall-with-a-sledgehammer levels of satisfying, but it was the best he had. And Afton's suggestion about the fabric softener had been helpful. He was getting to the actual wall underneath the layers of hideous wallpaper. After everything got stripped, it would need retexturing, which would lead to a whole new YouTube DIY rabbit hole. This was the nature of his weekends, especially on the ones Freya was in Edinburgh with Dayna.

He appreciated the opportunity to work out his frustrations on inanimate objects. It meant he could be calmer and more present with his daughter during the time they spent together. It also just gave him the chance to drop the mask and acknowledge that he didn't have everything under control. Least of all, the current situation with Afton.

Today was the first day he hadn't seen her this week, and he found he missed her. At Freya's insistence, it had become the norm for Afton to eat dinner with them each night. It made total sense. She was preparing their meals. If she *didn't* join them, it meant she didn't get to eat herself until a ridiculously late hour. It also meant she was there asking them both about their days, helping Freya process whatever had happened at school, giving him the chance for some adult conversation that had nothing to do with work or his divorce. Without concern for propriety because of his marriage, they'd been able to settle into a kind of easy friendship that proved they'd both been paying a hell of a lot closer attention to each other all these years than either of them had let on. Every single day, he found more and more reasons to *like* her. And when she wasn't directly there, she was calmly and quietly taking things off his plate, without his having to ask, making herself indispensable.

Like this morning. He'd slept in a little, given he hadn't gotten back from dropping Freya in Edinburgh until nearly eleven. By the time he'd stumbled out to the barn this morning, Afton had already been by to feed the goats. She'd even left a basket of freshly made scones on the counter for breakfast. The woman was still settling into her new flat, but she'd taken the time to take care of him, even when Freya wasn't around.

Hamish hated how quickly he'd come to depend on her. Both because he despised admitting his own inadequacies and because he had no idea how he could replace her when she moved on to whatever the next thing was. And she would move on. She couldn't stay the nanny forever.

He hated that, too.

With a growl, he wielded his scraper against a freshly soaked patch of scored wallpaper as if it had insulted his mother. The wet paper peeled off in messy strips. He'd exposed another four feet of wall by the time the knock sounded on his front door.

Wiping his hands on the ancient jeans he wore, he opened it to find Connor standing on the stoop. He carried a bag from The Village Chippy in one hand and a six-pack in the other.

Hamish eyed the beer. "A little early, aye?"

"It's after one, and Freya's with her mum. I figured you could use some guy time. We havenae gotten to hang out in ages."

As the scent of fried potatoes rose from the bag, Hamish's stomach growled. It was later than he'd realized. "Come on in."

Connor eyed the progress from the morning. "Still declaring war on that wallpaper?"

"I'm finally getting somewhere with it. Maybe my time would be better spent on one of the other projects that need doing, but this bothers me every time I step into the house."

"Seems like sound reasoning."

They wandered back to the kitchen—the only room other than the lounge that was more-or-less finished downstairs—and settled in at the table, unwrapping the fish and chips Connor had brought.

Now that food was in front of him, Hamish realized he was starving. "Thanks for this. I was all caught up in work and didn't realize how late it was getting."

"No problem." Connor popped a chip into his mouth and chewed thoughtfully, studying him. "You know, when I asked you what you were going to do about Afton, I didnae mean you should hire her as your nanny."

Ah ha. So this was the reason for his friend's unexpected visit. He'd known it was coming. It would've happened sooner if Connor hadn't been off on his honeymoon, then playing catch-up since he got back.

"That wasn't the plan. It was Freya's idea. And Afton volunteered. I canna imagine why. Especially not after I—" He cut himself off with a shake of his head.

Connor narrowed his eyes. "Not after you what?"

Hamish debated with himself, wondering if telling him would violate her privacy somehow. But hell, it was his life, too, and it had been so damned long since he'd been able to talk about his own shit with a friend.

"She'd come by the house to talk to me that first week she was back."

"To make amends, like she did with everyone else."

"Aye, that. But also... she... admitted she has

feelings for me. That she always had." His brain helpfully offered a picture of her face as she'd stood before him, eyes on her glass. *I left after the kiss because I couldn't stay here, knowing what that was like and knowing that I could never be with you. For better or worse, it's always been you for me.*

"Right, so she cares for you, and you're in love with her—I can only blame my own absolute obliviousness for the fact that I never saw it before. So I'm back to my original question. Why would you hire her as the nanny instead of, I dunno, asking her out?"

Hamish's hand fisted on his fork. "Because she deserves better."

Connor threw a chip at his head. "That is complete and utter horse shite. You're the best man I know."

"No, I'm not saying I'm not a good person. It's just, all her life, she's been second. You took her for granted. You thought you were going to marry her, and you were having all the fun before you got to that point. You convinced yourself you'd figure everything with her out after the fact." Something Hamish had raked him over the coals for that last day the banns had been read.

Seeing Connor's shoulders tense, he hurried to add, "I'm not trying to criticize you or tread over old ground, but that was the way things were. She was an afterthought. And right now, I am not in a position to put all of my focus on a new relationship. I have to put everything on my daughter. She deserves better than feeling like collateral damage in this divorce. So I shot Afton down."

Connor's brows climbed up toward his hairline. "And she still volunteered to help with Freya?"

"She did. I gave her an out, and she didn't take it."

"Did you want her to?"

"I dunno. Maybe? No. Being around her like this all the time... it's hard."

His friend paused, giving an uncharacteristic consideration to his words. "Do you think she said yes in hopes you'd change your mind?"

"I considered that briefly. But no. She seems to truly enjoy Freya, which is more than I can say for her own mother just now."

"Are we to the point where I can admit I never liked Dayna?"

"I dinna like who she's become myself, and I'm glad our marriage is over. But Afton is... she's everything Dayna's not. She overruled my protests and has walked in here, made my life better and easier. I've been able to finally breathe for the first time since all this started. Freya adores her in a way that concerns me."

"Why? I'd think having another positive adult female presence in her life would be a good thing."

"It is. To a point. But what happens when she goes? Staying here in Glenlaig long term isn't the plan. She's a chef. We dinna exactly have a lot of need for those around here. She's not going to stick around to be my nanny forever. This was just supposed to be temporary, to help me out and so she can earn a little money while she's figuring out what she wants to do next."

"Did you ever actually consider that if you gave her a reason to stay, she would?"

Only every single day since she'd walked back into his life.

"Aye, but she deserves the chance to follow her dreams, whatever they are. She gave up so much to actually be free to do that. I dinna want to limit her choices."

"Have you actually *had* that conversation with Afton?"

"Of course not. I dinna want to give her false hope. She has a right to move on."

Connor huffed a breath. "Brother, I love you, and I have never known you to be stupid before, but you're being thick as mince. You're deciding for her, which, I can assure you, is a mistake. And you're talking about being worried about Freya getting attached. Hell, you're both already attached. So what do you gain by keeping this distance? What do you gain by not at least trying? For fuck's sake—I'm finally out of the way. Dayna is finally out of the way. What's holding you back?"

Hamish didn't have a good answer to that. Because all his reasons were feeling thin and insubstantial. The truth was, he was afraid. Afraid that he wouldn't be enough for her. His wife had gotten all of him, and it hadn't been enough. Why should the scraps of him keep a woman like Afton happy? Which left him back to being twitchy.

Wanting to put an end to this line of questioning, he picked up his beer. "Did you just come over here to feed me and bust my chops, or did you come to do some work?"

Connor just grinned and clinked his bottle against Hamish's in a toast. "I'm your best mate. I can do both. And while we're at it, we should talk about Christmas."

"Christmas?"

"Yeah, it's in less than two weeks, and last time I checked, you haven't actually decorated."

"Oh, fuck."

NINE

Afton stared at the mountain of pots, pans, and other cookery implements in the sink, then took in the array of dishes that respectively simmered or cooled on the Aga. No question, she'd gone completely overboard with recipe development today. With Freya in Edinburgh with her mother for the weekend, she'd had a long stretch of time just for herself, and she'd just been so excited to finally have a kitchen of her own again. Sure, she'd effectively taken over Hamish's, and he'd gone along with all of her rearrangement. But it wasn't the same as cooking in her own space.

Of what she'd made, two of the dishes would probably go over fine with Hamish and Freya. She had a much better grasp of what he liked than she did his daughter. Admittedly, he could have an entirely different palate now that he was grown. Of course, so far, the two of them had been so grateful they'd seemed willing to eat anything. Afton wasn't sure that would extend to the rabbit and cabbage casserole. Which left her with the question of what the hell she was going to do with all this food?

A knock sounded on the door of the flat. Tossing aside her dish towel, she went to answer.

Sophie stood in the hallway between the flat the flower shop. "I'm really sorry to interrupt, but I need to know what that smell is."

"Oh, God. I'm so sorry. Is it disturbing your customers? Disturbing you?"

"No." She paused. "Well, yes, but not because it smells bad. What *is* that? It smells amazing."

Relaxing, Afton loosed a breath. "Oh, well, I've just been experimenting with some new recipes. Do you want some?"

"Yes!"

A couple of other women stepped out of the shop. Betty McPhee, who Afton knew from her mother's old knitting circle, asked, "Is there enough for us to try, too?"

Well, she'd wanted some guinea pigs. Best not to look gift ones in the mouth. "There is. If you've time enough to wait a few minutes, I can dish some up and bring it across for everyone to try."

"That would be lovely," Agatha Campbell declared.

"I'll be right over."

Hunting the cupboards, Afton found a tray and began dishing up multiple miniature servings of each of the offerings. This was a taste test. Adding utensils to the tray, she carried the whole thing over to Village Blume and set it on the empty front counter.

Feeling a little self-conscious, Afton began her presentation. "Here we have a braised venison stew with root vegetables and herbed dumplings. Ideally, it would be served with fresh crusty bread or oat-cakes, but I hadn't gotten that far yet. Over here is a leek and potato soup with smoked haddock and swirl of cream. Again, it should be served with warm buttered bread. And finally, a rabbit and cabbage casserole, with mashed parsnips and carrots."

Betty picked up a fork and went straight for the casserole. "You know, I'd heard you were doing some cooking as part of the job working for Hamish Colquhoun. But I had no idea you were making food like this."

"You can take the chef out of a restaurant..." Afton muttered.

"A chef, is it now?" Agatha spooned up some of the leek and potato soup and tasted. Her eyes immediately closed in that unrestrained expression of surprise bliss that Afton simply lived for. "Oh, and that's well earned, that is. This is delicious."

Sophie went for the venison stew. After just one bite, she moaned, and Afton grinned. "I may have to make food part of your rent. This is outstanding."

Betty took another bite of the rabbit casserole. "Would you consider doing any cooking like this on the side? The sort of thing we could pick up and take home when we dinna feel like cooking ourselves?"

"Like personal catering? Aye. I did a lot of that through cooking school. It's definitely in my wheelhouse."

"How much would you charge for such a thing?"

Afton hedged. "It would depend somewhat on the dish itself. The cost of ingredients and time—that sort of thing."

"Just give me an estimate."

She thought back to what she'd charged back in the States and did some mental math to accommodate for the exchange rate. She'd barely gotten the number out of her mouth before Betty announced, "Sold! Do you have any more of this?"

"Enough for three people. Four, if you were to add a side salad."

"Excellent. Can you box it up for me? It'll save

my aching back not having to get in the kitchen and figure out dinner tonight."

"This is such a wonderful idea," Agatha exclaimed. "How can we contact you to place orders? That kind of thing?"

Overwhelmed, Afton didn't immediately have an answer.

Sophie stepped in. "You could keep a sign-up sheet here. I'm sure each day would be different in terms of how much time you'd have around Freya. You could list a limited number of slots and options, and people could come back by later to pick things up on their way home."

"Aye, that would be amazing. Is it possible for me to take the rest of this soup?"

"I suppose so."

They all settled on a price, and Afton quickly returned to the kitchen to package up both dishes. There weren't enough storage containers, so she brought the dishes themselves well wrapped.

"I'm afraid I wasn't prepared for this, so all I ask is that you return the dishes when you're through."

"You can be sure I will."

They both paid cash and left with food and flowers.

Sophie was still shoveling in the stew. "I think you've got yourself the start of a nice little cottage industry here, as a job on the side, if you want it."

"I hadn't thought about doing personal catering here, but certainly it's an option." An appealing one, as it gave her the chance to try out more recipes and also to spread the word about the quality of her food among the villagers. If she were to open a restaurant, that word of mouth would be important. "I'm not exactly sure about permits and rules and things about that here. This was obviously a fairly under the table sort of affair."

"I wouldn't think that personal catering would be under the same rules as commercial catering, in terms of permits and such. It's basically a person-to-person transaction. If you didn't want to function on an ordering sort of basis, you could simply prepare a selection of offerings each day and people could stop by and just buy them on the spot. I've got an extra cooler in the back that's not really being used. We could put it out front and designate it for this."

"That definitely might cross some lines in terms of rules and regulations."

"Well, either way, there canna be anything against having a sign-up sheet here. You can decide what and how you want to handle it. With Christmas just around the corner, it's definitely the time of year people can use some extra help. Even if it's a time-limited thing, you could earn a tidy little sum."

Christmas. Right. Afton was doing her best not to think about that. Christmas was one of her least favorite times of the year. She had a standing offer to go back to the US to spend Christmas with her Tennessee family, as she had last year, but she couldn't see that a short visit would be worth the expense. Not when she didn't know how long it would be before she found a real job. Hamish paid generously for the nanny job, but it wasn't a long-term solution. Filling up the spare hours cooking for other people would certainly help with both distraction and padding her bank account.

"It's certainly something to consider. Thank you for the offer."

"Anytime. Since you fed me lunch, can I offer you a cuppa?"

"Sure."

When they'd settled in the back of the store, in what used to be the lounge, Afton took the time to study her friend. "Marriage agrees with you. You look really happy."

Sophie stretched out her long legs and beamed. "I am. I never imagined I could be this happy. And I never imagined it would be Connor."

"Really? I always knew he had a thing for you."

Sophie went brows up. "You did?"

Afton twitched her shoulders. "I dinna think he ever really considered doing anything about it because of the pact. But, aye. He always used to watch you when he didn't think anyone else was looking. You've always been one of his favorite people, so this—the two of you—makes sense."

Sophie sipped at her tea, a warmth in her brown cheeks that wasn't from the beverage. "Well, I happen to agree, as it turns out. And I know we've said this already, but we dinna know how to thank you for what you gave up to give us this. Even if that wasn't directly your intention. I canna imagine how hard it must've been to make that decision."

Uncomfortable with the observation, Afton hid her face behind her mug. "Desperate people do desperate things."

Seeming to pick up on her reluctance to continue that line of conversation, Sophie crossed her legs. "Speaking of people who had a thing for other people... What about you and Hamish?"

Afton almost bobbled the tea in her hands. "What? What about me and Hamish?"

"I just always suspected there was something there between the two of you."

"We didn't—we never—"

"No, no. You misunderstand me. I'm not saying anything ever happened. I know both of you better than that. But there's definitely always been a spark."

Thunderstruck by the observation, when she'd

thought she'd done so well hiding her feelings, Afton could only ask, "Did Connor know that?"

"Oh, I doubt it. We haven't talked about it."

Figuring Sophie was likely the safest person here she could discuss this with, Afton settled deeper into the chair. "Aye, there's... something. But it also doesn't matter. He doesn't have the bandwidth for anything and has said as much."

Sophie gestured with her mug. "I mean, you're helping with that."

Horrified, Afton shot straight up. "You dinna think I'm using Freya to get to Hamish?"

"No. I definitely dinna think that. But maybe he'll change his mind."

The panic receded a bit. "I canna afford to hang on to the idea that he might. We're just friends, and I'm okay with that. It's what we've always been."

But as she finished her tea, she couldn't ignore the flutter in her chest that said she was lying.

HAMISH INHALED a late lunch at his desk, staring at his work calendar and trying to sort out how he was going to take Freya to pick out a Christmas tree. She'd always wanted a live tree, and they'd never been able to have one because Dayna was allergic. He'd thought that was something good he could offer his daughter for this first Christmas after the divorce. But the holiday was a week away, and he hadn't done the first thing to decorate the house. She hadn't said a word about it, but he'd still felt like a right arsehole when Connor had brought up Christmas over the weekend.

How the hell had he let it all get away from him? Well, that was easy to explain. Everything had gotten away from him. He'd fully expected them to be doing Christmas with his parents and had relied too much on his mum being the driving force in decorating. But both of them were staying in Glasgow with Gran. He'd thought that he and Freya would join them there, but Dayna was being a hardass about the custody agreement and demanded that they do the handoff by noon Christmas day. It was the first time since the divorce that she'd seemed really excited to be spending time with Freya. Maybe the holiday had jumpstarted her maternal instincts again, making her realize everything she'd been missing out on. Hamish wouldn't risk derailing that by fighting about this.

At least he'd managed to do the Christmas shopping. Thank God for the internet. All the gifts had arrived and were hidden away. They'd need wrapping, and he'd get to that. Somehow. But he *had* to make sure they had something to put them under. Which meant he had to find time to get out from under work. But staring at how the last three hours of his day had been blocked off for client meetings, he didn't see how.

You cancel them, eejit.

That made his sense of responsibility cringe, but it was the holidays. Surely his clients would understand. There weren't even any details about the ones on the schedule today. Surely, they weren't so time-sensitive that they couldn't be changed?

He picked up his phone and dialed out to his assistant. "Marsaili, I'd like you to cancel the rest of my appointments today and reschedule, please."

There was a long pause on the other side. "I can start working on that, but your next one is already here."

Hamish closed his eyes. "This is the last one today."

"Yes, sir." He could've sworn he heard a smile in her voice. But what sense did that make?

He cleared away the remains of his lunch and straightened his tie before stepping out to meet his next client.

Afton and Freya stood in the reception area. The sight of them was so incongruous, he stopped dead in his tracks.

"What are you doing here? Is everything okay? Why are you out of school?"

"I'm fine, Da. I exempted out of my last exams, so Afton came to pick me up early."

"Oh." Wasn't that a thing he should've known about? Hell, maybe Afton had messaged him and he'd missed it. It seemed all sorts of details were slipping through his fingers lately. "That extra free time will be lovely. But what are you both doing here?"

"I needed to come by and drop off the food Marsaili ordered," Afton explained.

"Ordered?"

"I'm doing a bit of personal catering on the side."

"And thank God for it. You're going to help me impress my unimpressible mother-in-law."

That was when Hamish saw the big insulated bag on her desk.

"I even included instructions for how to plate it and the best way to make it look like it came out of your own kitchen."

"You're a treasure, you are."

Afton grinned, then turned that smile on him. It struck him momentarily speechless, leaving him wondering when the last time he'd seen her smile like that had been.

"We also came to kidnap you. It's time to go tree hunting."

The immediate lift he felt at her words faded

almost instantly. "I wish I could, but I'm booked with back-to-back clients all afternoon."

Freya grinned up at him. "We know. They're all us."

"What?"

"You didn't recognize half the characters from *Pirates of the Caribbean*?" Afton asked. "I thought for sure you'd remember."

"I..." He thought back to the names. Elizabeth Swan. William Turner. Jack Sparrow. It had been right there, and he'd been too frazzled to notice. Hamish laughed. "You two are sneaky."

"We figured this would be the easiest way to block out time without making you feel guilty about short-changing your clients. C'mon. Get your coat. Malcolm's waiting for us out at Lochmara."

Hamish did as she asked.

The day was frigid, with rare clear blue skies. Out at the estate, Malcolm was waiting in one of the farm trucks. They all piled in for a ride into the forest. Afton had grown up here, so she knew where the best trees were likely to be for harvest. But when was the last time she'd done this? Hamish watched her out of the corner of his eye, wondering what emotional toll this was taking. So far as he knew, she hadn't truly celebrated Christmas since her parents had been killed. Oh, she'd come to the friend-family dinner every year—

they'd all been sure to bully her into that. But she'd always seemed calcified in her grief this time of year, and eventually they'd all stopped pushing for more.

He wondered what her plans were for Christmas. Did she have any? The idea of her being alone for the holidays had always made him ache, and he hadn't been able to do anything about it because there'd always been Dayna. But nothing was stopping him from asking her now. He should check with Freya first, though. Just to make sure she was okay with it.

Afton had planned the perfect afternoon for Freya. They tromped through the woods, and she explained what made for the perfect live tree. She told stories about doing this with her parents growing up, and for the first time, her eyes weren't full of shadows.

"Never thought I'd see her be able to do this again," Malcolm murmured.

Hamish glanced at the other man. The two of them trailed after the girls as they considered and rejected more than a dozen trees. Too tall. Too fat. Too skinny.

"Talk about her parents? Christmas?"

"Aye. She wasnae ever able to do it before. Not really."

"Maybe getting away from Lochmara and the

daily reminders of her grief has finally allowed her to do some healing."

"Maybe. Or maybe having someone to share all of it with is helping her to remember the good times." The older man shot him a significant look.

Hamish's step faltered. Did Malcolm mean Freya or both of them?

"This one! Da! What do you think? Will it fit?"

"That there is a Nordman Fir," Malcolm explained. "About nine feet, I'd say."

Hamish eyed the tree. It was wide and full, and would likely take up a good portion of the lounge. But they had the room, and Freya was clearly in love with it. "I think we can make it work."

Freya cheered, and Malcolm pulled out the chainsaw.

It took another hour to get the tree back to the farmhouse and hauled inside. Thankfully, Malcolm had already come prepared with a tree stand. Hamish cut the twine holding the branches close and stepped back as they sprang open. Then the three of them stood admiring it beside the fireplace.

"That's going to be gorgeous all decorated up," Freya declared.

Hamish's belly sank. The decorations. "I... uh. I went to pick some up over the weekend, but as it's rather late, there wasn't much left to be had. A few strings of fairy lights. Some colored balls. I'm sorry.

With Mum and Da gone to be with Gran, it got away from me."

A light hand squeezed his shoulder. Afton. "Not to worry. I've got plenty of corn for popping and a boatload of cranberries to string. I'll mix up some hot chocolate, and we'll put on a Christmas movie marathon while we string garland."

Saving his arse again, per usual. Hamish looked to Afton, intending to thank her, and spotted the expression of uncertainty. "What is it?"

"Nothing. I just... I know that you've been really overwhelmed, and that the two of you might rather do your own thing—so feel free to say no—"

"Spit it out. Say no to what?"

Her fingers knotted together in a show of anxiety he hadn't seen in weeks. "It's just... among all the things that Raleigh and Kyla saved for me are all the Christmas decorations from my family. I haven't remotely finished unpacking, so there's no real room for a tree at my flat. I was just thinking, if you'd like, you could use those this year. If you want."

Hamish understood what this meant for her. That she'd make this offer. Be willing to unpack those memories for them.

"That would be awesome!" Freya declared. "And it makes sense it should be your tree, too, since you'll be here for Christmas."

Surprise chased away the anxiety as Afton

turned to his daughter, white-blonde brows arched. "I will?"

Now it was Freya's turn to look uncertain. "Of course. I mean, I thought you would. If you want."

Afton pulled her in for a tight hug, obvious tears glistening in her dark eyes. "I'm so very flattered that you'd want to include me. And I'd love to spend Christmas with you. If it's okay with your da." Her gaze met his over Freya's head.

"It doesn't seem right that you should be any-where else."

And Hamish was running out of reasons why that shouldn't be true every day.

TEN

The lights of Ardinmuir Castle stood out against the night, a beacon of warmth and history, both ancient and personal. Afton had once known this six-hundred-year-old castle as well as her own home. She'd been here as often as the MacKean siblings had been at Lochmara. But this was the first time she'd seen it since she'd been back. There were signs of restoration and upgrades everywhere. Subtle ones that guests wouldn't notice if they hadn't seen how it started. But the signs that they'd finally been able to afford those repairs said a lot about the success of their assorted business ventures.

Hamish parked the car beside all the others,

and the three of them climbed out, everyone gathering a dish or bottle of wine before they trooped to the kitchen door. Cheerful chaos greeted them, and for once, Afton didn't feel the need to hang back. She eased her way past where Charlotte and Malcolm were making eyes at each other, and around Isobel, where she was trying to sneak a taste of whatever Angus had created for dessert, to set the hot dish she carried on the counter.

"Afton, love. It's wonderful to see you." While still brandishing a wooden spoon at a laughing Isobel, Angus stretched out an arm.

Freed of her burden, she flowed into him, wrapping the old man in a hug. Kyla and Connor's great uncle had always been one of her favorite people. She hadn't seen him since he'd escorted her to the private room in the church the day of her arrival. "Angus. It's so good to see you again under less... strained circumstances."

With another tight squeeze, he eased back, taking both her hands in his. "It is, indeed. There's someone I'd like you to meet." He waved over another older man she remembered seeing in the room that day at the church. "This is my husband, Munro."

Afton gasped. "Husband? You went and got married while I was gone?"

"They bloody well eloped while Angus was off in Berkshire filming the latest season of *The Great British Bake Off*," Connor complained.

Her jaw dropped again as she turned back to Angus, whose blue eyes twinkled. "You were on *Bake Off*?"

"Made it all the way to the semi-final," Kyla announced proudly.

Angus just shrugged and continued to twinkle.

"Congratulations!" Afton hugged him again. "I admit, I fell off watching after they changed hosts. Clearly I've got some binge-watching to do."

"I volunteer as tribute," Freya announced. "*Bake Off* is my happy place."

Talk immediately turned to planning a watch party. Somehow, in the midst of that, the group began transferring bowls, platters, and dishes to the massive table in the dining room. And this was the first real sense of homecoming Afton had felt since she'd returned to Glenlaig. Having this meal, for this holiday, with these people—though their group had expanded quite a bit—was familiar. This friend-family dinner had been started by Angus all those years ago, that first Christmas after Afton's parents and the MacKeans had been killed. Being here again meant more to her than she'd realized it would.

Throughout the meal, conversation flew fast and furious. She didn't say much, content to observe. But, for once, it wasn't because she felt uncomfortable. She simply wanted to soak in the holiday cheer around her and enjoy the absurdly huge array of delicious food.

From the seat beside her, Hamish leaned close enough his shoulder brushed hers. "Okay?"

At his low, quiet voice, her head whipped toward him, and for a moment, all she could see was his mouth, mere inches away from hers. "Aye. Fine. Why?"

"You're just quiet."

She resisted the urge to point out she was usually quiet in large groups. He knew that. And he was checking on her, in that unobtrusive way of his. It was something he'd always done. Because he saw her, even when she'd tried to be invisible.

"I'm good." It was mostly true. She'd been accepted back into the fold, and she was finally starting to believe it. If she hadn't gotten everything she wanted for Christmas, she'd learned not to be greedy with her expectations.

At the head of the table, Connor clapped. "Okay, people, we have to decide something of vital importance." He waited until everyone's attention had swung his way. "Do we have dessert before or after the evening's entertainment? Isobel has kindly offered us a private concert."

"I couldn't eat another bite. Not for a while yet," Sophie protested.

"I could," Gavin announced.

"You have a hollow leg," Charlotte accused. "And you grew two inches in the last four months."

The boy patted his stomach. "Gotta fuel all that extra height."

From the corner of her eye, Afton caught Freya sighing in his direction. Oh, boy. Hamish was going to hate that.

By majority vote, they decided to give the dinner time to settle before tackling dessert. They made their way to the formal parlor, where a massive Christmas tree had been set up. At least twelve-feet tall, it glowed with white fairy lights that bounced off the colorful array of ornaments. It made Afton think back to earlier in the week when she'd decorated the tree with Hamish and Freya. It had been a lovely and unexpected night, an effort to give something back to these two wonderful people who were still hurting from the dissolution of their family. Offering up her family's ornaments had been an impulse of the moment. There was still an ache when she'd pulled them out and put them up for the first time since she'd lost her parents. But being able to share some of the stories behind them with Freya and Hamish had reminded her of a lot of wonderful memories.

While Connor played bartender and Ciara took non-alcoholic drink orders, Afton wandered over to admire the tree. When Hamish followed, she dropped her voice low enough only he could hear. "What sort of concert are we getting, exactly?"

"Oh, you didn't know?"

"Didn't know what?"

"Isobel is Elizabeth Duncan."

Afton's head whipped up. "*The* Elizabeth Duncan?" She'd been a fan of the violinist's music for years. But she'd never seen what the other woman looked like. Dimly, Afton remembered hearing something about a scandal surrounding her back in the summer, but she'd been so busy with her externship hours, she hadn't really paid attention. "But how—?"

"It's a long story."

More things she'd missed. And in that moment, Afton decided to let it go. She'd been gone for more than a year and a half. Clearly, a lot had happened. There was no sense in beating herself up over it.

"Mistletoe alert!" Freya crowed.

Afton looked around to see who'd been caught and found everyone staring at the two of them. She glanced up. A dark green clump of greenery with white berries dangled above her head. "Um..."

"You have to kiss," Freya announced. "That's the rules. It's terrible bad luck not to."

"So it is." Connor snagged his wife and bent her into a dramatic dip before taking her mouth, and Afton spotted another cluster hanging above them.

In fact, there was mistletoe hanging all *over* the room, in so many places it would be nigh impossible to avoid it.

Afton tried to joke it off. "You know, you're newlyweds. The mistletoe explosion was entirely unnecessary. We all expect you to kiss."

Sophie offered a breathless laugh. "Oh, I had nothing to do with this." She twined her fingers in Connor's hair. "Not that we're complaining."

One-by-one, all the couples in the room took advantage of being in proximity to that infernal greenery. And then they all looked back at her and Hamish.

Panicked, she looked up at him.

A wry smile quirked his lips. "A quick one to appease the masses?"

If he kissed her again, she wasn't sure she could keep up the mask in front of their audience. "Seriously, you don't have to."

He took a half step closer, and she tipped her head back to look up at him. "Those are the rules. And we wouldn't want either of us to be struck with bad luck." The low rumble of his words rolled over her, rooting her to the spot.

His big hand cupped her cheek, dragging her back to that hilltop all those months ago, when he'd done the same thing to wipe away her tears, and they'd both gone a little mad. The feel of those fingers, roughened from the work he'd done to make a home, was a shock against her skin. She wanted to close her eyes to absorb the sensation, but she didn't dare. Not when she saw all traces of humor drain out of his eyes, replaced with a wanting she knew was reflected in her own.

Bollocks.

All these weeks, they'd avoided this. Kept to their roles. Boss and nanny. Friends. She'd respected the boundaries he'd set. Told herself she was fine with it. That their friendship was enough, as it had always been.

But as he closed the distance between them, she knew she was lying.

The brush of his mouth was soft. He could've stopped there, with that whisper of a kiss. But he didn't. Instead, he lingered, as if unwilling to part from that bare taste of her. Afton sighed against his mouth, some long-held tension in her releasing. Forgiveness for both of them for that first, desperate, forbidden kiss. The guilt she'd carried all this time slid away, and she trembled, soaking up the sweetness of the moment.

Then his hand slid into her hair and the sweet turned molten as he hauled her closer and dove deeper. Every nerve in her body lit up, and she was so here for it. There was nothing forbidden here. No rules being broken. There was only an incredible, breathless want, echoed and returned tenfold.

When he lifted his head, she tried to follow and swayed, kept standing only by his arm wrapped around her. Only the thinnest rim of blue showed in his eyes as he stared down at her, mouth still parted. His chest rose and fell against hers, and she realized she'd fisted her hands in his jumper.

Enthusiastic cheering—Freya's—had heat rushing to her cheeks as she remembered their audience.

Oh God.

Afton forced her fingers to relax. With one last brush of his thumb along her jaw, Hamish stepped back, looking as shell-shocked as she felt. She had no idea what to do or how to respond.

At the sound of a violin being tuned, she turned blindly toward Isobel. "I'm really looking forward to hearing you play. I've been into your music for many years."

Isobel's eyes were dancing. "I hope I live up to the hype."

Of course she did. Elizabeth Duncan was an internationally famous musician. Getting this intimate performance was almost enough to distract Afton from the swirl of emotions inside her. Almost. As Isobel continued to play, it felt as if she somehow reached inside and pulled that swirl into the light, putting melody to the yearning that cut like a blade. Tears pricked Afton's eyes, and she sighed.

A light touch brushed her shoulder, and she turned to find Hamish reaching his arm along the sofa behind Freya, who sat between them. His eyes held a question. Afton was too wound up to be certain what it was. But she didn't shrug off his touch, instead soaking up the connection while it lasted.

By the end of the night, after music and dessert and gift giving, Freya was asleep on her feet. She leaned heavily against Hamish on the way to the car. He tucked her into the back, brushing a kiss against her temple as he buckled her safety belt. Afton's heart rolled over in her chest at the sight.

She said nothing when she climbed into the passenger seat. Nothing still, when he didn't turn toward town to take her back to her flat. He probably wanted to talk about the kiss. They *ought* to talk about the kiss. What it meant. What it didn't. Nascent romantic that she was, Freya's enthusiasm for the whole thing meant she was ripe for unrealistic hopes and misunderstandings. Afton knew Hamish would want to address that.

Back at the farmhouse, Freya didn't stir as Hamish parked. With what Afton knew was long practice, he scooped up her sleeping form and carried her to the house. Afton unlocked the door and followed them both up the stairs, watching as he laid her in bed and tugged off her shoes, before tucking her in with another kiss and a murmured, "Goodnight, Cricket."

He closed her bedroom door with a quiet snick and joined Afton in the hall. They stared at each other for a long, charged moment. Afton wondered if he'd kiss her again. God, she wanted that. Wanted the chance to touch and taste him without a time clock or an audience. Which was foolish. Because he was probably trying to find the words to let her down gently.

"Stay."

Afton's heart leapt at that single syllable. "What?"

"It's late. There's no reason for you to go all the way back to the village, just to turn around and come back out in the morning. This way, you can be here when she wakes up. You should be here when she wakes up."

"Okay." The word was a mere whisper because she didn't know what this meant and was too afraid to say more for fear of breaking the spell.

Hamish stepped past her to open another door. "We have a guest room. There's not much to it yet, but it's somewhere to sleep."

Reality grounded that brief flare of hope. He wasn't asking her to spend the night with him in his bed. He wanted to include her in the family Christmas. Probably because it was what Freya wanted. And that was fine. She wanted to be here. Wanted to be part of the ritual of a family, even if she was still a little on the outside.

"I'll grab you something to sleep in."

Afton stepped into the room, switching on the overhead light. After the dimness of the hallway, it all but blinded her. As he'd said, there wasn't much to the room. Just a bed and a simple table to one side. Not even a lamp or curtains. They hadn't had guests, so it hadn't been a priority on the renovation list. But that was fine. The bedding was clean and neat.

"Here." Hamish stopped in the doorway, offering a stack of clothes. He seemed reluctant to cross the threshold. Not wanting to give her the wrong idea? Or not wanting to tempt himself by being near her and a bed?

Wishful thinking, Lennox.

She reached to take the clothes. "Thank you."

He didn't release them immediately, his eyes dark as they searched hers. Then he bent forward to brush his lips over her temple. "Goodnight, Afton."

And though she wanted to grab him by the jumper and drag him into the room, she stepped back. "Goodnight, Hamish."

Then she shut the door and sagged against it with a sigh, wondering what the hell all of this meant.

AT TWO MINUTES until noon on Christmas Day, Hamish pulled into the driveway of the terrace house he'd shared with Dayna. He didn't see any other vehicle, so it seemed his former in-laws weren't here. Something in him relaxed a little. He hadn't seen them at all since the divorce and had no idea what they knew about the circumstances. He seriously doubted that Dayna had admitted to either of her image-conscious parents that she'd had an affair. Whether she'd blamed the split on him or not didn't really matter. He'd have been polite either way. But they'd hijacked Christmas Day for most of Freya's childhood, and he no longer had to pretend that he liked them.

The front door opened as he popped the boot.

Freya raced toward her mother. "Mum! Happy

Christmas!" She crashed into Dayna, and Hamish saw his ex-wife wrap around her, bending to kiss the head that wasn't too far below hers anymore.

Maybe this visit would go better.

He carried Freya's suitcase and the two paper bags of presents she'd wrapped herself and met the two of them in the entryway.

He passed the bags of gifts to his daughter. "Why dinna you go put those under the tree?"

"Okay!" She bounced into the family lounge to do that.

Watching her, he had a moment of nostalgia, remembering their first few Christmases, when she was wee. Before this house. Before Dayna bent to the pressures of her high-society family. Back when things were good.

They hadn't been good for a long time.

"Remember when she was two, and she was more excited by all the wrapping and ribbons than she was by the presents?"

Dayna chuckled. "That photo of her popping out of that enormous gift bag is still one of my favorites."

Hamish caught her smile and shared it. And for a moment, he saw the woman he'd loved enough to marry. From the lounge, Freya squeed with joy over the pile of packages already waiting under the picture-perfect tree. The room was draped in garland

and ribbon and all the magazine-worthy decorations that were the norm around here because Dayna's family cared about how things looked. It was all far more matchy-matchy and formal than he liked, but it would be familiar to Freya, and that was good. She'd had enough changes this year.

It felt strange being in this house where they'd shared a life. Where they'd built a family. Where they'd lost it. He'd loved the architectural details of the space, the history behind it. But without Freya as a full-time resident, it no longer looked lived in or comfortable. Everything was set up just so. It was a far cry from the hodgepodge farmhouse in Glenlaig, with the live tree taking up nearly half the lounge, loaded with popcorn and cranberry garland and someone else's ornaments. For now. There were new ones, too. Afton had seen to that. A collection of goat ornaments for Freya, and a tiny farmhouse that was a surprisingly close match to the actual house for him. To start their collection, she'd said.

This morning with her had been so much warmer and more comfortable, despite the horrendously early hour it had begun. Freya had pounced on Afton in bed to wake her. Then they'd all trooped downstairs in pajamas. Afton had, of course, been wearing one of his shirts and some flannel pants that were far too big. It shouldn't have been sexy, but it was. He hadn't considered that when he'd asked her to stay last night. They'd opened presents and eaten a strata Afton had put together the day before, which had been divine, as everything she made was. He'd completely over-done it on buying things for this daughter because the parental guilt was strong. But he'd also bought a few things for Afton. Some books by authors he knew she enjoyed. A few cookery implements he'd overheard her talking to Freya about. It had felt so good to have her there, to see her enjoying Christmas again. It made him glad he'd impulsively asked her to stay, even if he had wished she'd been sleeping beside him.

Okay, he hadn't been thinking about sleeping after that kiss.

Dayna's voice interrupted his train of thought. "Happy Christmas, Hamish. Thank you for bringing her all this way."

"Of course."

"I'm really looking forward to spending a longer chunk of time with her."

He prayed that was true. "I hope the two of you have fun. Are you going over to your parents' for dinner?" If she had other plans, he'd be shocked.

"Yes."

Freya bounced back into the entryway. "Did you get the ingredients I asked for?"

Dayna wrapped an arm around her. "I did. Are you finally going to tell me what they're for?"

"I'm making something to take to Christmas dinner with Grandma and Grandpa."

Hamish hadn't been aware she'd been working on this. He could just imagine how Dayna's parents, who had a chef of their own, would respond to their granddaughter making something herself. God, he hoped they were nice about it.

Dayna's lips quirked in amusement. "Are you now?"

"I am." Freya nodded with emphasis. "Afton taught me how to make it."

The amusement on his ex-wife's face chilled as she lifted her gaze to his. "Afton's back?"

Before he could say a thing, Freya leapt in, cheerfully babbling in that preteen girl sort of way. "Aye. She's my nanny, and she's awesome. She's a chef, so she's been teaching me to cook and helping me take care of the goats and—"

As their daughter continued to ramble, Dayna's eyebrows rose steadily higher. "The nanny?"

He felt compelled to explain. "Temporarily. Gran broke her hip, so both my parents are out of town dealing with that for a few months. I needed some help."

Her face softened with concern he knew was legitimate. Dayna had always been fond of his grandmother. "Oh, I didn't realize. How is Gran doing?"

"Prognosis is good. She's stubborn, which is in her favor. Keeps pushing to do more with physiotherapy."

"We'll be sure to call to wish her a happy Christmas. Unless you already have?"

"Just a brief chat this morning. I'm sure she'd love another call."

As Freya continued to chatter about Afton, Dayna shot him a measured look. "You'll have to tell me all about it."

Belatedly, it occurred to Hamish that perhaps he should have asked Freya not to say anything about Afton to her mother. It was too late now. The cat was clearly out of the bag, and Dayna wasn't happy. For years Hamish had known she resented Glenlaig and his attachment to village life. She'd hated all the time he spent with his friends and working on untangling the marriage pact. But for the first time, he wondered if maybe that resentment had been more about Afton. Perhaps she'd realized he felt something for Afton before he'd figured it out for himself.

Not exactly comfortable with that realization, he decided it was definitely time to leave. "You two ladies should get to your visit."

Freya squeezed him tight. "Bye, Da."

"Bye, Cricket. I love you." He leaned back just enough to tweak her nose. "See you next year."

His car felt incredibly empty when he got back into it. An entire week stretched out before him without his daughter. While a part of him looked forward to the silence, he was also dreading being there by himself. She took up so much space, brought so much life with her. When she was gone, he felt every bit of the weight of the crazy impulse that had driven him to buy the house, despite all the work it needed. That was the plan for this week. Work on the house. He'd closed his offices with that in mind.

But that wasn't the only thing he needed to address. The contract with Afton would be up for renewal late next week, after Freya was back. Hamish was almost certain she hadn't been applying for other jobs. He didn't want to lose her in their daily lives, but he also didn't want to be responsible for keeping her from her dreams.

Connor had a point. You could give her some other reason to stay.

He hadn't forgotten his friend's assessment of the situation or the questions Connor had asked. What *was* he gaining by not even trying for a real relationship with Afton? Because being around her every day, seeing how wonderful she was with his daughter, what a fantastic part of his life she could be... Even in just in the short weeks she'd been with him, he'd been able to breathe again. He'd gotten on enough of an even keel that he no longer felt as if he was spinning completely out of control. That made him wonder if they really could try.

He wasn't sure that was fair to her, but he had a three-hour drive to figure it out.

ELEVEN

Tired and happy, Afton let herself into her flat and carried the bags of presents she hadn't expected upstairs. After Hamish and Freya had left for Edinburgh, she'd gone over to Malcolm's and spent the day with his family. There'd been food and laughter and an abundance of love in the house—something that had been sorely missing for her and Malcolm both for many years. It had been an unconventional Christmas, but a good one.

Setting the bags aside, she dropped onto her loveseat, automatically scanning the room, noting the piles of boxes still waiting to be unpacked. She ought to open some. Get more of her things put away. But Freya would be gone for a week, so it didn't have to be today. Today, she just wanted to relax. The late night and exceptionally early morning were starting to weigh on her. And it wasn't as if she'd slept well just down the hall from Hamish, lying in bed, reliving that kiss. Fighting the completely mad urge to sneak into his room, into his bed. Which would have been insane, as he'd made it clear where he stood. It wasn't together with her.

But that kiss... That caress of her cheek before he'd let her go. The fact that he'd asked her to stay, even if it wasn't with him. All of it made her wonder if he was changing his mind.

Dinna be daft. That road leads to heartbreak.

Nothing had changed. His stance had nothing to do with a lack of attraction and feelings between them. Last night had proved that beyond a doubt. He'd made her ache and yearn, and Afton didn't know if she could keep doing this. Every day she was part of his life, she fell further. For him. For Freya. She'd told herself she could handle it. Wanting him and knowing she couldn't have him had been her status quo most of her life. But hadn't that been a big part of why she'd left in the first place? Because she couldn't handle knowing he felt something for her and couldn't or wouldn't act?

All her joy in the day faded.

She didn't know what to do. Leaving would hurt Freya, and that was the last thing she wanted. She'd come to adore the girl. And she didn't want to leave Hamish high and dry without some sort of help. But at some point, she had to protect herself. Had to start building a life that left room for finding a love of her own. That couldn't happen here.

A knock sounded from below.

She was hardly in the mood for company at this point, but she shoved to her feet, nonetheless. Maybe Kyla or Sophie was popping by with a plate of Christmas goodies. She couldn't think of anyone else who'd be showing up on her doorstep this late on Christmas Day.

Hamish stood on her front stoop, shoulders hunched against the cold. Even standing still, his body hummed with a restless tension. "Can we talk?"

Nothing about that boded well, but she backed up anyway. "Sure."

He stepped inside. It was the first time he'd been inside her flat. Remembering the mess upstairs, she moved into the kitchen and automatically reached for the kettle. "What do you want to talk about?"

"Last night."

Ah.

This was what she'd expected when he'd taken them straight back to his house last night. He'd want to set the record straight. Re-establish boundaries.

Ignoring the sting of disappointment, she ran water into the kettle and figured she'd get ahead of whatever careful lecture he'd devised. "I'm sure that was confusing for Freya. We can clarify when she gets home that it was just—"

"I think we should try it again."

Water splashed onto her hand as it jerked. Deliberately, she set the kettle aside and shut off the faucet, because she couldn't possibly have heard him correctly. "You what?"

His eyes met hers with an intensity that set her blood to pounding. "I want to see what's there when there's not an audience, not my marriage, not the marriage pact, nothing else in the fucking way."

It was exactly what she wanted. But this was so counter to what he'd said before that she couldn't just leap. She needed to understand. "Why?"

One corner of his mouth twitched. "It might have been brought to my attention that I'm being an idiot."

Despite her own twanging tension, she laughed. "Oh? By whom?"

"Doesn't matter." He took a step toward her. "The last few weeks have shown me how things could be. They've shown me so many of the things that were missing in my marriage, and I've had a significant drive to think about the fact that my holding this line and not being willing to follow up on feelings we both have is just depriving all of us of something that could be pretty wonderful."

Instead of throwing herself into his arms, Afton held herself very still as she stared up at him. This was too important, and she didn't want to misunderstand. "What are you saying?"

He blew out a breath, running a hand through his thick, dark hair. "I know I'm a package deal. I know that, contrary to everyone else's belief but maybe not yours, I dinna have my shite together. I dinna have a hundred percent to give you when you deserve a thousand." He took another step, until he was only a hand span away. "But I canna ignore what I feel when I'm around you. I canna ignore how we could be together. So I'm saying that, if you're willing, I'd like to give this a try. If you don't, I completely understand—"

Before he could backpedal further and retract the offer, Afton surged forward, closing the distance between them and finding his lips with hers. Finally. *Finally,* he was offering exactly what she'd wanted.

His arms came around her, his mouth crashing against hers in desperate relief. Every wall they'd erected to cage their feelings crumbled. Every chain of careful restraint they'd forged for years snapped. They touched and took, bodies straining to get closer, as they sank into the fever of need.

As his hand closed over her backside, pressing her against his erection, Afton pulled back only long enough to gasp, "Take me upstairs."

Hamish seemed to come back to himself, shaking off a little of the delirium. "That wasnae... We dinna have to... I got carried away."

She framed his face. "Hamish, if my life has taught me anything, it's that time is precious, and you never know how long you have. I dinna want to waste any with you. We've been waiting for years. Isn't that long enough?"

For a long moment, he searched her face. She let every ounce of wanting show, praying he wasn't going to choose irrational nobility here.

When he boosted her up, she sighed with relief, wrapping her legs around his waist and settling her core against the bulge behind his fly. She'd expected him to lead her upstairs. Being carried was even better. It hit at dozens of fantasies she'd entertained over the years. Anticipation had liquid heat pooling between her thighs, and every step he climbed caused a friction that set little fireworks zinging through her blood.

Through long, drugging kisses, she managed to direct him to her bedroom, where he lowered them both straight to the mattress. She moved restlessly beneath him, every inch on fire and wanting more. Wanting everything.

Holding on to her virginity hadn't been a planned thing. When she'd been caught up by the marriage pact, she hadn't seen the sense in getting serious with other guys, and she wasn't wired for casual physical intimacy. That hadn't changed since she'd freed herself, so there'd been no one else she'd wanted this with. To find herself finally on the cusp with the man she'd loved most of her life was an exquisite gift she hadn't expected.

Hamish's hands slid beneath the hem of her jumper, sliding it up until it got caught beneath her shoulders. He rolled so she straddled him and tugged the top off. Appreciating the position, Afton bent to take his mouth in another greedy kiss, rocking against his hips to chase the high she knew he'd bring her. His fingers unclasped her bra, slipping it off. Then those callused palms were on her breasts, thumbing her nipples, and she moaned, arching into his hands.

"God, more."

"So lovely." Jack-knifing up, he closed his lips around one nipple.

Afton cried out, driving her fingers into his hair to hold him in place as his tongue swirled and tugged. An answering tug pulled low in her belly, and she continued to rock, seeking that friction, wanting the fullness of him.

Hamish rolled them again, shifting to unfasten

her trousers, all while continuing to worship her breasts. His hand slid inside to cup her sex, and she arched into the shocking warmth of that possessive touch, inviting more. When one finger parted her folds to slip inside, she gasped and widened her legs.

"So fucking wet." His voice was a rumble against her breast.

"More. Please, more."

He added a second finger, and that warmth and fullness were so much better than the toys she'd become so adept at using. As her hips began to rock again, he found her rhythm, driving her higher with his fingers and mouth and tongue, until he pressed his thumb against the bundle of nerves at the apex of her thighs, and she detonated.

The orgasm left her wrecked and still needy as his thumb continued to circle her clit, drawing out the aftershocks. He trailed kisses up from the valley of her breasts, along her collarbone and the length of her throat, before finding her mouth again.

Afton willed her arms to lift, to wrap around his shoulders and tug at his shirt, but she couldn't find the muscle control to lift them that far. Instead, she managed to hook her fingers at his waistband and unbuckled his belt, lowering the zipper so she could curl her hand around his hard, hot length and return a little torture.

"Fuck!" he gasped.

"That is the general idea. You're far too clothed."

His hand between her thighs stilled, and he dropped his brow to hers with a groan. "I dinna have a condom."

"I have an IUD." She'd gotten one before her wedding that wasn't, and there'd been no sense in having it removed.

He lifted far enough to look down at her. "I havenae been with anyone since my divorce. And I got checked before to make sure I was clean."

"Okay." She brushed a kiss to his stubbled jaw. "Then be with me now."

He rolled away, and Afton's heart froze in her chest. Then he started stripping, yanking his shirt up and off with one hand before shedding his jeans and boxer briefs. Naked, he crawled back onto the bed and dragged down her trousers and underwear, until she lay completely bare under that burning blue gaze. On his knees above her, he gave himself one long stroke.

God, that was hot. Some other time, she wanted to taste him, to explore every inch and find out what drove him wild. But right now, she wanted him inside her.

Afton parted her thighs and reached for him. He settled over her, into the cradle of her hips, until his erection nudged her entrance. There was no fear, no anxiety. Because this was Hamish. And he was finally going to be hers. She arched up, taking the tip of him inside, encouraging him to sink deeper.

Lacing their fingers, he kissed her and pressed inside.

Afton gasped as he slowly filled her. She'd thought she'd understood what it would be like. But no amount of toys had prepared her for this fullness that was right at the edge of pain, for the warm weight of him on top of her and the way her whole body seized, as if he were a key sliding into a lock. That sense of completion had emotion clogging her throat. Then he began to move, and the wave began to build once again.

She'd read romance novels for years, falling into fantasies. As a single woman, she'd embraced the self-assisted orgasm and all the shades of pleasure that could go with it. She hadn't shied away from exploring her own body. But none of it compared to the feel of his big body moving with hers. She didn't know if it was the difference in having a partner or if it was because it was Hamish, but she climbed faster and higher as he plunged.

Their skin slicked with sweat, and they both groaned as they strained toward that final crest.

"Harder," she gasped.

Hamish picked up the pace and shifted the angle so that the base of his cock rubbed her clit with every stroke.

"Oh God, yes. There!" Her head fell back, her whole body arching to take him deeper still. Incoherent sounds of pleasure spilled out as he pushed her toward the finish.

And suddenly she flashed over the edge with a scream, her body clamping around him. On a bellow that might have been triumph, he followed after her.

***

HAMISH LAY CURLED AROUND AFTON, staring at the miracle of all that white blonde hair spilled out on the pillow beside him, his body still humming from his release. If not for the rise and fall of her chest against his, he might've wondered if they'd killed each other. He was already wondering when they could do it again. His fingers stroked along the flare of her hip.

"I love these extra curves you've put on."

Afton roused herself enough to purr at that, so he let his hand continue to wander, exploring the texture of her impossibly soft skin.

"I had no idea you'd be a screamer."

Her heavy-lidded eyes blinked open, and she

stretched against him, all that bare skin brushing against his cock as one hand lightly scratched his chest. "Neither did I. I really didnae have a clue how much better a man-made orgasm could be."

More than a little horrified, he stared down at her. "You've never had a partner give you an orgasm?" What the hell kind of selfish men had she been sleeping with?

One shoulder twitched in a shrug. "I told you there's never been anybody serious."

What did that have to do with a partner taking care of her properly? Unless she meant there hadn't been any partners at all...

Hamish stilled. "Was this your first time?"

Those eyes went from half-mast to fully awake, and new tension replaced the languid satiation of her body. "Aye."

Oh God.

He played the whole interlude over again through that filter, wondering if he'd been too rough. He knew she'd come, but what if—

Afton's hands framed his face. "I'm not some naïve innocent, Hamish. I have lots of toys, and I know how to use them."

That snagged his interest. "You do?"

She traced a finger over the words inked on his pec. "*Rely on yourself and you will not be disappointed.* I was supposed to marry a man I didn't love. I wasnae about to leave my satisfaction in his hands, no matter what sort of reputation he'd earned." Her eyes came back to his, unapologetic and aware. "I know what I like."

The idea of her sharing those preferences with him, of being the only man to fulfill her fantasies, was an incredible turn-on. But that wasn't the point.

"That is definitely a fascinating line of inquiry I'd like to pursue later. I just would have handled all this differently if I'd known it was your first time."

Her lips curved in a feline smile that had him imagining them wrapped around him. "I have no complaints."

He didn't let himself get pulled in by her teasing or his clearly horny imagination. "Still. Did I hurt you?"

"No." She rolled closer to brush her lips over his in a soft, gentle kiss that belied everything they'd just done to each other.

As he looked into her beautifully flushed face, he understood he very much could still hurt her. Because while being with her was wonderful, he was still conflicted. And now that the first wave of lust had been sated, all the concerns he'd shoved to the side were bubbling back to the surface.

His change in mood must've shown because the pink faded from her cheeks. "Hamish, I swear to

God, if you're about to tell me that was a mistake, I'm going to kill you."

"No." He followed the assurance with another kiss, because he definitely didn't want her to believe that. "It's just... What comes next? I'd love nothing more than to keep you in this bed for weeks. To take all the time we need to catch up on everything we havenae allowed ourselves to talk about or feel all these years. But I canna just lose myself like that. I have responsibilities."

"Freya."

He stroked her cheek, hoping to find a way to explain all this without wounding her more than he already had. "I dinna know how this will go. I dinna want her seeing us together and making assumptions and getting attached."

Afton's face and tone softened. "Hamish, she's already attached. And frankly, so am I. Wouldn't you want that from the woman you're involved with?"

"Of course. I just... She's had so much disappointment, and I dinna want to disappoint her again, if you ultimately leave." He spit the words out fast, hoping she'd assume he was only talking about his daughter. But he didn't know if he could take it if Afton decided to leave after this.

Eyes serious, she framed his face. "I dinna want to leave. I've waited my whole life to be with you. I never actually believed it could happen. Why would I walk away from this?"

"But your job—your dream. I dinna want you to give all of that up because you chose to stay here just to take care of us." As he said it, another horrifying thought occurred to him. "And God, I hope you dinna think that's what this is about. Not that I dinna appreciate everything you've done for us. But that's not why I want you to stay."

"I appreciate the clarification. I didn't think that, for the record. And I happen to enjoy taking care of the two of you. I've been on my own for so long, I've never really had anyone to take care of before. I mean, there was the estate, but that's not the same. It's not so personal. Anyway, my dream was never to leave." She took a deep breath, clearly bracing herself for an admission. "I want to open a restaurant here."

"You do?" The idea of it had never occurred to him. Glenlaig was small. He'd assumed there wasn't a need for a chef here. Certainly, there wasn't a ready-made position. But if she opened a restaurant, that would be something else altogether.

"I didn't just decide to train as a chef on a whim. Well, not exactly. I spent most of my time away in Tennessee with the people who helped me escape."

Hamish listened as she told him the whole

story. How she'd made it to Glasgow without her car. How she'd gone to visit the Greysons after she'd left Las Vegas. How she'd met Athena Reynolds. And how she'd fallen in love with farm-to-table cooking.

"Raleigh already went with me to speak to a lot of the crofters. They were incredibly receptive. And because of Sophie, I've sort of fallen into an informal, personal catering gig, which has done wonders to get the word out about my food. So far, the village seems excited by what I've offered, so I can only hope that they'd be supportive of an actual restaurant. I mean, there are a million details that would have to be figured out, and all of it would be a long process. But it's something I think I can really do. And it means that I can stay, so I'm invested in making it work. Because you and Freya are worth it."

All his marriage, Hamish had been the one who'd had to bend. That Afton was willing to do whatever she had to in order to stay meant more to him than he could say. And opening a business was something he could sink his teeth into.

"That's brilliant, Afton. And I can absolutely help with the search for a space and the permits and dealing with the village Council and all those headaches. Cutting through red tape is my love language."

She laughed. "I know."

He cuddled her close, relieved that he wasn't going to have to let her go when they'd only just come together. But that was only one hurdle. "We do still have to decide what to tell Freya and when."

"You're her father. That's your call."

Hamish considered. Much as he wanted to dive into this headfirst and shout his joy to the world, experience warned him to tread with caution. "I think it's probably best that we keep this on the down-low, for now. I dinna want her to think that I brought you on as her nanny just because of this."

Afton shoved up into a seated position, her expression horrified. "Oh God. You dinna think she'll believe I offered to help just to get close to you?"

"I dinna know. I hope not. I'd hope she's got a better sense of you than that. But I dinna want to risk it. So I think we take our time publicly."

She eased herself back down on the pillow, relaxing again. "Okay. And privately?"

Hamish ran a hand down her bare torso, gripping her hip. "Privately, we still have a week alone. I think we should make the most of it."

Her eyes flared with heat. "Mmm, I agree. But we do have to feed the goats."

He blinked at the non sequitur. "The goats?"

She smiled. "Aye. The goats out at your farm, where no one can see your car or mine."

Meaning if they fell into bed and didn't come up for air until New Year's Day, fewer people would be the wiser. He could work with that.

"You should pack a bag."

"I think that's an excellent idea." With a swift kiss, she scooted away from him and opened the closet.

"Afton?"

"Mmm?"

"Pack your toys."

TWELVE

"I will never be able to look at a drop cloth without getting hard ever again."

With a breathless laugh, Afton collapsed down onto Hamish's chest, nuzzling at the scruffy line of his jaw. "Then it's a good thing we've essentially finished painting the last of the house."

He combed his fingers through her hair. "You have paint in your hair. Again."

"Worth it." She propped herself up enough to rake her fingers through his as well, noting the splotches of cool blue. "So do you."

The remains of their final worksite surrounded them, along with all their clothes. Fortunately, during all their exertions, they hadn't knocked into the paint tray or the open can still perched on the ladder. Really, it was a miracle they'd gotten as much work done on the house as they had, considering they'd been positively insatiable. She might have come late to sex with a partner, but they'd sure as hell been making up for lost time. It had been *glorious*. Too bad tonight would be the last of it for a while. Because of that, they'd rejected multiple invites to assorted ceilidhs, electing to stay in and ring in the New Year together—naked—as Freya would be home tomorrow.

Hamish's stomach let out a mighty growl.

Grinning, Afton sat up. "You clearly worked up an appetite. Let me feed you."

"I willnae say no."

They cleaned themselves up and tugged on the bare minimum of clothing—unbuttoned jeans for him, his shirt for her—and wandered down to the kitchen. She stared at the contents of the fridge, mentally flipping through recipe possibilities before she began pulling out ingredients. Since she was without her usual sous chef, she put Hamish to work washing and peeling some potatoes while she tackled some onions, peppers, and mushrooms. Home fries would be just the thing with some streaky bacon. She'd developed something of an addiction to them while she'd been living in Tennessee.

Absently, she hummed while she worked.

"You look so relaxed when you do that."

Afton shot him a saucy wink. "I think you had a lot to do with that."

His grin was cocky as hell, and she loved it. "Aye. But just in general, watching you cook these past weeks. It's made me wonder—why cooking? Why the chef thing? I never knew you to have any special interest in it beyond doing the necessary for living. Not professionally, anyway. Was it just that you fell in love with the process when you took Athena's class?"

She grabbed one of the knives she'd honed to proper, professional sharpness and began to dice the bell pepper. "There was some of that, aye. But, in a way, it was about control. Cooking gave me control at a time when I had very little. I love the predictability of it. Love knowing I can combine ingredients in a particular way and get a consistent result. That's comforting to me after a lifetime of being denied control over one of the most important parts of my life."

He nodded. "That makes sense."

"I fell in love with the creative side of it, as well. Because, while combining things in a certain way gives me a consistent result, I can always find different ways to put ingredients together to create something new and wonderful. And it turns out I really enjoy cooking for the people I care about.

That's part of why I want to open a restaurant here."

His hand trailed down her spine in a gesture as much soothing as arousing as he brushed a kiss to her temple. "I'm glad your Tennessee family gave you that."

She smiled, pleased he understood what the Greysons and her friends back in the US were to her. "Me too."

He went back to the potatoes. "How big or small?"

"About a quarter inch dice. We want them to cook quickly."

"Understood." Grabbing one of the other knives, he went to work. "Did you work in restaurants while you were over there?"

"I spent six months doing an externship at a high-end restaurant in Nashville, as part of my training program, once I finished apprenticing with Athena."

"Is that what you want to do here?"

"No, not specifically. Food can be a great equalizer. I think a lot of haute cuisine, while it absolutely shows off skill and the quality of ingredients and whatnot, can also feel very inaccessible." It was a belief she and Athena had in common.

"Inaccessible how?"

"A fancy restaurant with twelve courses on tiny

plates is not going to fly with the audience here. We are meat and potatoes people in the Highlands, and we believe in solid portion sizes. But I also want to create cuisine that's more elevated than what's on offer at The Stag's Head or Village Chippy. I want to create a restaurant that's somewhere people can go for date night or for celebrations. We dinna really have that here."

"No. We don't. What would you serve?"

She'd thought a lot about this as she'd studied what was on offer at the market these past few weeks and begun more in-depths talks with the crofters who were raising meat or growing produce to sell. "That would vary. It would be a seasonally focused menu that changes regularly, depending on what's available. I won't be able to source ingredients exclusively from the area because of the shorter growing season, but I'd like to use as many local products as I can."

"That sounds lovely. I know Ewan does a little of that at the pub, but not to this extent. What about the rest of it? How big a place and all that?"

With the speed of many, many hours of practice, she diced the onion. "That's hard to say. I'll have to do a lot of maths around the cost of ingredients, staff, the cost of the space itself, to sort out how many tabletops I'd need to have and turn over a night to cover all the expenses. There's a lot that goes into the whole thing. And there's a very thin profit margin in restaurants. Most of the money comes from drinks, which is not my thing. Not that I won't hire a bartender because, of course, I will. I'd like to focus a little more on wine. And, of course, I can incorporate local gins and whiskies since those have been on the rise in popularity. I'd have to find someone who wants to run that side of things. For me, it's all about the food, so I've got to figure out how to make all of that work in a way that's going to be sustainable in a village of this size."

He nudged the cutting board full of potatoes in her direction and leaned back against the counter. "I presume it's cheaper to retrofit a space than to build one outright."

Afton added the potatoes, onion, and peppers to a skillet, soaking up the satisfying sizzle of oil. "Probably."

As she cooked, he continued to ask questions, clearly working through logistics in that very organized brain of his. It was one of the many things she loved about him.

Plating up the home fries and some over-easy eggs, she leaned over to brush her lips to his. "I appreciate your enthusiasm, but I'm not going to rush this. Most restaurants fail within the first year. I'm determined not to be one of them, so I'm going to take the time to do the research and figure out all the details so that I do it right. Because I dinna want to waste the money, and I dinna want to lose something else that's mine."

He tugged her into his arms and laced his hands at the small of her back. "Well, you're no' going to lose me."

Because he was hers. That was what he was saying. And after the past week, Afton couldn't stop herself from believing it. He'd seen what they could be together, and he'd embraced it. So had she.

Moved, she tipped her mouth to his in a lingering kiss. One kiss turned to more, heating her blood anew. His callused hands slid beneath the hem of the shirt she'd swiped to cup her bare backside, drawing her against his fresh erection.

"Will that food keep?" he growled.

"It'll reheat." More than on board, she switched the heat off on the stove before her hands went to his jeans and began to draw down the zipper as he backed her toward the island.

The doorbell rang, and they both froze.

"Who the fuck is here at this hour?" Hamish demanded.

Afton glanced at the clock on the microwave. They'd lost track of time. "It's after midnight. First footers. We should've expected this. It's Hogmanay." And here they were, more than half naked, on the verge of having sex in the kitchen. "Oh, God, go answer the door. I need to find clothes."

Hamish gestured to his bare chest. "Like this?"

Afton stripped the shirt she wore up and off, tossing it at him and watching his eyes go molten.

"I'm going to kill whoever's at the door so you dinna have to cover any of that back up."

With another laugh, she gasped, "Later," and streaked out of the room, bolting for the stairs.

It took her more than a couple of minutes to find all the clothes he'd stripped off her in the freshly painted room upstairs, but she tugged them on, hoping she didn't look as sex-crazed as she felt.

Voices sounded from the entryway as she drew near.

"You finally got rid of that God-awful wallpaper." Connor. Of course, it would be Connor.

"Aye, we've gotten a lot accomplished this week," Hamish answered. "I think most of the painting is finished."

"Just some last touchups on the trim upstairs left," Afton added, coming in to join him.

"Ah, that's why you've both got paint in your hair." Sophie nodded sagely.

Hamish's tone was dry. "That is, frequently, something that happens when you paint."

"True," Connor admitted. "I just thought it

might have something to do with the fact that both of your shirts are on inside-out."

They both glanced down, verifying the truth of his assessment.

As Afton spotted the tag on her t-shirt, her cheeks caught fire. Hamish swore.

Connor beamed. "Gotcha."

Well, there was no reason to keep pretending now, was there? Afton sighed. "I suppose I should thank you for all the mistletoe."

Connor just continued to flash that delighted little-boy grin. "Oh, that wasnae my idea. I just helped."

That left her wondering whose idea it *had* been. Charlotte's? Maybe Malcolm's? He seemed to have softened into an almost romantic under her influence.

"We're just glad it worked," Sophie put in, beaming almost as bright as her husband. "You both deserve this."

"Seriously. I'm glad you decided to stop being a numpty about the whole thing."

Connor had been the one to call Hamish out on being an idiot? Afton wasn't sure how to feel about that.

Hamish sobered and tucked her to his side. Knowing this was some of the last easy, open affection for a while, she snuggled in. "Well, we're keeping things quiet right now. Freya gets home tomorrow, and as far as she's concerned, we're taking things very slow."

After a beat of hesitation, Connor pressed his lips together and mimed twisting a key. "Your secret is safe with us."

"We didn't come over to interrupt your private time. We wanted to bring you some of Angus's millionaire shortbread and wish you a Happy New Year."

Connor held up a bottle. "And we brought whisky to have a drink."

"Well, since you were kind enough to bring your own, come on in," Hamish invited.

THE MOMENT HAMISH opened the barn door, Paul Hollywood head-butted his thigh hard enough it would probably leave a bruise.

"Shite! What's wrong with you, you lunatic?"

Beside him, Afton repressed a laugh. "He didn't appreciate the delay in his breakfast because we slept in." Inserting herself between them, she crooned at Paul. "We're sorry, love. I'll make you some fresh goat mix today with extra molasses. How's that?"

The traitor nuzzled her like the gentlest lamb.

Not that Hamish really blamed him. He'd been doing the same first thing this morning, as it would likely be the last time for a bit, given Freya was due back at noon.

He'd missed the hell out of his daughter, but he also dreaded her arrival. By his own decree, it meant he'd have to repress all those natural urges toward open affection around Afton. After a lifetime of doing exactly that, a week of being free to be with her in any and every way had been heaven. Locking all that back down was going to suck. But he still thought it best to gauge his child and see how the week went before they changed anything in terms of their relationship status.

They went about finishing up the barn chores, putting out feed, mucking pens. Hell, even shoveling shite was better with Afton by his side.

"I was thinking I'd make lasagna for lunch to welcome Freya home."

"Oh, she'll love that."

"I'll get started when we're through here. There should be plenty of time to assemble it so she doesn't realize I'm sneaking in extra vegetables."

The sound of a car drew them both to the barn door.

Dayna's sedan bumped up the drive.

"I thought she wasn't due home until noon," Afton murmured.

"She wasn't."

"Go ahead. I'll finish here."

With a growing sense of dread, Hamish walked out to meet them. Maybe it was fine. Maybe they'd just gotten an early start this morning. Maybe Dayna had something she had to do later.

But the moment the car came to a stop, Freya flung open the door and stumbled out. She bypassed his open arms and ran straight for the house. The flush of her sweet face indicated she was either crying or had been.

The moment his ex-wife climbed out of the driver's seat, he fixed her with the glare he normally reserved for the courtroom. "What did you do?"

"I didn't do anything." Everything about her suggested annoyance and irritation. "She was ready to come back here at the crack of dawn. I just gave her what she wanted."

"Why is she upset?"

Dayna opened her mouth to speak, then her gaze slid past him, toward the barn. Presumably to Afton, given how her expression hardened. "This is all your fault. Filling her head with nonsense. Acting like her parent."

Hamish sent up a silent prayer of thanks that Freya was already safely inside. He'd known Dayna would take issue with Afton's presence in both their lives, but were they really going to do this in his front garden?

Afton changed trajectory and came to stand beside him. If she was bothered by his ex-wife's vitriol, she didn't show it. "I dinna know what you're talking about."

"What the hell are you on about, Dayna?"

Dayna's lip curled in clear disdain. "Defending her as always." Her gaze cut between the two of them. "Well, I can see she didn't waste any time when she returned, weaseling her way back into your bed."

Hamish clenched his fists to hold back the torrent of fury he wanted to unleash.

Afton angled her head, displaying all the poise she'd learned as a baroness. "That would suggest that I'd been in his bed to begin with, which I wasn't, as I was expected to marry someone else. Some of us took the prospect of those vows far more seriously than others."

Dayna flinched as if she'd been slapped. "You always wanted him," she hissed.

"Aye. I did. And just because I treasure everything you were fool enough to throw away doesn't give you the right to come here and attack me or do anything else to upset Freya. You made your choices, Dayna. Now, you've got to live with them."

In a gesture of clear dismissal, Afton turned her

back on them and headed into the house, leaving Hamish with his ex-wife.

She stared at him in white-faced outrage. "You're really with her now."

"Who I am or am not in a relationship with is none of your concern. Our marriage is over. Because of a deliberate act you took." Wanting this conversation over as well, he walked past her and reached into the car to open the boot.

As he retrieved Freya's things, Dayna crossed both arms over her middle. "It would have been over anyway as soon as she came back from wherever she's been. Because she was finally free of that blasted pact."

Because there was probably some truth to that, Hamish spared her a glance. "Maybe. But I wouldn't have gone about ending things in the most hurtful way possible. Goodbye, Dayna."

Like Afton, he left her standing by the car, carrying Freya's things into the house and locking the door. He didn't think she'd walk in. Probably she'd be burning rubber to get out of here as fast as possible. Hamish didn't bother to check before he dumped the bags at the foot of the stairs and went in search of his daughter.

She was in the family lounge, curled up on the sofa with her head in Afton's lap.

Afton stroked a gentle hand over her long, dark

hair. "Do you want to tell me what's wrong, Cricket?"

"My mother is a bitch." Her voice was muffled against Afton's legs, but the words came clear enough, and they made Hamish's heart squeeze. What the hell had happened to prompt his gentle daughter to say such a thing? Because they seemed to be having a moment, he held back in the doorway.

Afton's hand didn't still, and her tone didn't change. "That's not a very kind thing to say."

"She's not a kind person. She said all sorts of horrible things about you."

For a moment, Afton pressed her lips together. "Your mother has never been fond of me."

"She claimed you were after Da, as if she wasn't the one who cheated on him."

Hamish jolted. She knew? How? He'd always been very careful not to discuss any of that with Dayna when Freya was around.

Afton's voice remained soothing. "You know that has nothing to do with you, aye?"

"Of course not. I'm just so tired of all the crappy holidays with Nana and Granddad."

Hamish finally stepped fully into the room. "What about your grandparents?"

Freya shoved up. It was obvious she'd been crying, which absolutely gutted him. She wiped at the tracks of her tears. "They were having this New Year's Eve party. Mum acted like it was going to be this fun thing and took me shopping for a new dress and everything. But really, they just wanted to trot me around like some sort of pedigreed dog meant to perform. But only to be seen and not heard. I wanted to stay in, just us, and have family time, and they wouldn't give me that. It was all about business and connections. Afton said I'm not obligated to do things I dinna want to do that dinna feel like me. This didn't feel like me. I'm not a trophy. So I locked myself in my room and refused to go."

When had they had that conversation?

Afton winced, but he just shook his head. He wasn't upset with that piece of advice. He was furious with his ex-in-laws for making everything about them. As usual.

Afton patted Freya's leg. "I'm gonna leave you and your da to talk and get started on some lasagna for lunch."

Freya sniffed, looking every inch like the little girl she still was to him. "That's my favorite."

With a kiss to her brow, Afton rose. "I know."

When she left, Hamish opened his arms, and Freya cuddled in. There was so much to unpack from that conversation, but he zeroed in on the thing he was most concerned about. "I didn't realize that you knew about your mother."

"It's not like I want to talk about it."

"I get that." And he understood she wanted to drop it, but he needed to know a little more. "How did you find out?" He was deathly afraid that Freya had seen her with David before the divorce.

She jerked her thin shoulders. "I hear things. It doesn't matter."

He supposed it didn't. She knew, and there was no taking that away. Perhaps the parents of one of Freya's classmates saw Dayna out with David and were talking about it where their kid could overhear. For all that Edinburgh was a city, it was a very small town in certain circles.

"What *do* you want to talk about?"

"She hates Afton. Like *really*."

Hamish wished he was surprised that Dayna had gone there. "Aye. I know. She always has. She was never okay with how much time I spent here and trying to find a way to end the marriage pact."

Freya huffed and sat up, outrage scrawled across her features. "What kind of person is going to be resentful of you doing the right thing?"

"An unhappy one." It was the kindest truth he could give her. "Your mum and I had been unhappy for a really long time, and at the end of the day, that is why we got divorced. I know that's been hard on you."

"No."

He looked at her in surprise. "No?"

"We got to come here. This gets to be home. If the price for that is that I have to go hang out with her every couple of weeks and spend the holidays there, I dinna regret it."

God, she was so much his child.

He squeezed her shoulders. "I'm still sorry you're having to deal with your mum when she's upset. That shouldn't fall to you."

"Her problem." Freya pulled away, clearly done with all of this. "I'm home now, and I wanna go help Afton make the lasagna."

For a few minutes after she walked out, Hamish sat, marveling at the wonder of his child. Dayna had said God-knew what, in an effort to turn Freya against Afton, and it had backfired magnificently. That said a lot about how Freya would likely take the news of their relationship. But she'd had enough upheaval for now. He could let it ride for a while. She needed Afton for her right now.

As he wandered into the kitchen and saw them working together at the counter, side-by-side, his heart squeezed in his chest. Freya was smiling again. Maybe it was time to accept that Afton coming back into his life was the miracle he and his daughter had both needed.

THIRTEEN

Freya was back in school, and they'd all settled back into their former routine, with Afton on nanny duty, predominantly seeing Hamish first thing in the morning before she took Freya to school, and in the evenings for dinner before going back to her flat and her very empty bed. After a lifetime not having to share, she'd had no idea it would take her so little time to get used to sleeping with someone else. She'd slept more deeply having Hamish wrapped around her than she ever had in her life. Part of that might have been because of the extensive physical exertion prior to sleep, but it wasn't just the sex. He made her feel safe. Protected. After being on her own for so long, Afton didn't take that for granted.

But she understood Hamish wanting to take

things slow regarding them and Freya. Particularly after Dayna had apparently done her level-best to poison Freya against Afton. That might have back-fired spectacularly, but caution made sense, so they were both putting Freya first. In the meantime, Afton had filled her days in the kitchen, continuing to receive orders for personal chef catering and toy with menu ideas.

She was in the midst of an experiment with some Southern casseroles she'd learned from Athena, when a knock came on her door. Giving the filling a good stir, she lowered the heat and went to answer.

Sophie stood in the entryway, Connor by her side. "What is that incredible smell?"

Grinning at the predictable question, Afton stepped back. "Come in. You can try a bite."

The two of them trailed her inside and back to the kitchen.

Connor peered over her shoulder into the bubbling pan. "What are all those little black specks?"

"Poppyseeds. While I was in Tennessee, I got introduced to Southern casseroles. Poppyseed chicken is a favorite for brunches and luncheons." She spooned a bite of filling onto a couple of the rich, buttery crackers she'd baked. "Over there, this would be baked with the crackers crunched on top of the filling, but for mid-project taste testing, this is what you're getting. Careful, it's hot."

Connor, predictably, shoved the whole thing into his mouth, then began making pained noises and muffled, "Hot!" sounds. Sophie took a more delicate approach, nibbling slowly.

"Oh, this is wonderful. I wonder if it could be adapted as an appetizer to be served on the crackers?"

Afton considered. "I dinna know. Maybe. The sauce would have to be thicker, so it didn't just turn the crackers to goop."

Connor pointed to the pot. "Can we take one of those home with us? With the crackers?"

"You'll have to get one another day. These are spoken for."

"Damn."

Afton patted his arm. "I promise, I'll make you one." Her amused smile faded as she took in their rather grave expressions. "Is something wrong?"

Sophie bit her lip. "Not exactly wrong. We have a potential tenant who wants to sign a two-year lease."

"Oh." It was all Afton could say because she'd forgotten that she was essentially on a week-to-week basis with keeping the flat. She'd let a lot of things drop since she'd fallen into this domestic setup with Hamish and nannying Freya. It was hard to make any kind of plan, not knowing what exactly came next and when with Hamish. There was tons of research still to be done about the viability of her restaurant. And none of that made an iota of difference in the moment because she'd promised when she moved in that this very situation wouldn't be a problem.

"Right. Well, when are they needing to move in?"

Connor cringed. "Next week. It's the new doctor coming to join Doc Albright's practice."

Bollocks. When she'd agreed to get out in a hurry, she'd had only the bag she'd brought with her from the States. She hadn't expected to be moving an entire flat's worth of furniture.

"Well, then I suppose it's a good thing I haven't gotten too much further in my unpacking."

"We didn't want to put you in this position, but a two-year lease..." Sophie trailed off, clearly miserable.

Wanting to put her friend at ease, despite the situation, Afton squeezed her shoulders. "This was the agreement, Soph. It's fine. I canna make that sort of commitment, and you need a tenant. I knew that going in."

"But where are you going to go?"

That was a damned good question. One she didn't have an answer to. Maybe she could see if

Malcolm's old duplex was still vacant out at Lochmara.

A knock came on the door before it opened again. "Afton?"

"Hamish? I'm in the kitchen."

"Of course you are. I—oh, hey Con. Sophie."

Afton tipped her face up as Hamish bussed her cheek. "I thought you were in court this morning."

"Got rescheduled, so I find myself with a bit of free time."

Afton's brain immediately dropped the current problem and began offering suggestions for what they could do with that free time. Which would require getting rid of their company.

But Hamish was focused on Connor and Sophie. "What's going on?"

"We've found a long-term tenant for the flat. She wants to move in next week," Connor explained.

"Ah." Hamish nodded as if this was no big deal. "Then it's a good thing I have half an empty house."

Afton whipped her head up to stare at him, her thoughts of a late-morning quickie dissipating. "What?"

"I feel like this is a good opportunity for us to vacate the premises, so you two can discuss that." Sophie turned her husband toward the door and pushed. "Just let us know what you need, Afton."

The pair of them beat a hasty retreat and shut the door behind them.

"Are you seriously asking me to move in?"

"I have the space. Including more than one guest room."

Guest room. So this wasn't moving in with *him*. Wasn't an advancement of their relationship. Afton squashed the flare of disappointment and tried to be rational.

"Is that a good idea? You wanted to keep things quiet, and I agreed, but I dinna know if we'll be able to pull that off as easily if we're living in the same house."

"It makes the most sense. We've got plenty of space—all those rooms that still need filling. And it'll save you the commute of having to come out to get Freya if you're already there." He pulled her into his arms. "Consider it a trial run. Even if you're not in my bed, we'll get to see more of each other, and it'll be an opportunity to see how Freya reacts to us spending more time together."

That seemed like a step in the right direction, and there really was nowhere she'd rather be than with the two of them.

Still, she wanted to be certain he was sure. "People will talk, whether I'm in your bed or not."

"Let them. It doesn't matter what anyone thinks but us."

"Okay. Then I guess I have a lot of packing to do this week."

"Good. We'll round everyone up to help move things again." He glanced over at the stove. "How far are you from being able to walk away from all this?"

Definitely on the same page with having some one-on-one time, she strode over and turned the burner off under the remaining pots. "I just need to transfer this filling to containers and let them cool before I add the topping and pop them over to Village Blume for my clients to pick up."

"Do that. We're going to the pub for lunch."

Wait. What? "Isn't it a bit early for that?" It wasn't even eleven yet.

"That's the point. We need to get there before the midday rush."

She arched a brow. "Are you under the impression there's going to be wall-to-wall customers on a Tuesday?"

He grinned. "No. But we have a meeting."

"With whom?"

"You'll see. Finish with your food."

Afton scowled a little as she transferred the poppyseed chicken to the waiting aluminum trays and set them on the counter to cool. "A meeting was definitely not what I had in mind when you said you had free time this morning."

Hamish boxed her in against the counter, his front pressed to her back as he nuzzled her neck. "Mine either. But it's important. We'll get takeout when we're through. I dinna have to be back at the office until one."

She hummed with pleasure, dropping her head to the side to encourage more. "Promise?"

"Absolutely," he rumbled.

She danced out of his hold and headed for the stairs to go retrieve her purse. "Then, by all means, let's be off. The sooner we go, the sooner we'll get back, and the sooner I'll have you all to myself."

***

BECAUSE IT WAS ONLY a few blocks away, Hamish and Afton walked to The Stag's Head. He didn't take her hand in his, though he wanted to. And maybe it didn't matter. As Afton had said, once she moved in, people would talk. But not yet. Not before he spoke to his daughter himself. It was fast by most people's standards, and he wouldn't have suggested it if Afton wasn't losing the flat. But it made little sense for her to find yet another flat with short-term lease options, when ultimately he hoped to be taking things to the next level and asking her to do exactly this. He'd have preferred she be moving in directly with him, into his room and his bed, on a permanent basis. And that he was even considering that when he was less than a year divorced was probably kind of crazy. But was it really that insane when he'd loved her in some form all his life?

The focus right now was on making sure she could stay, and this morning's meeting was his first step in that direction.

"It's ten-forty in the morning," Afton protested. "They aren't open yet."

"I know. We're expected."

Jason McKinnon looked up from where he was doing some sort of prep behind the long, polished bar and nodded a greeting. Isla Boyd and Zo Bassey, two of the servers, were in the process of flipping the chairs from the tabletops to the floor.

Laura Craig, half-owner of the pub, stepped out of the office in back. "Hamish. Afton. If you're looking for Ewan, he willnae be in until later."

"We're actually here to see Dom," Hamish explained.

"Ah, he's in the kitchen. Go on back."

At her words, Hamish saw Afton's curiosity pique. They walked down the hall and through the swinging door, into the domain of Dominic Bassey, Zo's father and the longtime cook for the pub. Dom moved like a dervish at the long stainless-steel prep table, chopping onions and carrots. A wide smile stretched across his dark face at the sight of them. "Well, now, it's good to be seeing your faces."

"Thanks for meeting with us, Dom. You remember Afton?"

"Mostly by reputation." He winked. "Don't worry. All good. Hamish tells me you're a chef?"

Afton cast him a little side eye as she answered Dom. "Newly minted. I certainly dinna have your experience."

The older man laughed. "I'm no *chef de cuisine*, just a man with a lot of hours at the stove. We've all gotta start somewhere, and I'm hoping you'll start here. See, I've got a problem."

"What's that?"

"My wife and I have been married for thirty years. Our anniversary is coming up, and I really want to surprise her with a four-day cruise. She's always wanted to go, but I've never been away from the kitchen that long. Hamish said you might be able to help me with that."

Because Afton still looked uncertain, Hamish leapt to explain. "I thought you could come in and take over his kitchen for a few days so Dom can take his wife on holiday. Pinch-hit, to borrow an expression from the Americans."

She smiled. "I'd be delighted to help and take over your kitchen. But there's the matter of my existing job." She turned her attention to Hamish.

"What about Freya? If I'm here, I canna be ferrying her about or tending to the rest of my nanny duties."

"It's only for part of a week. We'll sort it out." Hamish was extremely motivated to do whatever was necessary to make this restaurant scheme a success.

"Well, if that's the case, then count me in. Do I need to learn the full menu by then?"

Dom continued to chop carrots. "Well, you could do that, sure. Or you could create some custom menus for your time in the kitchen. I heard about your idea of opening a farm-to-table restaurant. I think it's a brilliant idea. We've tried to do a little of that here, but with all the pub staples, a lot of what we offer still isn't. I think the concept would go over really well."

Hamish interjected. "I thought it would be a good opportunity for you to introduce your food to a broader audience in the village."

"That would be amazing." Afton frowned, her brows drawing together in an expression Hamish knew meant she was working through the details. "When would this be happening?"

"Well, I've not booked the trip yet, but probably in a couple of weeks."

"Okay. What sorts of ingredients would I have to work with?"

"If you want to work with our usual suppliers, I

or Laura can get you that list. But if you really want to do the farm-to-table experiment, I expect that'll depend on what you can source."

Afton bit her lip, thinking. "I'll need to make some calls. At this time of year, I'll still need a lot of basics from your regular suppliers. But I can get back to you both with some menu options. How far out do you put in orders?"

Dom glanced at the clock.

Afton's gaze followed. "Almost time for service. Here, pass me a knife. I can chop while we talk."

As the two of them continued to discuss the details, both of them dispatching vegetables with a speed and alacrity that astounded, Hamish watched Afton light up. This really was her element. He wished they could be more open about their relationship because he really wanted to kiss her right now. Wanted to taste that joy on her lips. But there'd be time for that yet. He didn't have to be back at the office until one.

As Afton and Dom came to terms about their arrangement, Isla swung through the kitchen door with the first of the lunch orders. "I need a fish and chips and a cottage pie."

"We'll talk more. I'll get those menus together and be back with them later this week."

"Sounds fantastic. I'm gonna go book that trip

and give my wife the surprise of her life. Hamish, thanks for thinking of this solution."

"Any time." He gave himself a mental pat on the back for thinking of it when Ewan mentioned recently that Dom was looking for a temporary replacement. He'd been feeling so out of his depth, so off-kilter being the one needing the help instead of the one offering. This made him feel a little more in control again. "Before we go, could we put in a take-away order for our own lunch?"

"Sure thing. What'll it be?"

"Whatever's easiest," Afton put in. "We've taken up enough of your prep time."

"Girl, you're about to be part of this kitchen family. Dinna go all formal on me now."

In the end, they left with two portions of the cottage pie that had just come out of the oven. The walk back was faster because snow had begun falling yet again.

"Thanks for this. I'm grateful for the opportunity."

"I'd have done it for anyone, but I have a vested interest in the success of your future restaurant. I thought this would be a great way to get your name out there in the community about something other than the marriage pact or being a runaway bride."

She glanced up at him through lowered lashes as they reached the flat. "I appreciate that, too. It's a lot to deal with over the next couple of weeks. When I agreed to move out in a hurry, I only had what I'd brought with me from the States. I dinna know how I'm going to get all of this moved."

They stepped back into the flat, stomping off snow and carrying their takeaway into the kitchen. "We'll all help. It'll be fine."

She set the bag of food on the table and stepped into his space, lifting her arms to loop around his neck. "You're a good man, Hamish Colquhoun."

He skimmed his fingers across her cheek and down the column of her throat. "Good of you to notice, Miss Lennox."

"Did you mean what you said about not needing to be back at the office until one?"

His blood heated. "I did."

"Then leave the cottage pie for now and come upstairs so I can properly express my gratitude."

How could he possibly argue with that?

FOURTEEN

By the time Hamish left to go back to work, Afton had throughly thanked him for his efforts, and they were both considerably more relaxed. She had only a couple of hours to make a plan before she had to go pick up Freya from school, and she made the most of them, multitasking by calling various crofters in the area to inquire about availability of ingredients, while she began packing. The fact that she'd been too busy to do more than break down the original boxes ended up playing in her favor.

Armed with a mental list of ingredients and an estimated volume of diners from the pub, Afton's brain was spinning with possible menus as she waited in the pickup line at Freya's school. Then her young charge was flopping into the front seat, and Afton was immediately distracted by the other major change coming up. Not that she said anything to the girl about moving in. That was entirely Hamish's purview to talk to her about.

As Freya continued to chatter about some debate being had between Aileen and Esme about whether a boy in their class had a crush on Esme, Afton only listened with half an ear. She was too wound up, worried about how the child would react to her becoming a true part of the household. Worried, too, about whether she'd be up to the task of running a full kitchen on her own for several days. She'd worked in a busy commercial kitchen before, but not by herself. Dom had no sous chef. As he'd explained earlier, the waitstaff and their dishwasher, Archie Watson, pitched in to help prep ingredients as needed. But all the actual cooking would fall to her.

She was still on autopilot as they dealt with the goats. At least until Sue made a forceful bid for her attention via a head-butt to her midriff.

"Oof!"

"Is everything okay? You seem awfully distracted today."

Afton straightened and really focused on Freya where she stood, putting out hay in the next pen.

The girl's posture was stiff, her shoulders a little rounded with an unease she couldn't quite hide.

Pushing everything else from her mind, Afton smiled. "I'm sorry for worrying you. Everything's fine. I'm just excited and a little nervous. I'm going to be taking over the kitchen at the pub for a few days, while Dom takes his wife on an anniversary cruise. They're giving me free rein to cook what I like, so my brain is spinning with menu options."

"Oh! That's exciting. What do you have to work with?"

"Leeks, Brussels sprouts, venison, potatoes and carrots, of course. An array of other root vegetables. One of the crofters at Lochmara is willing to butcher a pig for the occasion."

Freya went a little pale. "Butcher?"

"That is where meat comes from, Cricket."

The child cast a glance at the goats, pausing to rub Mel along the cheek. "I think I'm glad we dinna have that kind of farm animals."

Best not to mention that these were technically meat goats. "Fair enough. Anyway, I can certainly get my hands on fresh fish as well."

"Sophie might have some fresh herbs growing in her greenhouse."

"Oh, that's a good thought." Afton made a mental note to call her later to ask.

The pair of them finished their barn chores and retreated to the house, Freya offering more suggestions for the menu. She'd been a quick study about food, and Afton had enjoyed her enthusiasm.

As they washed up from the barn, Freya announced, "I'm cooking dinner tonight."

"Oh, you are?"

"You've been teaching me. I want to try."

Afton couldn't think of a reason to say no. "Okay. Let's figure out what you can make with what we got on hand."

They settled on chicken piccata, as it was a quick dish that would leave Freya ample time to get to her homework. Afton supervised as Freya thawed and prepped chicken breasts and gathered up the rest of her ingredients. She was painstakingly mincing shallots when Hamish got home.

He stopped at the counter, eying the spread. "What's going on here?"

"The sous chef has requested control of the kitchen tonight. I'm supervising. She's doing a very thorough job."

"I see."

The doorbell rang. Hamish started to turn, but Freya waved him away. "No, no. I'll get it. You stay."

She walked out, wiping her hands on a dish towel.

"She's up to something," Hamish observed.

His suspicious Dad-voice amused Afton. "Clearly."

"Have you said anything about the other thing?"

"No. That's on you."

He sucked in a breath and nodded, clearly anxious about the conversation. "Okay, I'll address it over dinner."

Afton prayed it went well.

A few moments later, Freya strode back in with an armful of flowers.

Suspicion lit Hamish's gaze, though his tone was mild enough. "What's this? Did someone send you flowers?"

"No. I just had Sophie drop some off. I thought they'd look nice on the table."

"You... had Sophie drop off flowers," he repeated.

"Aye. Presentation is important." She began hunting around in the cupboards for something to put them in.

Lips twitching, Afton explained, "We've been talking about the restaurant and how presentation is a big part of the meal."

"You eat with all your senses," Freya added.

"Ah."

She'd evidently taken the conversation to heart,

as she folded napkins and even dug out some candles from somewhere to add to the tablescape with the flowers in a stoneware pitcher. Afton was touched by all the effort and wondered if they had a budding restauranteur.

"What kind of wine goes with chicken piccata?" Freya asked.

Afton considered. "Something white. A Sauvignon Blanc or Pinot Grigio. Maybe a Chardonnay."

Freya began dredging the chicken cutlets in flour. "You should open one for you and Da."

"I think we have a bottle of Sauv Blanc... somewhere," Hamish muttered.

"I've got it." Afton slid off her stool and found the wine in the rack, covered in dust. Whites were not his usual drink of choice, but it would pair well with the meal, and she thought perhaps he could use a little loosening up. After pouring them both a glass, she returned to her sentry post in the kitchen, offering directions and pointers from time to time as Freya followed the recipe.

The kid was a natural. Once she had all her ingredients out and thawed, she managed to get the meal cooked and plated in a little over fifteen minutes, complete with lemon slice garnishes and capers. "Sit!" she ordered.

Afton and Hamish took their places at the table, and Freya served them both with a flourish.

Taking in the plate that was more visually appealing than a lot of the restaurant fare she'd been served, Afton smiled. "This looks marvelous. Well done, Cricket."

Freya made a dramatic bow, a dishtowel draped over one arm. "Enjoy your meal."

She did an about-face, as if about to leave the room.

"Where are you going, young lady?" her father asked.

"The chef doesn't eat at the table with the customers."

Hamish chuckled. "Sit. Eat. I want to talk to you."

Freya's playful mood immediately vanished, and she sat without food.

Wanting to allay any apprehension, Afton interjected, "You're not in trouble."

"No. You're certainly not." Hamish gave her a Dad-look. "Should you be?"

"No, sir."

"Just checking." He took a deep breath. "You enjoy having Afton around, right?"

She visibly brightened. "Obviously."

"Well, she's losing her flat because Connor and Sophie found a long-term tenant. She needs a new place, so I thought she might move in here with us. If it was okay with you."

Freya pumped her fist in the air, a smile stretching her cheeks from ear to ear. "Of *course*, it's okay with me! I've been hoping for this!"

Hamish blinked at her. "You have?"

"Well, of course."

At the implied *Duh* in her tone, Afton took another look at the table and the meal and the flowers and the obvious effort Freya made for what was probably supposed to be a romantic dinner. For two.

She's parent trapping us.

The realization slammed into her, and her heart went squishy at the idea that Freya wanted the two of them to be together.

Hamish obviously hadn't caught on to what was happening. "It'll certainly be more convenient for all of us to have her here. There's plenty of space, and she'll have her own room.

Freya's face screwed up. "Her own room? Why wouldn't she stay with you?"

"With—" He trailed off, taking another long look at the table and finally cluing in. "Is that what all this is about? You're trying to get me and Afton together?"

Exasperated, Freya threw up her hands. "For a smart man, you're being really dumb, Da. You're perfect for each other. You both have feelings for each other. Why dinna you just admit it?"

Wait, how did she know that? Were they that obvious?

"What makes you think that?" Hamish asked cautiously.

Freya leveled him with a very adult *please* stare. "I may have heard you talking about it that first day Afton cooked for us."

The day I came over to confess my feelings. Oh God.

Hamish stared at his daughter, clearly struck speechless.

Freya took advantage of their shock and shoved back from the table. "I appreciate everything that you do for me, Da, but you also deserve to be happy. So, stop using me as an excuse and get out of your own way." On that mic-drop statement, she picked up her plate from the counter. "I'm going to eat in my room."

Then she was gone, leaving Afton and Hamish in the ringing silence.

Afton was the first to recover her voice. "Well…"

"She was eavesdropping." Hamish scrubbed both hands over his face. "She must've been home the whole time."

"That seems to be the case." She tried to recall the rest of that conversation but couldn't remember much aside from the fact that he'd admitted he felt for her, too, and couldn't act on it.

Beside her, Hamish went rigid. "God, that's how she found out about her mother."

She laid a hand over his, understanding his upset that he might've been the source of that information. "It's a lot to process. Maybe we just enjoy this nice meal that your very sweet daughter made with the very best of intentions, and table that discussion for later."

He met her gaze and turned his hand up to squeeze hers. "Aye, okay, let's do that." Releasing her hand, he cut into the chicken. "I guess this answers the question of how she'd react to the idea of us as an us."

"I guess it does." Freya wanted them together. She was one hundred percent on board. Would Hamish be? She tried not to allow herself to get overexcited or pushy.

"So what do we do now?" he asked.

Afton lifted her glass and held it up for a toast. "I, for one, think we should take her advice."

After a long moment, Hamish lifted his own glass and smiled. "Then I guess I ought to be clearing out some drawers."

HAMISH GATHERED around the poker table that had been set up in the library at Ardinmuir with Connor, Raleigh, Malcolm, Angus, and Munro. Now that Isobel's tour was over and his duties as head of her security were through, Ewan was back, as well. They'd skipped the monthly game in December, between Connor and Sophie's wedding and all the holiday busy. Angus—official master of the kitchen at Ardinmuir—had outdone himself with the spread of appetizers and sweets to fuel the night. Each of them had a small plate by their place, piled high with the first round of selections.

Connor slapped Ewan on the back as he sat. "Good to have you back, Cousin."

"Good to be back. The tour was... interesting, but Isobel's happy to be home. She's nesting. And while Havoc is sad not to have dozens of people adoring him on the daily, he's glad to have the room to roam."

"I still canna believe you took that massive beast on tour," Malcom muttered.

"If you'd seen his face *and* Isobel's when I suggested it was impractical and perhaps he ought to stay home, you'd understand."

Raleigh grinned. "Ain't love grand?"

The usually stoic former Royal Marine smiled back. "It is, indeed."

"How's the new agent working out for her?" Hamish asked. In the wake of helping extract Isobel from her previous abusive agent and manager, he'd been the one to step in as acting agent for several months, until she'd found someone else she felt she could trust. He'd been happy to help, but thrilled when he was able to take those additional duties off his plate.

"Cordelia is fantastic. She respects Isobel's vision and *listens*. And she's rabid about protecting Isobel from any more predatory contracts. She's not even batting an eye at Isobel's plans to avoid touring for a while as she rerecords all those early albums."

"That's wonderful." Munro settled in with his food. "Will she be spending time in London or Glasgow to do the recording?"

"No. She's booked time at a remote studio in the Hebrides for now. But we're in talks with an architect to put an addition onto the house so she can ultimately record at home."

Raleigh passed out the poker chips. "Oh, that's big, adding onto your house for a woman. When you planning on making you two official?"

Ewan blinked. "We are official."

"I mean, when are you gonna pop the question and marry that girl?" Raleigh paused. "Or did you elope while on tour, like Angus and Munro did down in Berkshire?"

"No. And I dinna ken. We're committed. I'm no' in a hurry to push her into anything. You've all just got weddings on the brain."

"Hard not to when Malcolm's coming right behind us," Connor pointed out. "Just a few weeks to go."

"And I canna wait." The contented sigh proved that Malcolm Niall was a changed man since Charlotte had come into his life. The estate manager had a lightness to him that Hamish had never seen. The unconventional family life he'd fallen into with Raleigh's second mother and their foster son suited him down to the ground.

As Malcolm began shuffling cards, Hamish bit into a savory mini mushroom tart bursting with Gruyère and caramelized onions. "Mmm, I've missed this, for sure. Well done, Angus."

"Thank you, lad. Though I'd wager you're eating rather well these days." The old man's blue eyes twinkled.

Connor eased back in his chair. "Speaking of, is Afton settling in okay?"

They'd finished moving all her things from the flat over the previous weekend, and he had cleared out some drawers and wardrobe space. There hadn't seemed much reason to stick to his original intentions for total propriety when his daughter was apparently perfectly aware of their feelings for each other and was in full support of their relationship. God knew he loved having Afton in his bed, even just for sleeping.

"Well, we've got boxes everywhere again, courtesy of everything Raleigh and Kyla packed up for her from the estate. But that's fine. I had half an empty house to fill. She'll get unpacked, eventually. Right now, she's entirely focused on menus for her upcoming stint at the pub."

"Customers are already talking," Ewan reported. "We'll definitely have plenty of traffic to try her food."

"That'll make her both happy and nervous." She'd been obsessively testing recipes for days. His freezer was full of her efforts.

Angus picked up the cards he'd been dealt. "How is Freya taking all of this?"

Hamish rearranged his own hand into some semblance of order. "She's delighted, considering evidently she's spent the last two months trying to parent trap us." At the silence that followed, he glanced up from his cards to see guilty expressions on every face at the table. "You knew?"

Raleigh laughed. "Son, we were all in on it. How do you think there ended up being all that mistletoe at Christmas?"

Speechless, Hamish could only stare. "How

could you... What... I don't..." He didn't know where to start.

All of them? They'd *all* had a hand in his daughter's machinations?

Entirely unrepentant, Connor shrugged. "You and Afton make sense, and you wouldnae get out of your own way, so Freya asked for our help. We agreed with her. The question is, did it work? I mean, we all ken you two are together, but are you openly together?"

"Aye, at this point we are." There'd been no announcement about it, and they were still being discreet when in the village, but they'd stopped hiding at home.

"Then the real question is, are you happy?" There was an urgency in Connor's tone, as if he was really desperate for the answer to be yes. And maybe he was. He'd found his happiness, so he wanted all the people he cared about to find theirs.

"Of course I'm happy."

Connor's eyes narrowed. "Why dinna I believe you?"

Hamish sighed. "It's not that simple. I keep expecting to wake up and find out that it's all some kind of dream. Or for Dayna to find out and cause problems. Which, let's face it, is going to be inevitable, because she's going to lose her shite. She's always hated Afton. Has always felt like Afton was a threat."

Raleigh tossed in some chips. "Well, that hardly matters now, since y'all are divorced."

"It *shouldn't* matter now, because we're divorced," Hamish corrected. "But Afton is a part of Freya's life. Dayna does have something of a say. And finding out that I moved her in, not only to the house, but in with me, is not going to go over well."

The Texan winced. "Lord, I hope you had the good sense to remind Freya not to say anything to her mama about that."

"We did have a discussion about what is and is not appropriate to talk about with her mum. And she's so supportive, I don't think that's going to be a problem." Though it made Hamish incredibly uncomfortable to ask his daughter to withhold information from her mother.

"That's good, aye?" Ewan prompted.

"Aye."

"So, what's the problem?" Connor prodded.

"I think the bigger issue is that Freya adores Afton, and the feeling is mutual. They have a great relationship. The kind of relationship that Dayna only wishes she had with Freya. But they're just not alike enough. Freya reminds me so much of Afton when she was young. The two of them clicked from the very beginning. On top of which, Afton gives her the time and attention she craves. She's a good parent."

Realizing they were all staring at him now, Hamish twitched his shoulders. "Oh, don't look at me like that."

"You're already thinking about her in that way?" Munro asked.

"She's been my nanny for two months. Of course, I've been thinking about her in that way."

"So what are you gonna do about it?" Raleigh challenged. "Are you just gonna kind of rock and roll along and let things take their natural course, or are you thinking about locking that down before something else can go wrong?"

"Locking it down how?"

Malcolm met his gaze across the green felt table. "Marry her."

His blunt delivery was like a football to the chest, squeezing Hamish's lungs. Not that the thought hadn't crossed his mind. Since Afton had walked back into his life, it was impossible *not* to imagine how the three of them could be a family. It was a fantasy he hadn't allowed himself to really indulge. But now...

He could see it. So clearly, he ached with the wanting.

"I've been divorced for less than a year."

"So?" Raleigh demanded. "When it's right, it's

right. Why should you have to wait some prescribed period of time if y'all make each other happy?"

It was a fair question, one Hamish didn't have an answer to. One that haunted him long after the poker game had passed and he lay in bed that night, with Afton snuggled in beside him, the silk of her hair brushing his chest.

He'd fought so hard to try to keep things slow with Afton because he'd rushed into things with Dayna. In part, that had been because he was running away from something else. From the feelings for Afton he hadn't known what to do with. From a temptation he could never act on.

With Afton, he'd be rushing *toward* something. Grabbing on with both hands to the thing he'd known he wanted, before he'd even been able to fathom a circumstance where he could have it.

He'd spent his whole life playing by the rules, finding resolutions for others within those rules. But didn't he love the challenge of finding the loopholes? Of finding ways to circumvent the very restrictions placed on people? He'd fallen into it because he'd wanted to find a way to free Afton and Connor from a ludicrous expectation. And he'd found it. An exit option with an exceptionally high cost.

But she'd come back.

And she was free.

So was he.

There was finally, at long last, nothing stopping them from being together. Even his own daughter thought he was being foolish for not giving in. So maybe it was time to take everyone else's advice and be reckless, for once.

Afton was absolutely worth that risk.

FIFTEEN

Just a few hours left.

Afton wiped her sweaty brow on the sleeve of her chef's jacket and scanned everything currently cooking on the commercial range. Those lamb chops would need to be turned in a minute, and the latest batch of turnips was nearly done for the next round of mash. There were only two bowls of venison stew remaining, and the roasted winter squash soup wasn't going to last much longer, either. They were already out of the mussels in white wine, and she needed to put together a fresh batch of apple cabbage slaw. With one eye on the chops, she turned to the counter to begin peeling more apples.

She'd known running a kitchen on her own

would be a big challenge, and she'd deliberately created menus that included dishes that could be made in large quantities at once, like soups, chowders, and pies. But the point had been to show off the slightly more refined options for the local ingredients she'd sourced, and she'd overestimated her capabilities without a proper sous chef to assist. Every day had gotten a little bit worse as word spread and more people showed up to try her food.

People had loved what she'd made. That part of this experiment had been an overwhelming success. But she *hated* the scramble of juggling everything herself on this scale. If nothing else, it one hundred percent brought home the fact that to have her own restaurant, she'd need to budget for a certain amount of in-kitchen staff just to keep up with the volume of orders. She had nothing but mad respect for Dom's capabilities on that front.

Isobel swung through the kitchen door, which hadn't ceased to be a surprise all week. Afton still couldn't quite believe that this internationally famous musician was picking up a serving tray to help out, even if she had spent the summer hiding out from her abusive former agent by waiting tables.

"I need a venison stew, another of the lamb chops, and one order of the mussels."

"We're out of the mussels." And damn it, she should have planned better.

"Okay, I'll let them know. What are the options?"

Remembering the lamb chops, she lunged for the frying pan, flipping them. They'd be past properly medium rare. Cursing herself, Afton closed her eyes and took a deep breath. *Just a few more hours.*

"Are you okay?"

"Aye, I'm fine." Pretending was something she'd gotten very good at in the past ten years.

Turning her attention back to the original question, she considered what she could whip up quickly. At this point, it wasn't even about sticking to the local ingredients. She'd cook out of the pub's regular stores just to see that people got fed. "If they're in the mood for other seafood, I can make some lemon garlic prawns or blackened tuna steak."

"I'll let them know."

Afton pulled the lamb chops and set them aside, starting fresh ones. These she kept an eagle eye on and seared to perfection before plating them with the waiting roasted root vegetables. She'd just ladled up the last two bowls of stew, adding the crusty sourdough on the side, when Zo swung into the kitchen to load them on her tray.

"Mussels are out," Afton told her. "So's the venison stew. I can make another batch in the pressure cooker, but that won't be ready for an hour. Can you update the menu board?"

"You've got it!"

Whirling like a dervish, she spun to the walk-in cooler and began gathering more ingredients. There were pork chops. She could put together a quick brine, and they'd be ready to sear by the time the lamb ran out, which wouldn't be long. And she could put together a smoked haddock chowder to replace the winter squash soup.

"Archie, scrub up these potatoes and carrots."

"Yes, Chef." The young man leapt to do her bidding as if her voice was a whip.

If he was this jumpy with her, he'd never have survived working with Athena. The thought of her mentor had Afton shaking her head as she mixed up a quick brine for the pork and began dicing the remaining venison for more stew. And to think Athena actually *enjoyed* this kind of pressure, this chaos. Afton was pulling it off, but truly, it was awful.

With grim determination, she browned chunks of venison, sautéed onions, and roasted garlic, developing layers of flavor with every step before she added everything to the pressure cooker and set it to cook in between prepping other orders. They ran out of the lamb chops, but the pork was a popular substitute. And the smoked haddock chowder had come with at least two requests for the recipe. Afton got through her final shift by putting one foot in front of the other, focusing on filling one plate at a time.

She was outright shaking with exhaustion by the time the flood of orders slowed to a trickle. It was Laura who shoved her onto a stool and made her eat some of the chowder in the lull. It truly was delicious, considering it had been a throw-together.

"There now. That's put a little color back into your cheeks." Laura nodded, satisfied. "Come on out to the dining room."

"For what?"

"To be introduced and take a well-deserved bow over your accomplishment."

Afton wasn't feeling accomplished, but she knew how to put on a polite, happy face. She slid off the stool, checking to make sure nothing would burn while she was gone, before following the older woman into the main part of the pub. Ewan, who'd been manning the bar all night, gave a piercing two-fingered whistle that brought the din of conversation to a screeching halt.

"Thanks for that, Ewan. Everyone, I'd like to introduce you to the artist of the lovely food you've been eating this week. Please give a warm round of applause for Chef Afton Lennox."

The cheers were loud and long. Afton had to admit to herself that their enthusiasm and approbation felt fantastic, despite everything else. It gave her just enough energy to get through the last of her shift, packing up any leftovers to send home with the staff and otherwise helping to clean and set the kitchen to rights, because cleanup was part of the job, and she wasn't leaving a mess for Dom.

Hamish and Freya were waiting in the dining room when she finally came out.

He swept Afton into his arms, spinning her in a circle, beaming with excitement. "This week was an absolute triumph!"

She wasn't sure she'd go that far. That people loved her food was, in and of itself, a triumph. But after this week, she wasn't at all sure about her dream of a restaurant. She'd need to give the whole thing some very serious thought. Not that she'd tell Hamish she was having doubts. He was so very proud of himself for having come up with the idea. And it had done exactly what he'd intended for it to do, introducing a broader chunk of the village to her food.

"What do you want to do to celebrate?" Freya asked.

Slumping against Hamish, Afton finally let go of the last of the frenetic energy that had kept her moving these past few hours. "Honestly, I'm completely shattered. I really just want to go home and have a glass of wine and maybe a bath. Except I'm not completely sure I wouldn't pass out in the tub and drown. So maybe just the wine."

Hamish tightened his arm around her and brushed a kiss to her temple. "That can absolutely be arranged."

***

"YOU REALLY DIDN'T HAVE to duck down in the seat." Hamish glanced over to where Afton was readjusting herself into a normal position in the passenger seat and felt like an absolute arse.

"The last thing I want is for Freya to have to navigate all of Dayna's vitriol over the subject of you and me. Obviously, eventually, she has to find out, but not right now. Freya's already stressed enough about this visit."

"Fair enough. I still think you're going above and beyond." And that she'd do it for his daughter made him love her all the more. It made the surprise he had planned all the sweeter. "We should probably get some dinner."

"Aye. I'm definitely going to want something before we drive all the way back home."

Hamish loved the sound of home on her lips, knowing she meant his house, his bed, his family. "Actually, we have a stop to make before dinner."

"Oh, okay. Well, it's early yet. Restaurants will be open for hours more here."

Blessedly, she didn't ask questions as he navigated the familiar streets of New Town to the Airbnb he'd booked. When he pulled into the drive of the converted carriage house, she looked around, clearly expecting some sort of retail establishment or an office of some kind.

"What are we doing?"

"I'm surprising you."

"Oh?" The corners of her mouth tipped up. "With what, exactly?"

Hamish took her hand in his. "You worked so damned hard at the pub this week, and you've been so tired, I thought it would be nice for us to have a weekend away. So I booked an Airbnb through Sunday. This way, we don't have to drive all the way back to Glenlaig tonight, then back again on Sunday to pick up Freya. We have the whole weekend to explore the city and everything it has to offer on the culinary scene, if that is what you desire." Plus, he needed the break himself. The mediation attempt with Lewis Anderson's wife had failed, and they'd be going to court as soon as the judge fit them on the docket.

Afton's brown eyes lit with pleasure. "That's wonderful, but I didn't pack anything."

With a smile, he lifted her hand to his lips. "That's okay. I did."

He retrieved their bags and located the hidden key to let them into the building. The flat wasn't huge, but it was charming, full of historic architectural details he knew she'd love. As they climbed the narrow stairs to the second floor, he sprang the second surprise. "Ordinarily, I'd have asked you where you want to go, but as anything that falls into the category of gourmet requires reservations, I took the liberty of making some at Whisky & Thyme. If that's not somewhere you'd like to go, we can make other arrangements—"

"That's Chef Iain McLeod's restaurant! I absolutely want to have dinner there. God, I hope you packed something nice for me to wear."

Hamish passed over the garment bag and duffel full of the rest of her toiletries and supplies. One of the benefits of having been married as long as he had was that he knew all the accoutrements she'd need. "Hopefully, what's in here will pass muster."

Taking them, Afton disappeared into the bathroom. While she changed, he did the same. Of course, he'd worn a suit to work today, but after the three-hour drive from Glenlaig, he was more than a little rumpled. She'd be a knockout in the dress he'd packed, and he wanted to match. He was fastening his cufflinks when she stepped out of the bathroom, a vision in a dark, shimmering blue dress that reminded him of nothing so much as a star-studded Highland sky. Her pale blonde hair was twisted up in some complicated updo, with strands escaping to frame either side of that lovely face. Damn him, all he wanted to do was strip her out of it.

"I'm wishing I made later reservations." His voice was barely above a growl as he took her in.

With a feline smile, she strolled over in the heels that put her almost level with his mouth. She tapped his cheek. "Later." The single word was a promise. One he'd absolutely collect on. "For now, you promised to feed me."

"So, I did." Still, he lifted her hand again, pressing his lips against the thump of her pulse in that delicate wrist, darkly delighted when it leapt.

They took an Uber to the restaurant. The moment they walked in, Afton tried to look everywhere at once, taking in all the dark wood and elegance. It was the most excited he'd seen her in a while. She'd been dimmer this week, which he'd attributed to her simply being exhausted from the pub gig. There was nothing dim about her now. She fairly glowed like a candle as the maître' d led them to their table with a view overlooking the moonlit Firth of Forth. They could just see the outline of Carlton Hill in the distance.

Afton stroked the menu like a lover. "This all looks absolutely amazing."

"Order for both of us."

"Really?"

"This is your area of expertise, and I trust you know my palate."

The early twenty-something server looked almost awestruck as Afton turned her beaming smile to him. Hamish knew exactly how he felt. But she'd be going to bed with him tonight. Wasn't he the luckiest bastard in the city? He only half listened as she reeled off a multi-course meal for them both. He was too busy admiring her.

"And if you can just pass along to Chef McLeod that I'm a friend of Athena Reynolds, and I've been very much looking forward to trying his food, I'd appreciate it."

"Of course, Miss. Your name?"

"Afton Lennox."

"Yes, Miss."

As he scurried away, Hamish settled back into his seat. "Athena knows him?"

"Sometimes it feels like she knows everyone in the foodie world. She has a lot of connections. If I'd wanted to find a position in the city, I could have. But I'd never be happy here. It's too big, too crowded. I need my green hills and mountains."

"I certainly understand that."

They paused as their wine was delivered. Again, Hamish deferred to Afton, who sipped and approved the choice.

When they were alone again, she leaned toward him. "Were you happy here all those years?"

"Edinburgh is my city. There are a lot of things I loved about it. The culture, the restaurants, the museums. I have a lot of friends and colleagues here. And all my earliest memories of Freya involve this city. But, at the end of the day, I'm grateful to finally be home."

"Fair enough. What do you miss the most?"

"Longer city hours made it easier to get things done around the workday. And the wide array of cuisines. Though you've certainly helped with that. The nightlife. Not that I've actually engaged much in the nightlife for years, as I have a child. But I enjoyed it when I had the chance."

"Would you like to take advantage of the nightlife while we're here? Find a club or... something?"

Hamish knew perfectly well that wasn't her scene. She'd go if he wanted, just to make him happy. But he was far more interested in making them both happy. He leaned forward, lacing his fingers with hers and dropping his voice low as he rubbed a thumb over that fluttering pulse point. "Actually, what I'd really like to do is take you back to our Airbnb, strip that dress off you, and worship you as you deserve for the rest of the night."

Her eyes were nearly black as she leaned close enough they shared the same air. "I one thousand percent support this plan."

Sexual tension snapped between them, potent enough Hamish gave serious thought to whether they could find somewhere private to relieve the edge.

"Miss Lennox."

At the deep, rumbling voice, they both sat back. A man in a black chef's jacket stood beside their table. Hamish knew he was Iain McLeod, even before Afton's eyes went round.

"Chef McLeod. Oh, my goodness, it's an absolute pleasure to meet you, sir."

The older man shook her hand. "The pleasure is all mine, I assure you. Athena's spoken highly of you."

"Athena's spoken of me? To you?"

"Aye. She has. She says you're newly returned to Scotland and looking for work."

"Oh, well, I'm exploring my options, considering opening my own place. I'm so flattered she'd mention me."

"Lot of work. If you want to pick my brain about it sometime, just let me know. I'll leave my contact information with your check."

"That would be... amazing! Thank you, Chef."

"Think nothing of it. I need to get back to the kitchen. I just wanted to pop out to meet you. Enjoy your meal."

As McLeod strode away, Afton turned wide eyes on Hamish. "He knows who I am!"

"So it seems. Sounds like he'll be a good contact as you're sorting out the details for your place."

She took a hefty swallow of her wine. "It's going to take me a little while to get over all the inner fangirling I'm doing right now."

Hamish grinned. "To be fair, that wasn't part of my surprise, just a happy accident. But I'm pleased it could add to the evening."

Afton covered his hand with hers. "Seriously, Hamish, this weekend is wonderful of you. This meal, just... everything. You've given me so much, and I want to say thank you."

In the grand scheme of things, this weekend was so little. But seeing how happy it made her, Hamish wanted to give her everything. Wanted to give her forever.

Damn it. He was going to have to buy a ring.

SIXTEEN

"Miss Lennox, Mr. Colquhoun. So glad to meet with you today. We're all verra excited by the prospect of you opening a restaurant here in the village."

Afton shook the estate agent's proffered hand and flashed a smile. "I appreciate you taking the time, Mr. Harrison."

Afton's enthusiasm for the restaurant project had been renewed after her weekend with Hamish in Edinburgh. They'd visited multiple restaurants of different sizes and styles, and she felt she had a better handle on what she'd actually like to do. The absolute truth of the matter was that the size and scope of the pub was far larger than what she wanted or could handle. No way could she afford to hire that much staff—in or out of the kitchen. So the goal was something smaller, more intimate. How big would depend on a variety of other details, like how much renovation would be required, as there was certainly nothing in Glenlaig that already had a commercial kitchen. That costly necessity would eat up a decent chunk of her budget, even before it came to the finer details like decorating the space. Add to that, to maximize profits, she really needed to be able to shoehorn in a small bar, and her options were going to be limited. But she and Hamish had discussed all of this at length over the past couple of weeks. He'd taken a true interest in what she needed for the restaurant and had asked lots of good questions that brought her more clarity.

She'd spent a lot of time driving to all the villages within a half-hour radius, exploring what other dining options existed. None of them had anything like what she wanted to offer. That could be a blessing or a curse. She could draw customers from all those places, providing an elevated dining experience where currently none was on offer. Or those same prospective patrons wouldn't even consider it because it was out of their milieu. She'd already decided before that she wouldn't be going high-end. The general populace wouldn't be able to afford those sorts of prices, and the sort of high-brow gourmet cuisine they'd had at Whisky &

Thyme wouldn't fly with everyday people. Her goal was to elevate the familiar and give them an experience. A place to go for something special. Celebrations. Date nights.

"Our first location is just off the high street. We can walk to that one before we go look at the rest."

"Oh, I didn't realize there were any vacancies so near the high street." Afton had walked the length of it often.

"Just one and recently. It's not quite what you're looking for, but as the location is so good, I thought it worth showing you."

Afton braced herself. She knew the ask she was making, trying to find anything truly suitable for a restaurant in their small village. The question was whether "not quite" was even remotely close to what she needed. Still, she determined to look at the spaces on offer with an open mind.

When Mr. Harrison stopped in front of the Furry Friends Highland Haven, Afton struggled not to ask what the hell he'd been thinking. She put on her best Baroness polite smile instead. "A former pet services facility?"

"A pet spa, actually. The fact that she made it as long as she did is frankly a miracle in a village this size. I know it's unusual, but let's take a look before you say no. It has a lot of space, which is something you did say you needed."

Hamish caught her eye and rolled his, but they shrugged and followed Harrison inside. He hadn't lied about the space. But massive renovations would be required. The front of the shop was small, meant only to serve as a reception area. The back was full of empty kennels and storage space, with a large indoor area covered in Astroturf that had presumably been the play area during the snowy winter months. The flow was all wrong, and the acoustics were terrible. The whole place would have to be gutted. She didn't have the budget for that, even if she could get the permits to do it. When Harrison named the figure, Afton just laughed. It seemed more polite than the "What the actual fuck?" that was on the tip of her tongue.

"Next, please."

The second location was a few blocks further, off another side of the high street. A familiar building that also gave her pause, and not in a good way.

"The old Village Blume location?" Hamish asked. "You can't seriously be suggesting one of John Milligan's old properties. Everyone in the village knows he was a terrible landlord."

"He was, aye. But Theo Gordon is the new owner, and he's been rectifying all that. Come see."

Well, the contractor was well respected. That gave Afton a little hope as they stepped inside. The walls had been ripped out and replaced with fresh drywall. The formerly leaky ceiling had likewise been yanked, replaced with a beautiful pressed tin that Harrison informed them had been reclaimed from somewhere or other. The higher ceiling made the space feel bigger and more open. But not big enough to house an entire commercial kitchen and a bar in addition to a dining room. The building would be better suited as a coffeeshop. Somewhere with lots of foot traffic that didn't need to stay.

"I'm afraid it's still far too small for my purposes."

Harrison hummed a noncommittal note. "There are two more on my list. Let's go."

She held her tongue on the drive, but she was wondering if this venture was doomed to fail before it even started. That fear grew bigger as they toured the third location, which had poor ventilation and an electric system that she doubted would hold up to the burden of a commercial kitchen without massive updates. And the fourth had so little curb appeal, she didn't even want to go inside for fear of what awaited. The structural issues there would also zap her budget.

"Well, that's disappointing." Her tone was mild, masking the inner devastation. What if she had to look at a different village? There were others not that far, but opening a restaurant would already require such long hours, and she didn't want to lose out on her time with Hamish and Freya.

"Well, I have one more that is, perhaps, an option. It's not currently zoned commercially, but the Council could likely be convinced. It's a mile or so outside the village proper."

Without much hope, Afton climbed back into Harrison's car.

When he drove out to the old vicarage, she straightened. The old stone house sat on an open tract of land with views out to the mountains to the east. There was ample space to put in a parking lot, and she could immediately envision an outdoor dining space with patio seating for the warmer months, when business would theoretically pick up from the tourist trade.

"The house hasnae been a vicarage for the past forty years, as the parish elected to sell the property. It's been a private home for most of that time. Two-stories, with lots of rooms, and, of course, a kitchen. Though I'm certain modifications would have to be made to accommodate your needs there."

They stepped inside a high-ceilinged entryway that she recognized as of a similar era to the manor house at Lochmara. Two rooms opened off to either side, with large windows and plenty of space. Her brain immediately fit five to seven tables in each. As they walked through, she considered the space. The two levels weren't ideal from an accessibility stand-point, but she'd seen such things work before. Like many homes of the period, the rooms on the lower level flowed into one another, with pocket doors allowing each to be closed off. That could serve well for private party dining or to create a section that was specifically a bar. The kitchen would need near gutting. The layout was nothing at all like she'd need for proper efficient flow. But the rest of the house would require far less work to make ready, and the historic character could absolutely play in her favor. The upstairs was full of more small bed-rooms. Space she could either open up for dining or block off to turn into a rentable flat. While she had no designs on being a landlord, having rental in-come could help offset the lean months.

"It could work. What's the price?"

Harrison named it. The figure was more than she'd hoped, but not stratospherically so. And this was the only option he'd shown them that was even a remote possibility.

"Well, I'm definitely interested. But, of course, that's pending the Council agreeing to rezone the property."

Hamish, who'd been a largely silent presence during this exercise, finally spoke. "I can help with that. Both with whatever paperwork the Council requires and with the actual presentation at their meeting. It would be no different from going before a judge. I know how much you hate public speaking."

"Their next meeting is in three weeks," Harrison supplied.

"Think you can get your business plan together by then?" Hamish asked.

"Aye, I think so." It would be a lot, but she could pull it off.

"Then I'll see it done." He smiled at her, and she was pleased to see his confidence coming back. Beyond that, he looked happy. She couldn't help but feel she'd had a lot to do with both those things.

What a difference a couple of months had made. She'd found her place with him, with Freya, and she would find it in the village. For the first time in longer than she could remember, *she* was happy. She didn't feel alone anymore. She loved this man and knew he loved her. Maybe neither of them had specifically used those words, but they'd both talked around it, mostly out of an abundance of caution because they both had fears about pushing this too hard, too fast. He was a cautious man by nature, especially in the wake of his divorce. She'd waited so long for this future she'd never allowed herself to dream about. He could take as much time as he wanted to declare it to the world. She was content with what they had because with him was where she was supposed to be.

They stayed a little while longer so she could take some measurements of the space. Then Harrison drove them back to his office. He promised to be in touch if any other offers materialized before the Council meeting next month. Then Hamish walked Afton back to her car.

"I know you have client meetings this afternoon."

"And you'll have to pick up Freya."

"See you at home before we leave for Malcolm and Charlotte's rehearsal dinner?"

His smile this time was unrestrained and lit up his eyes with joy, as they did every time she called the farmhouse home. The same joy she felt being able to say it.

He brushed a quick kiss over her lips. "See you at home."

And as she watched his long strides eat up the pavement toward his office, she couldn't help but think that everything was coming up roses.

AS MANY WEDDINGS as Hamish had helped with since Kyla and Sophie started Ardinmuir Event Planning, he never quite got used to seeing the castle bustling with people. Multiple vehicles were parked in the crushed gravel drive, with event staff scurrying about, finalizing details before this evening's ceremony. Knowing how important this wedding was to Charlotte, for whom this was the first trip down the aisle, Hamish and Afton had elected to pop over and offer their assistance with whatever was needed. For all that Charlotte and Malcolm had planned for a small wedding, between her extended family, who'd flown in from Texas for the nuptials, and local friends and family, there were still approximately seventy guests expected. He'd gotten the chance to meet Charlotte's father and the rest of the Vasquez clan at last night's rehearsal dinner and found them all boisterous and delightful, much like Charlotte herself.

Afton shut her car door. "Where do you suppose we'll find Sophie and Kyla?"

"Best guess is the great hall. If not there, someone there ought to know where they've gone off to."

With the familiarity of long friends, they let themselves into the castle and wove through the labyrinthine corridors until they made their way to the great hall, which was generally the location for most ceremonies, at least during the colder months. Their friends were in the corner of the big room, in deep discussion about something. Hamish could see the tension in their body language, even before they got close enough to hear Kyla insist, "We canna tell Charlotte."

He stepped up to join them. "Canna tell Charlotte what?"

Kyla turned wide, distressed eyes on him. "The caterer was in an accident on the way here."

Afton closed the circle. "Is she okay?"

"She's..." Kyla raked a hand through her long red hair. "Well, not fine. She broke her arm. They're transporting her to the hospital, but she should be fine. But we have no food. I mean, she wasn't doing the cake, thank God. So we'll at least have that. But we have to feed seventy people in six hours, and we have nothing else."

Oh, shite. Not wanting to exacerbate the situation, Hamish kept his tone mild. "Ah. I see why you canna tell Charlotte."

"Can't tell Charlotte what?"

Everybody froze at the familiar Southern drawl. Charlotte stepped up to join them, Malcolm on her heels.

Sophie made a halfhearted bid to change the subject. "You're not supposed to see each other before the wedding!"

But the fierce Latina woman who had a habit of mothering them all wasn't about to be deterred. "Can't tell Charlotte what? What's going on?"

No one spoke as they exchanged looks, all of them clearly saying, "Not it!" for breaking the bad news.

Afton stepped into the silence because she was magnificent. "There's been an accident with the catering van. The caterer will be okay, but we're going to have a change in menu."

Malcolm muttered a low curse and stepped closer to his bride, pressing a hand to her lower back in silent support.

Charlotte's lip wobbled, and her big, dark eyes filled. A passionate woman, she had a tendency to cry at the drop of a hat. Hamish had seen her happy tears more often than anything else. This was definitely not that.

"But—"

Afton took her hands. "I promise, it's going to be okay. I will make it okay." Without taking her eyes off Charlotte, she addressed Kyla and Sophie. "Is there a list of food allergies from the guests? The number of vegetarian and meat dishes?"

"Yes, of course. I'll go grab it." Ciara, who'd been lurking who knew where, took off running.

"Can I raid your spice cupboard?"

Charlotte blinked at her and nodded. "Yes, of course."

With one last squeeze of her hands, Afton

stepped back. "I'll need someone to drive me out to your house."

Hamish stepped up. "I can—"

"No, I need you to go back to our house and pick up my knives and my dress for the wedding. I'll change here."

"I'll take you," Malcolm said.

"Good. I'll be making calls on the way." Her mind was clearly already engaged in sorting the details.

"What can we do here?" Sophie asked.

"Do you have a pressure cooker?"

"I do."

"Pull that out, and see that the counters are as clear as you can make them. I'm going to make a list of ingredients for someone to run into the village to pick up from the market. I was just there yesterday, so I've got a solid notion of what they'll have."

She continued whipping out orders like a five-star general, pausing only to wave Hamish on his way. "Go!"

Properly chastened, he got moving with a salute. "Yes, Chef."

He drove back to the house, surprising Freya when he swung through the door.

She looked up from where she'd been taking advantage of the quiet and reading on the sofa. "What's going on?"

"Food emergency for the wedding." He explained what had happened, and his daughter immediately leapt up.

"I can help. I know how to chop things."

Hamish wasn't at all sure whether she'd be a help or a hinderance, but it seemed likely that all hands were on deck to salvage the situation. "Go pack your dress and such for the wedding. We'll probably need to change there."

She bolted upstairs.

He was right behind, striding into the room he now shared with Afton. Signs of her were everywhere, in the books on the bedside table, and the little jewelry case on the dresser. The scent of her surrounded him as he gathered up her dress and makeup, before grabbing his own suit and meeting Freya downstairs. She already had Afton's knife roll. They loaded into the car and headed back for Ardinmuir.

He couldn't have been gone for more than forty minutes, round-trip, but by the time he returned, the kitchen was a hotbed of activity. Afton's hair was twisted into a knot on top of her head, and she was clearly running a dozen things at once. The massive center island was covered in ingredients that had clearly been dropped off from the crofters themselves. Angus and Munro were sorting through those. Multiple pots bubbled on the Aga, and as he watched, Afton tossed several rough-chopped onions into a massive roasting pan with what he thought might be a couple of pork shoulders and some kind of broth or marinade. She covered the whole thing with foil and slid it into the waiting oven. With focused efficiency, she turned toward the next task.

Hamish couldn't help but take a moment to admire her. She was clearly in her element, in full control, and it was sexy as hell.

She spotted him in the doorway. "Knives!"

He handed over the roll. "Where do you want us?"

Her face softened for just a fraction of a second as she spotted Freya. "Bless you for coming, Cricket."

His daughter drew herself up to her full height. "Of course, Chef."

"Okay, we're doing mini empanadas filled with Highland beef and cheddar, smoked salmon tostadas with avocado cream, and black bean and crowdie quesadillas for the appetizers. For mains, we're making pulled pork sliders with Scotch Whisky barbeque sauce, grilled chicken fajita skewers with a Scottish herb marinade, and vegetarian haggis enchiladas with green chile sauce. For sides, roasted potatoes with chipotle aioli, Mexican rice pilaf, and citrus-dressed roasted carrots with cilantro."

Hamish stared at her. "You're doing all that in six hours?"

Afton checked her watch. "Five now. Chop-chop. We've got a lot of work to do."

SEVENTEEN

Afton looked around the castle's kitchen, checking the status of every dish, many already completed and only waiting to be plated and served. A few other things were still in the oven or bubbling on the hob. But she'd done it. She'd pulled together a full meal for seventy people in less than six hours. The buzz of achievement overshadowed the exhaustion. Oh, she hadn't done it without help, though she'd sent all her stand-in sous chefs on to get ready for the wedding more than half an hour ago. The distant sound of music told her it was time to get ready herself, so she didn't miss the ceremony.

Locking herself into the bathroom off the kitchen, she stripped down, hastily washing her face and cleaning off the perspiration with a wash-cloth before slipping into the dress Hamish had brought. Bless him, he'd even thought to pack clean undergarments. A smart move, as she'd definitely sweated through what she'd been wearing. Her hair was still bundled up in a knot for cooking, but there was nothing to be done about that right now. She spent a single minute on her makeup, swiping on eyeliner and mascara, and adding a little lip gloss. Her cheeks were still flushed from the work and from the deep sense of satisfaction that she'd been able to give this to Malcolm and Charlotte.

Today had been worlds away from her experience cooking at the pub. This was the sort of cooking she truly loved. A limited menu with lots of pre-prep. Not that there'd been an enormous amount of time for that prep, but it was still different from cooking for actively waiting customers at a restaurant. She didn't know how much of that feeling was because of the personal nature attached to today, and that was something she really needed to give some thought to later, when she had time to breathe. Now definitely wasn't the time.

Slipping into her heels, she hurried through the castle, grateful that she'd grown up here and knew how to sneak into the great hall without having a repeat of what had happened with Connor and Sophie's wedding. There were multiple entrances and a secret passage or two that led into the space, and she intended to use one of those. She knew for a fact that Kyla and Sophie had oiled all the doors that had any kind of access to the room because it was useful for event staff to be able to slip in and out without making noise during any event going on.

Father Grant was already speaking by the time she emerged behind one of the curtained sections on the sides. Afton edged out just far enough so she could see. Malcolm and Charlotte stood at the altar. Gavin's lanky frame was straight and proud where he stood beside Malcolm as best man, and Raleigh stood likewise beside Charlotte as her man of honor, unable to hold back a grin. She spotted Hamish and Freya near the front on the groom's side. As if sensing her eyes on him, Hamish looked over. He patted the empty seat next to him. But she didn't want to risk stepping out and disrupting anything, so she just shook her head. She'd have to leave before the recessional anyway, to get back to the kitchen. She didn't want to get caught up in the exodus of guests.

Afton had never been a particular fan of weddings. It was hard to be when she'd never looked forward to her own. There'd always been a little edge of bitterness that everyone else got to marry for love, and she was stuck in an antiquated marriage pact. But now she was free to do as she wished. To choose who she wanted. And, of course, she wanted Hamish. She'd always wanted Hamish. More, now she wanted his daughter and the little family unit they'd made these past couple of months. Standing here, watching the ceremony, it was impossible not to wonder if they'd eventually end up here.

Maybe it was fast. They hadn't dated. She'd moved in after a matter of weeks. But none of that changed the fact that they'd been friends for a lifetime, and her feelings for him had lasted just as long, as had his for her. It was only that they were finally getting the chance to act on them. And, while perhaps some aspects of their relationship had been fast, she knew Hamish wasn't likely to move quickly toward anything permanent because of Freya. That was completely fair. He might even be a little gun shy of the idea of another marriage, though they certainly hadn't discussed it.

What was he thinking as he was sitting there, watching this wedding? Was he remembering his own wedding to Dayna? She certainly did. It had been painful as hell to watch him make those vows in that posh Edinburgh hotel, at a high society wedding that hadn't fit him in the least. At the time, he'd done a great job of convincing them all that he loved Dayna. Afton had wanted him to be happy, and if that woman and that life made him happy, who was she to say anything against it? She hadn't had the right to intervene. It wasn't as if she could have offered him an alternative. What would she have said? *I think I know you better than you know yourself.* That was ridiculous, even if it had been true.

"Do you, Charlotte, take thee, Malcolm..."

Shoving away bad memories, Afton focused on the couple at the altar. Seeing the two of them together, she was struck again, as she had been with Connor and Sophie, how she could truly tell the difference because they all truly loved each other. She hadn't seen that at Hamish and Dayna's wedding all those years ago. Her heart swelled with joy that Malcolm was getting a second chance at love and that Charlotte had found him. The two of them were great together. She hadn't known Malcolm was capable of looking this happy.

"Do you Malcolm, take thee, Charlotte..."

Feeling eyes on her, Afton shifted to find Hamish watching her. As Malcolm made his vows to love, honor, and cherish, she found she couldn't look away from Hamish. There was an intensity in his gaze that, somehow, made the connection weighty and necessary. Her heart began to pound because somehow this silent communication they were having felt like its own sort of vow. Emotion clogged in her throat, and her eyes filled. He hadn't said the words. Neither of them had used the word love. They'd both danced around it. But as he smiled, she felt his promise that he wanted this with her. Someday.

That was enough for her.

"I now pronounce you husband and wife. You may kiss the bride."

Afton jerked her attention back to the front in time to see Malcolm frame Charlotte's face and kiss her with a passion she wouldn't have thought him capable of. Everyone cheered and began to clap. That was her cue. Afton melted back into the shadows and slipped away again to go finish with the rest of the food for the reception, feeling lighter and more buoyant than she had in years.

***

"THIS FOOD IS INCREDIBLE." Hamish's father forked up another bite of the vegetarian haggis enchiladas. "I was mostly just glad we made it back in time for Malcolm's wedding, but now I'm doubly so. I had no idea Afton was so talented."

Beside him, Freya picked up her third pulled pork slider and grinned. "And we get her all to ourselves."

"At least until she opens her restaurant." Hamish wasn't sure how much she'd want to cook at home once she was cooking full time for work.

"Well, I think it's a marvelous idea." Niamh fixed her son with a significant look. "As are the two of you."

Hamish shifted in his seat. He hadn't precisely hidden the fact that he was *with* Afton from his parents—there was no way to do that when someone in the village would've spilled the beans—but he had the impression Freya had been a lot more chatty about the specifics of their living arrangement.

Apparently ignoring his discomfort, his mother's expression went soft. "I'm so glad you found your way to each other. Despite how everything was for her growing up, I always hoped for this."

"You did?"

"You two always suited."

Before he could figure out what to say to that, someone at the head table started tapping a glass for attention.

Malcolm shoved back his chair and stood. "I ken we're already done with speeches, but I have one more thing to say. Earlier this morning, we got notified that our original caterer was in an accident on the way here. She's okay, but the food was ruined, and she ended up with a broken arm. Afton Lennox was here when we got the news, and she stepped in and put together this beautiful meal we've all been enjoying. Charlotte and I just want to acknowledge her amazing contribution to our day and say a very public thank you. Afton, take a bow."

Hamish spotted her standing just beyond the head table. Color streaked her cheeks as everyone present burst into cheers and applause, perhaps none louder than Hamish himself, who let out a two-fingered whistle. She'd pulled off a freaking miracle, so she deserved every single accolade. With a dignified nod of acknowledgment, she gave a scant bow, then accepted a bear hug from Malcolm and Charlotte.

As the music started up again, and people began heading for the dance floor, Afton wove her way toward their table. At least she tried. Guests kept stopping her, presumably to compliment the food, given the smiles and nods she offered in return.

"Perhaps you should go rescue the poor girl," Niamh suggested.

Hamish was already out of his seat, closing the distance. Afton's head was angled toward Hettie Fraser, whose gnarled little hands waved as she spoke. The woman was eighty if she was a day and had been married to her husband William for over sixty years. Hamish had heard Sophie refer to them as #RelationshipGoals and couldn't say he disagreed. Six plus decades with the love of his life sounded pretty damned good to him, too, which was why he'd found time to drive up to Inverness last week to see a jeweler. He wouldn't ask her here. Tonight was all about Charlotte and Malcolm. But he was definitely thinking about it as he slipped his arm around Afton's waist—a move Hettie definitely didn't miss. "Mrs. Fraser. I'm sorry to interrupt."

"Young Hamish! Good to see you've come to your senses. We're glad to have you home in the village."

"I'm glad to be home."

Afton leaned into him. "Mrs. Fraser was just telling me about her family's recipe for Scottish Stew with Oat Dumplings."

Hettie nodded. "Passed down from my granny and from hers before that."

"I'd be so honored to make it."

"I'll write it down for you. In the meantime, go spend some time with your lad, there." Her dark eyes twinkled.

Her husband leaned over, nodding toward the dance floor. "You young people should dance while your bones will let you."

"That is a fantastic idea, Mr. Fraser," Hamish told him.

The old man winked. "I've been known to have one or two about keeping my lass happy."

"We should all definitely learn from your example. Excuse us."

Hamish steered Afton away. "Have you eaten? I haven't seen you sit down for hours."

"I ate in the kitchen. It's fine. Did I see your parents over there?"

"Aye. They made it in time for the wedding. Gran's doing really well, and they've got her set up with home health for the rest of her recovery."

"Oh, that's wonderful. I know they're so glad to be home."

As they approached the table, Niamh rose from her seat and opened her arms. "Afton, dear, it's so good to see you."

With only a moment's hesitation, Afton walked into her arms. "Welcome home."

"That's supposed to be our line to you." Niamh pulled back far enough to look into her face. "You're finally where you're supposed to be."

Afton seemed puzzled by that until his mother looked over at him. Fresh color stained her cheeks, and she turned shy. "Aye, well..."

"Dinna embarrass the girl, Niamh." Hamish's father stood and took his turn in the hug train. "Next thing you ken, she'll be talking about more grandchildren."

As Afton's mouth fell open, Niamh raised a finger. "I want it noted, that *I* wasnae the one who mentioned it!"

Graham seemed to replay what he'd said.

"Whoops. Sorry. We're just happy to see you two happy."

"I... uh... Thank you."

Realizing he absolutely needed to rescue her again, Hamish grabbed Afton's hand. "If you'll excuse us, I want to dance with my date."

As luck would have it, the lively salsa number rolled into something low and slow when they stepped onto the dance floor. Hamish gave a little tug, spinning Afton into his arms.

She laughed. "Where did you learn to do that?"

"Because of all the society events I've been forced to attend over the years, I got forced into dance lessons."

"I definitely won't complain about reaping the benefits." Her hands slipped over his shoulders, fingers toying with the ends of his hair. "I didn't realize that you'd told them about us."

"We said we weren't hiding. Plus, if I didn't tell them, someone else would. And that was news better coming from me."

"Fair."

He nuzzled her temple, inhaling the scents of spice and the subtle sweetness of the perfume she'd dabbed on hours ago. "Tonight was a triumph."

She hummed a noncommittal note.

"Seriously. The base goal was to make sure there was food at all. You delivered something exquisite and meaningful. Malcolm and Charlotte will never forget it. And neither will the rest of the village. Everyone's talking about the restaurant."

"That's all premature. The Council still has to agree to rezone the building before I can even get started."

"Just three weeks. I canna imagine they'll object. It's too good an opportunity for the village."

"I dinna have the bandwidth to think about it tonight."

"Fair enough. I just wanted you to know how proud I am of you. Proud, too, to be here with you on my arm."

Her lips curved. "You're sweet."

As she swayed against him, moving with every subtle shift of his body, he was feeling a lot of things. Sweet wasn't one of them. Because he couldn't resist, he lowered his mouth to hers for a long, lingering taste. They'd all been too busy today for anything more than the business at hand. But now... now he wanted to savor her. And, in a very caveman sort of way, he wanted to announce in no uncertain terms to everyone here that she was his. Afton melted against him, her hum of pleasure vibrating against his chest. It was so easy to get lost in her. To forget about everything and everyone.

The music had shifted by the time he lifted his head. Another hot Latin song that had what seemed like all Charlotte's relatives out of their seats and gyrating. When Afton made to step back, he only grinned and shook his head. "Uh-uh." He shifted his hold on her. "Try to keep up."

She did, following his lead for every spin, twist, and dip. Having her this close, with his blood pumping to the beat, made him think a whole host of thoughts that weren't audience friendly. Feeling a little reckless, he considered whether he could talk her into sneaking out and up to one of the myriad of empty bedrooms in the castle. Then the song ended, and he spotted Freya and his mother standing mere feet away.

Hamish promptly tried to wipe the lust off his face.

"I wanna go home with Nan and Grandda. Can I, Da?"

"Of course you can. I know you've all been missing each other." There, that sounded appropriately paternal, even if he was a tad breathless.

Niamh wrapped an arm around Freya's shoulders. "We'll stop by your house on the way to pick up an overnight bag. It's been ages, so we're absolutely stealing her for the rest of the weekend."

If Hamish didn't know better, he'd have thought his mom was playing wingwoman to give him alone time with Afton. Given his father's remark, maybe she was. Much as he appreciated their approval, he preferred not to think too hard about that. But he definitely intended to take advantage either way.

They danced for another half hour, long enough, by his estimation, that his parents could've made it to the house and left again. "Do you want to get out of here?"

Afton's eyes flashed with barely banked lust of her own. "Aye."

They made their excuses, said a final congratulations to the bride and groom, and beat a hasty retreat.

After the noise of the reception, the farmhouse was weirdly quiet.

Afton slipped out of her heels as soon as they stepped through the door. "I want out of these clothes."

"I expect that can be arranged."

She huffed a laugh. "I'm not even waiting for you to do it. Everything's sore, now that I've stopped."

"Then how about I draw a bath for two and pour us some wine? I can rub your feet."

With an expression of pure longing in her eyes, she sighed. "That, Mr. Colquhoun, is a deal."

"Go on up and change into whatever you like. I'll open the wine."

With his mind on seduction, Hamish took his time selecting the wine. Something bold and red.

Earthy. He opened the bottle and set it to breathe, as he gathered up some candles for mood lighting. She deserved some romance, after all. Piling the candles in a basket with a couple of glasses, he grabbed the open bottle and went upstairs, thinking about music to add to the ambiance. He'd make love to her until she was boneless and sated, and maybe then he'd find the right words to ask her to be his forever.

He stepped into the bedroom and stopped in his tracks. Afton had made it out of the dress. It lay draped over a chair in the corner. Her shoes were tossed on the floor. She'd shrugged into her favorite cotton robe and evidently sat down on the bed—where she'd toppled like a tree and fallen fast asleep.

Of course, she'd be exhausted after the day she'd had. He should've thought of that. With a rueful smile, he set the basket aside and moved to the bed. She didn't stir as he carefully unfastened her earrings and the necklace she'd worn. Nor did she rouse as he worked the duvet from beneath her and tucked it around her. Pressing a kiss to her temple, he murmured, "Sleep well, my love."

He crossed to the dresser, putting the jewelry back into its little case. Then he indulged himself for just a few moments, pulling out the ring from where he'd hidden it in his sock drawer. He wanted to see the diamond on her finger. Wanted to know she was his. But he'd been waiting all his life. It would keep a while longer.

Putting the ring away, he stripped off his suit and crawled into bed beside her.

EIGHTEEN

There was something to be said about being comfortable in silence with someone else. From her position at one end of the kitchen table, Afton made another note about restaurant supply costs for her business plan, while watching Hamish at the other, prepping for a court appearance tomorrow. The horn-rim glasses gave him a scholarly, sexy look that was hella distracting. But although Freya wasn't due back from Edinburgh for another hour or two, she didn't give in to the urge to seduce him. He'd said little about this case other than it was a custody battle, so she understood it hit close to home and he wanted to do the best by his client that he could. Still, it was nice to be in the same space with someone else, without the burden of talking or keeping up any appearances. Peaceful.

She'd made good strides on the business plan. The price of some things would no doubt change by the time she was able to purchase the rectory and finish renovations. But this gave her a clearer notion of what kind of overhead she could expect. That, in turn, would allow her to sort out the number of tables and the price point of the menu itself. It was a lot of maths, when all she really wanted to do just now was cook.

All part of the process.

She'd just opened up a new tab in her browser to see what sort of prices she could find on the commercial kitchen appliances she'd need, when they both heard a car coming up the drive.

Hamish took off his glasses. "I suppose Dayna's early."

"That's not usually a good sign in terms of how their visit went."

"No. I guess we should brace ourselves for whatever storm's about to hit."

As he spoke, the front door opened. "Da! I'm home!"

Something thumped—Freya dropping her bag, probably—then she was trotting into the kitchen, her mother on her heels. Afton could feel the cloud of rage without Dayna saying a word.

Uh-oh.

Freya bolted to Hamish, wrapping him in a hug and offering a smacking kiss. "Hi."

"Hi, yourself. Good weekend?"

"Fine." There was no underlying tone of belligerence, which meant it was likely Dayna who'd preempted their original arrival time.

Freya scooted around the table to hug Afton. "What's for dinner?"

Afton squeezed back. "I haven't gotten that far yet. Did you have something in mind?"

"Pork chops? The ones with the braised apples?" she asked hopefully.

"I'll have to check the supplies, but I think that can be arranged."

Dayna remained standing a dozen feet away. "Why don't you go upstairs, love?" The affection of the words was undermined by the tightness in her voice. "I need to speak to your father."

Afton already knew this was going to be about her. She wondered if Freya had said something to tip her off or if someone else had broken the news.

"But I just got home. I dinna want to go to my room."

Recognizing the mulish set to Freya's chin, Afton intervened. "Have you finished your homework for tomorrow?"

When Freya's gaze met hers, she did everything

she could to transmit a plea, because she knew this was about to get ugly. "Why dinna you go upstairs and check your planner, aye?"

With a scowl, Freya huffed out a breath. "Fine." She left the room, stomping up the stairs with a combination of temper and likely an effort to prove she'd changed locations, when Afton had already long since figured out she'd sneak back down them to eavesdrop so she didn't get left out of anything.

Dayna's hands curled into fists, her eyes blazing. "How dare you?"

Hamish set his reading glasses aside. "What are you on about?"

"How dare you move her into the house with *our* daughter? Into your bed with Freya right down the hall?"

Afton rose. This was certain to escalate, and Freya didn't neat to be witness to it.

As she moved to leave the kitchen, Dayna whirled on her. "Where are you going?"

"I'm going to remove your daughter from the premises so she doesn't hear whatever it is the two of you are about to say to each other. This is between the two of you."

Dayna looked as if she were going to argue, but Afton ignored that and exchanged a look with Hamish. He nodded, his jaw set in grim resignation for the confrontation he'd put off as long as he could.

As expected, Freya sat about a third of the way up the stairs.

"Get your coat, Cricket. We're going."

Since she still wore her shoes, they had only to grab their coats off the hooks on the wall by the front door. Dayna's raised voice followed them outside.

"What the hell were you thinking? We have a young and impressionable daughter. How dare you put the needs of your dick ahead of her?"

Afton winced. Yep, this would be just as bad as she thought. Amending her initial plan of hiding in the barn with the goats, she nudged Freya toward her car.

"Where are we going?"

"You'll see."

They didn't speak as Afton drove on autopilot toward Lochmara. If Freya wanted to talk about the weekend, she would. Afton's primary goal was to give her a safe space, so she took the girl to the place that had always been hers.

No one was around as she parked outside the big stone barn on the estate. She had no idea where Raleigh was. Up at the house, perhaps. Or elsewhere in pastures, as the work of a farmer was never done. She'd gotten to know him well enough these past months to know he wouldn't be upset with their presence.

"What are we doing here?"

Afton pocketed her keys, striding toward the heavy wood door. "All my life, when I was upset and needed to get away, this was my safe space." Despite its size, the door opened easily, and they slipped inside. "I'd come here and hang out with the animals or hide up in the hayloft. Actually, if nobody's cleared it out, there's probably still the chest of blankets I kept up there."

The scents of hay and leather and the warm musk of horses wrapped around her, comforting as an embrace. It was the first time she'd been in here since she'd come back, and something inside she hadn't realized was still ruffled settled. Motion-sensor lights flickered on as she made her way slowly down the familiar center aisle. The occupants of the barn shifted, poking out their long noses to investigate the visitors. Afton recognized old faces and saw quite a few new. She wished she'd thought to grab carrots or apples before they'd come.

Moving to the nearest stall, she let the black mare sniff her hand before scrubbing her head beneath her forelock. "Hello, Madge. Remember me?"

Madge pressed firmer into her touch and

groaned in pleasure, wrangling a laugh out of Afton.

Freya stepped up to the stall, not touching the mare, but leaning on the rail. "I dinna understand why she's so angry."

Afton took a breath and tried to find the right words that would be honest without condemnation. "I dinna know what to tell you, Cricket. I know that your mother very much dislikes me and has always felt I was a threat."

"To what? Their marriage is over. She didn't want him. She wanted that other guy. I'm not even sure if that's still going on. He hasn't been around when I've been there."

Afton wondered if David had broken things off with Dayna. Was she now rethinking her position and wanting Hamish back? Filing that away to talk to Hamish about later, Afton gave Madge one last scratch and moved toward the next stall. "She's worried about you. Worried about the example we're setting."

Freya threw her hands up. "What example? The example of a couple who cares about each other and respects each other and gets along and has things in common? Oh, the horror!" She added jazz hands for emphasis.

Clearly, the sarcasm was strong with this one.

"You know your father and I care about each

other, and we both care tremendously about you and want to do what's best for you, aye?"

"I know. I just dinna want Mum to ruin something else."

She wrapped an arm around Freya's shoulders, giving an affectionate tug on her braid. "No matter what comes out of the conversation your parents are having right now, you're not going to lose me."

Freya burrowed into her, speaking in a voice so small, Afton barely heard it. "You were the mum I always wanted."

The words hit Afton like a sucker punch. Throat tight, she wrapped both arms around the girl in a bear hug. "You're the daughter I never knew I always wanted."

They stood like that for a long time, until a firm nose nudged her between the shoulder blades. Stumbling a little, Afton managed to keep Freya upright as she turned and felt her heart roll over in her chest. The white mare glared at her with familiar baleful eyes, dancing back when Afton reached out a hand to touch her.

"I deserved that."

Freya joined her at the stall door. "She's beautiful."

"This is Queen Titania."

"Was she yours?"

"Titania belongs to herself alone. But, aye, technically, she was mine. As part of the estate, she belongs to Raleigh now." And because of that, Afton hadn't gotten up the heart to come see her after all this time. Clearly the mare's memory ran long, and she hadn't forgiven the abandonment.

The sound of happy barks heralded someone's arrival. Dugal raced over, bouncing around the two of them, his tail whirling like a helicopter. Raleigh strode after him.

"Hey! What are y'all doing here?"

"Hamish and Dayna are having a... discussion. Dayna didn't take the news of our involvement particularly well, so we thought we'd vacate the premises."

"Ah." There was a wealth of understanding in that single syllable. "Well, if y'all have the time, you want to go for a ride?"

Freya brightened. "Really?"

"Sure. No time like the present. Icarus would love to get some exercise."

Freya stepped across the aisle to the gelding and held out her hand.

At the sound of Raleigh's voice, Titania abandoned her sulk and stuck her head out of the stall, nudging him with demands for attention. Afton watched with a little jealousy as her mare let him scratch her behind the ears.

"You want to take her out?" Raleigh's lips quirked. "Assuming she'll let you."

"I'd love to make things up to her, if I can."

"I'm planning to breed her in the spring."

"Really?"

"She's got incredible bloodlines. Be a shame not to. That's one of the areas I'm wanting to expand for myself, because the horses are where my heart is." He stroked a hand down Titania's neck, but kept his eyes on Afton. "When I do, if she's amenable, maybe you can have her back. Keep her here."

Afton stared at him. "Oh, I couldn't."

"Please, you gave me so much. And I know how much it hurt me when my stepmama sold my horse out from under me. I know how much you love this temperamental girl, and how much it would've hurt you to leave her. If you two can come to terms, I say she's yours."

Afton's heart began to thud. He was offering a blessing she'd never expected to have again. Raleigh Beaumont really was the most generous man. "Well, I guess we'll see if I can woo her affections back, then."

The cowboy grinned. "I'll get some saddles."

As he strode away, Afton let herself into the stall. It was a risk. Titania was high spirited and definitely had a temper. But they'd been friends once. Afton held out her hands and began to croon in a low voice. "I'm sorry, my sweet darling. I would never have left you if I'd had a choice. You have every right to be angry with me."

The mare's ears twitched.

"I tried to send you the best possible replacement, and it's obvious you adore him. That's fair. But I'd love it if we could find our way to being friends again. I swear, I willnae leave you again."

Ever so slowly, Titania edged forward, extending her head until it bumped against Afton's shoulder as if to say *Fine, but you have a lot of adoration to make up for.*

With a low laugh, she stroked down Titania's neck and scratched her chest in exactly the spot she knew the mare loved. "I missed you, too, girl."

<hr>

HAMISH GAVE up on sleep shortly before five. Slipping out of bed, he made his way downstairs, through the darkened house to the kitchen, where he overrode the timer on the coffeemaker. Might as well try to finish getting through all the case notes he hadn't made it through yesterday, courtesy of his ex-wife losing her shite. At least Afton had been able to get Freya away before things truly devolved. Things had been said on both sides that neither of them could take back. Hamish wasn't proud of that. But Dayna was threatening to take him back to court over custody of Freya, arguing that he wasn't providing a good home environment for her. As if he and Afton had been inappropriate around her, when they'd never even been intimate beyond a kiss when his daughter was in the house.

He wasn't worried Dayna would succeed. She hadn't fought for Freya in the first place, and a judge would take that into account. On top of which, he could provide a dozen witnesses who could testify to exactly how good Afton was for Freya, including Freya's teachers, and, if necessary, Freya herself. Not that he wanted to put his daughter through the trauma of being forced to talk about her strained relationship with her mother on the stand. That wasn't something he thought either Freya or Dayna would ever get over. If she took him to court, more than likely a judge would consider this to be exactly what it was—an ex-wife upset that her ex-husband was moving on with someone else. Even if she was the one who'd had an extramarital affair to begin with. The extramarital affair their daughter knew about.

Not that he'd thrown that at Dayna during their argument.

Throughout the whole thing, he wished he'd already proposed to Afton. There seemed no quicker way to shut this whole argument down and prove that her being in their lives was not a temporary state. Certainly, being engaged already would be an additional weight against Dayna's claim that he was being irresponsible and putting Afton ahead of their daughter. But he didn't want to bring it up *now*. He didn't want to start that next phase of life with Afton because of this threat. It felt like that would taint their new beginning somehow, and he didn't want to risk it.

So, he didn't know what to do. Was Dayna making empty threats simply because she was angry, or was she serious? Hamish didn't know. And he couldn't afford to devote any more time to thinking about it today because he was due in court this morning to represent Lewis Anderson regarding the custody of his sons, and his client deserved so much better than the three-ring circus that was currently his brain.

Taking the first cup of coffee to the table, he sat down with his case notes and tried to focus on refining his arguments. Two cups of coffee later, Hamish knew he wasn't at the top of his game. This case felt far too personal. But a fight with his own ex-wife was hardly adequate grounds to ask for any sort of delay from the judge. Lewis Anderson was counting on him.

Afton came down a little before six, wrapped in

her soft, cotton robe, her hair plaited in the messy braid she'd slept in. She leaned over him, wrapping her arms around his shoulders from behind and squeezing, her cheek pressed to his.

"Are you okay? You were restless last night."

"No. Not really. My head isn't in this case, and my client deserves better."

There'd been no opportunity to talk with her about what had gone down yesterday, as they were both well aware of Freya's predilections toward eavesdropping, and this wasn't a conversation he intended to have with her around. It was bad enough she'd heard any of it before Afton managed to get her away. Plus, she'd been in such a good mood when she'd returned, full of talk about the ride Raleigh had taken them both on. He hadn't wanted to ruin what had clearly turned into a pretty good day.

"You are a brilliant lawyer, Hamish. I have faith that you'll do your absolute best to see that justice is done."

He didn't know that there was such a thing as justice in cases like this. As Lewis had said in their first meeting, someone was going to lose and miss out on large chunks of their sons' lives. But he appreciated her attempts to make him feel better. Pressing a kiss to the arm she had wrapped around him, he said, "Thanks for the vote of confidence."

"I'll make you some breakfast. You'll function better with food."

A little of the tension drained out as he watched her putter around the kitchen, putting on some bacon and chopping veggies for what would probably end up being omelets. As the thunk of pipes announced Freya was up, Afton turned her attention toward prepping lunch for school.

"Will you be back to the office for lunch, do you think?"

"I dinna know. I expect we'll be in court most of the day and break just long enough to pick up something near the courthouse. Dinna worry about me on that front today."

Accepting that, she continued her work, sliding a steaming and beautiful omelet in front of him a few minutes later. As she started to step back, he snagged her hand, bringing it to his lips for a kiss.

"Thank you."

It wasn't what he wanted to say. He wanted to spill out how much he loved and adored her. But he didn't want her to think it was only because of the domestic partnership support she offered. She simply made him feel loved and supported in all things. He wanted that for his daughter, too.

With a smile, she cupped his cheek. "You're welcome."

Freya came clattering down the stairs.

"I've got an omelet with your name on it. What do you want in it?"

"Sweet. Mushrooms, bacon, that fussy French cheese, and peppers."

"As you wish. It'll be ready when you're finished feeding the goats."

She clattered back out to find her boots.

The morning went faster then, as they all fell into the semi-chaos that was the usual routine. Hamish finished his breakfast and went to dress. He came down just in time to kiss both his girls goodbye before he left for court. Afton pressed a travel mug with more coffee into his hand.

"Bless you."

"See you tonight."

"Have a good day, Da!"

"I'll certainly try."

His positive mood lasted until he met Lewis Anderson outside the courthouse, dressed in an ill-fitting suit and looking bloody uncomfortable and anxious. It was hard not to let the other man's anxiety infect him, when he was so worried about the same thing with his own child. But as they stepped into the courtroom, Hamish shoved it all out of his mind, determined to do the best job possible.

At the front of the room, Darla Anderson sat with her attorney, a middle-aged white woman with graying red hair and a weary expression. Antagonism cracked around Lewis's soon-to-be ex like lightning, and she watched the pair of them walk down the center aisle with clear resentment.

Lewis, for his part, nodded and said a polite good morning.

"Good morning? How can you say that to me, Lewis? When you're trying to take my children from me? Why are you fighting so hard? How can you take children from their own mother?"

Lewis's broad shoulders bunched. "How can you take them from their father? You could find a job somewhere closer. Somewhere we can both share custody."

"You could move," she challenged. "They've need of stonemasons nearer to Glasgow."

This was exactly how the attempt at mediation had devolved. Neither of them wanted to give an inch.

Hamish stepped between them, placing a hand on the other man's shoulder. "Reel it in."

Behind him, Darla's counsel warned her in a low voice to keep it together.

"Anderson v. Anderson. Judge Eliza Wallace presiding. All rise."

At the court clerk's announcement, they all shuffled behind their respective seats and came to attention as the judge stepped into the courtroom.

A no-nonsense woman, Judge Wallace surveyed

the lot of them with sharp gray eyes before settling into her chair behind the bench. "You may be seated."

Putting on his game face, Hamish prepared to do his best to get his client what he wanted.

NINETEEN

Hands full, Afton jerked her chin toward the happy glow of Lochmara's kitchen. "Get the door, will you, Cricket?"

Freya raced ahead to let them all inside. Per usual, cheerful chaos greeted the three of them as they stepped into the kitchen of Afton's childhood home. It hurt a little less each time, and she thought, eventually, she'd come to see it with nostalgia instead of pain. Multiple greetings rang out on all sides.

As she and Hamish moved to place their covered dishes on the counter with all the others, Ciara announced, "I have news!"

Everyone turned toward her.

When she said nothing, only stood with her

eyes sparkling, Afton pressed, "Well, dinna keep us in suspense. What's the news?"

The young woman raised her glass of wine to her brother. "I'm officially giving you my two weeks' notice at the pub."

"Nooooo," Ewan groaned.

His sister just grinned and leaned back against the counter. "Be grateful I gave you any."

"Ingrate." With mock severity, Ewan glared at Sophie and Kyla. "This is all your fault."

The women exchanged a look and shrugged. "Sorry. Not sorry," they chorused.

Kyla shrugged one shoulder. "We can finally afford to employ her full time."

"Which she richly deserves," Sophie added. "We couldnae do all this without her."

"It leaves me short a server, without a lot of time to find someone else."

"I didnae go to uni with an eye toward serving pints the rest of my days," Ciara told him. "You knew this was temporary."

Isobel tucked up against Ewan's side and brushed a kiss to his cheek, not at all cowed by his grousing. "I'm not due to record again for another month. I can pitch in until you find someone else."

That would never *not* feel weird to Afton. But she loved that Isobel was both willing to help and that everyone in the village simply accepted her.

She was their Isobel. Who also happened to be an internationally famous musician.

Ciara continued to sip at her wine. "For the record, I told Laura already, so she's on it."

"Oh, so I'm the last to ken, aye? I see where I fall on the priority list."

Impish to the last, she twinkled at her brother. "I didnae want to deprive anyone of seeing your face when I told you. Prime entertainment, that."

"You're a menace," he pronounced.

"Aye, well, this menace *also* has a second date."

Ewan straightened, broad shoulders seeming to get even broader. "With who?"

"His name is Brodie Drummond. He's from Braemore."

"Why's this the first I'm hearing of it?"

Afton almost snickered at the heavy dose of side eye Ciara shot him.

"First, because my love life is none of your business. I'm well past the age where you get to play protective big brother on the men in my life. Second, because I didnae want to curse it, as the dating pool here is verra shallow. He brought me flowers two days after our first date and asked me out again. I think he has potential."

Charlotte wrapped an arm around her shoulders. "I'm happy for you, sugar. That certainly seems a good start."

She and Malcolm had returned from their honeymoon in Mexico last week, after an additional week in Texas to meet the family who hadn't been able to fly in for the wedding. Chatter turned to the party thrown in their honor, and Connor put a drink into Afton's hand.

"Thanks."

He jerked his head toward Hamish, who'd crossed to speak to Raleigh. "He okay?"

Afton was glad she wasn't the only one who'd noticed he seemed off. He'd been quiet and withdrawn since his confrontation with Dayna. The two of them hadn't had an opportunity to really discuss it, without fear of being overheard by a certain eavesdropping tween. All he'd said about the situation was that he was handling it. She had no idea what that meant. What exactly was he handling? Dayna's bad attitude? Was there something else they needed to worry about? She didn't like not knowing, but didn't feel like he was in a place where she could press him on it.

Checking to see that Freya was in conversation with Gavin on the other side of the noisy kitchen, Afton lowered her voice. "Honestly, I'm not sure. He had a run-in with Dayna about us. It didn't go well."

"Never thought it would. Is that all?"

At a loss, she could only shrug. "Work's been a

little rough, as well. A case or two is feeling very personal. If you get the chance, you should round him up for a boys' night. See if you can pry whatever's wrong out of him."

Connor tapped his long-neck bottle to her wineglass. "You've got it." With a smile, he wandered over to Raleigh and Hamish.

As she watched, Hamish took Lily from Raleigh and lifted her high overhead, making comic faces before lowering her low enough he could blow raspberries on her belly. The baby giggled, a joyful sound that seemed to visibly loosen something in him even as the sight of the two of them struck Afton like a fist to the feels. She knew Hamish was a good father. She'd had ample first-hand evidence of it these past months. But she hadn't really gotten to see him like this in years. Not since Freya was wee. And even then, not often, as she'd kept her distance. Seeing him so easy with a baby was just—

"It's enough to make your ovaries explode, aye?"

At the sound of Sophie's voice, Afton jolted. "What?"

Sophie just sent her a knowing smile. "Men and babies. Maybe Connor and I should think about getting started on one of those. Lily could use a cousin."

Speechless, Afton could only stare. She was saved from the awkward moment by the sound of a kitchen timer and Kyla's announcement that the main course was ready. Then began the great migration of all the food to the dining room, where they settled around the table, minus Angus and Munro, who were off visiting friends from their stint in Berkshire for *The Great British Bake Off*.

"So Afton, are you ready for tomorrow's meeting with the village council?" Charlotte asked.

Afton passed a bowl of roasted vegetables. "Ready might be a strong word. My business plan is finished, and it's solid. I've spoken to my mentor and another chef friend of hers, and they both agree that my numbers and premise are reasonable. There's not really anything more I can do to prepare."

"It's going to go fine. The council has no reason not to approve the rezoning. Having a restaurant like that would be nothing but a boon to the village." Hamish's tone rang with familiar confidence, something that he'd been lacking of late.

Hearing it again, Afton relaxed. She knew all the challenges of single parenthood and the transition from corporate to family law had shaken his faith in himself, especially after what he felt was a poor performance in the initial meeting with the judge for that custody case he was working. But he'd done as much or more prep for this presentation than she had. As he was the one doing most of the talking, she was glad he felt good about it.

"Well, I say we raise a glass to your future success." Connor lifted his.

Afton raised a staying hand. "I dinna think we should get ahead of ourselves. Toasting already feels premature. It hasn't happened yet. Celebrating already seems like a bad omen or something. I dinna want to curse anything. Because if they say no, I'm dead in the water. There's no other building anywhere in the village or immediate vicinity that would suit, and I certainly canna afford to build one. Not without going through all the trouble to find investors, and I dinna really want to tackle that."

Sophie frowned. "What will you do if they say no?"

"I have no idea. I've put so much effort into planning this, it's hard to think past it to anything else."

"What about a food truck?" Gavin suggested. "One of those wouldnae have the same zoning restrictions or whatever, aye?"

Afton considered. "Well, it's a thought. The kind of cooking I'm wanting to do is a few steps above your typical burger van, but it may be that it could be adapted. And the mobile component means I have more ready access to all the villages in the area, I suppose. Either way, I can continue the personal catering I've been doing. It's not a full-time gig, but it's keeping things level until I figure something else out."

Kyla and Sophie exchanged a considering look.

Before either of them could speak, Hamish insisted, "You're not going to have to do something else. This is going to work. Trust me. I won't let you down."

Afton squeezed his hand and leaned over to brush her lips against his cheek. "You never have."

"THANK YOU FOR YOUR PRESENTATION, Mr. Colquhoun."

At the dismissal by George Davidson, head of the council, Hamish gathered his notes and resumed his seat beside Afton in one of the uncomfortable chairs at the periphery of the room. Despite the fact that he'd been forced to limit his remarks to five minutes, he felt good about the whole thing. The entire proposal, comprising both Afton's business plan and his own arguments regarding the benefit the restaurant and rezoning would bring to the village, had been provided to the Council ten days prior, so each council member could review it before the meeting. It had also been made available to the public, so anyone interested enough had gotten a chance to read the entire thing. The purpose of his speaking today was to provide all the high points for those in attendance, prior to the council's debate and vote on the issue.

As village council meetings were generally held mid-afternoon on weekdays, attendance was usually poor. Today, nearly every seat in the small council room was filled. Granted, that wasn't *that* many people above and beyond their friends, who took up half the seats that didn't already belong to council members. Still, Hamish hoped the show of local support would be in their favor.

As council members began their debate over the merits of the proposal, he took Afton's hand in his. She had on what he thought of as her Baroness mask, face unperturbed and unruffled, as if nothing touched her. He knew better. She was counting on this rezoning application going through. So was he. This restaurant was how she got to stay in Glenlaig, stay in his life and Freya's and still pursue her dream.

"I agree with everything Mr. Colquhoun said. Farmers across the UK are experiencing unprecedented hardships. Scotland is no different. This proposal allows for a form of diversification that will help local crofters, which in turn, helps sustain a piece of Scottish history."

"Fair enough, but let us not forget that we arenae debating whether a restaurant is a good idea. We're specifically debating the rezoning of this specific parcel of land, so let us stay on topic."

Hamish frowned. That glossed over a huge chunk of his argument. The reasons for rezoning were entirely based around the benefits the restaurant would bring to the village. That meant the restaurant was central to the entire discussion. He resisted the urge to call out, "Objection!" This wasn't a court of law, and he wouldn't advance their cause with the interruption. But as debate continued, with more than one council member voicing concerns about the prospective harm a commercial business would have on the rural character and scenic beauty of the site, he realized that this rezoning petition wasn't going to be as clear cut as he'd anticipated. All he'd heard from people was enthusiastic support of the restaurant idea. But perhaps he didn't have a balanced view of the issue. His confidence began to strain as debate shifted well away from the specific benefits of the restaurant—additional dining options for the area, more employment opportunities for locals, and alternative revenue streams for struggling crofters—and settled heavily on worry about light pollution to the area and how much land would be claimed for a car park. Additional concern was raised about the prospective ruination of the historic character of the building itself.

Hadn't they read the proposal? They'd covered this in detail.

When one council member began to argue that perhaps the site would be better utilized for other purposes, it took everything Hamish had to hold on to his temper and keep from interrupting. What the bloody hell other purpose did they have for it? To his knowledge, no one had submitted a proposal for anything else. He'd done his due diligence and checked.

"Do any other council members have anything else to add?" George checked the room. "Seeing none, let's put it to a vote. All in favor of rezoning the property as commercial?"

Five of the twelve council members raised their hands.

"All opposed?"

The remaining seven lifted their hands.

George pounded his gavel. "Rezoning application denied."

They'd lost. *He'd* lost.

His logic should have been irrefutable. The points against the rezoning were hazy at best, with no solid evidence that it was a bad idea.

And still. He'd. Lost.

Afton's hand was limp in his. She said nothing.

When he glanced her way, she didn't seem to react at all. Shock, he guessed.

A pair of worn loafers stopped in front of them. Alan Mitchell. "Better luck next time, aye? You'll find the right site."

Eleanor Ross joined him. "Aye. This wasnae a no to the restaurant. We all still think it's a marvelous idea. Just not there."

Afton remained polite and noncommittal, that reactionless mask firmly in place.

God, he hated that mask.

Connor stalked over. "This is utter shite."

Afton just lifted one pale hand to stay his temper. "Not the place, Con."

"Perhaps we should all reconvene at the pub?" Sophie suggested.

"Aye, that sounds good," Afton agreed. With a squeeze of his hand, she rose from the chair, graceful as any titled miss.

Neither of them spoke on the drive. What could he say? He'd promised Afton he'd do this for her. Sworn he'd get this pushed through. And now... now her livelihood wasn't an option. There'd been some half-assed suggestions tossed out at family dinner last night. But she hadn't seemed excited about any of them. A food truck didn't lend itself to the sort of cuisine she wanted to prepare.

Which left them where exactly?

Right back to where he'd been before they'd even gotten together, wondering what the hell he had to offer her that was sufficient inducement for her to give up all her dreams. Because he didn't see an option here that didn't involve that sacrifice, and he very much worried he wouldn't be enough for her. That she'd wake up one day and decide she wanted more than this small town life they were living.

The pressure made his head ache, a situation not improved when they walked into the pub, where the early evening crowd was already gathered. On autopilot, he walked back to the private room reserved for events or family. A couple of minutes later, Ewan came through the door with a tray full of drinks. God love him.

Hamish took the whisky and tossed it back, knowing it was a crime to shoot it all at once but needing the burn to clear his head. As the others began updating Ewan and Ciara, he pulled out his phone to check messages. At the end of business, he wasn't expecting much. But he found one from Marsaili stating that he was expected in court tomorrow morning with Lewis Anderson, as the judge would hear final arguments before handing down the decision regarding the custody arrangements as part of the divorce decree.

Fuck.

"I have to go."

Afton's face creased with concern. "Everything all right?"

"No. I'm due in court tomorrow morning. I've got to go into the office to prep. I'm sorry." About so very many things he couldn't say.

"It's fine. Will you be home for dinner?"

"Probably late. Dinna wait on me."

"I'll keep you a plate for when you get home."

He jerked a nod and started to turn, but Afton stepped into his path, wrapping her arms around him and looking up into his face. "It'll be okay. We'll figure something out."

Because he knew she needed it, he brushed a kiss to her temple. He couldn't tell her it would be okay because he no longer knew that, and he wasn't in the business of lying. "I'll see you later."

She squeezed him again and let him go, but he didn't miss the look of concern in her big brown eyes.

Knowing he had a job to do, he ignored it and left for his office, where at least he could lick his wounds in peace as he prayed not to disappoint someone else this week.

TWENTY

"Have a good day, Cricket!"

"See you tonight!" Freya shot Afton a quick wave and shut the car door.

Well, that was one family member off for the day and in decent spirits. Afton couldn't say the same for Hamish.

He'd gotten home late last night, after Freya had gone to bed. After mechanically inhaling the dinner she'd saved for him, barely saying a word, he'd turned in himself. If he'd truly slept, Afton hadn't noticed. He'd been up and out well before dawn.

More prep for court today? Or was he avoiding her?

Hamish was a man to whom most things in life

had come easily. Oh, not that he hadn't worked for anything, but he was a naturally gifted and intelligent lawyer, and he'd earned a reputation as being one of the best in his field. She understood he was taking this council defeat very personally. She'd seen the look of utter disbelief on his face when the vote had been taken. The one thing he'd been confident and excited about in the past few months had just taken a nosedive, and he blamed himself.

For her part, Afton was a lot less upset about it than she'd expected. She had no idea what the answer was, but a part of her had been a little relieved when the rezoning failed. Which she'd wanted to tell him, to reassure him that this wasn't the disaster he was making it out to be. But she really wanted another option to present, even if it wasn't fully fleshed out.

Since their relationship had changed, they'd fallen into this weird hybrid domestic partnership, where she was both the nanny and the girlfriend. He was still paying her, which felt weird. And, of course, he was covering most of the living expenses. Afton wanted a way to support herself more effectively than she had been. One that didn't depend on him. Both because she needed to prove her capability to herself, and because she didn't want him thinking he had to save her. He didn't need to take that on. She could save herself.

She just had to figure out how.

Nothing had presented itself by the time she got back to the house, but the cars parked in the drive put it out of her mind. Kyla and Sophie climbed out as she did.

"Good morning. To what do I owe the pleasure of your company?"

Kyla shouldered a leather satchel. "We have a business proposition."

"Color me intrigued. Come on in."

Afton let them into the house and led them back to the kitchen.

"Wow. You and Hamish have truly gotten a lot done since the last time I was here," Kyla observed.

They'd finished almost all the interior projects by now, spreading out the furniture that had come with her, such that each room was actually furnished. Afton hadn't quite gotten around to finishing with the unpacking, courtesy of all the time spent on the business plan and the actual renovations, but it was coming along. "He just needed some extra help from someone who wouldn't listen when he said no."

Kyla laughed. "Aye, that sounds about right."

"It really looks like a home now instead of a construction zone," Sophie added.

They chatted easily, in the way of old friends, as Afton made tea. It was a lovely interlude she didn't take for granted after all her time away. Because they were there, she plated some of the lemon poppyseed scones she'd made over the weekend and added them to the tray she brought to the kitchen table.

"So, why are you really here?"

Kyla settled back with her mug. "Nobody expected the rezoning to fail yesterday."

"Hamish certainly didn't. He's really torn up about it."

"It sucks, but the thing about it is… it opens up another potential opportunity." Sophie snagged a scone. "We actually thought of this sooner, but you were going full-steam ahead on the restaurant, and we didnae want to distract you."

"With what, exactly?"

"You stepped in and performed a miracle for Charlotte and Malcolm's wedding, and you did it beautifully," Kyla began. "We've run some numbers, looking at what the cost savings would be of having an on-site caterer rather than needing to go outside the area to pull someone else in. It's an extra burden to bring outsiders in, as they frequently have to come from a fair bit away, depending on the size of the event. We mostly pass the cost of that on to the clients, but if we were able to be a true one-stop shop for all the things in-house, we could offer them better prices and a better experience overall."

"Added to which, we wouldn't have to worry about what happened with Malcolm and Charlotte happening again," Sophie put in. "Obviously, that's not something that happens all the time, but the potential for it is there. I dinna know what we would've done if you hadn't been there."

As they spoke, a buzz of excitement began to fizz in Afton's blood. "Okay, so what are you saying, exactly?

"We want to bring you in as a full-time caterer. The salary itself isnae likely to be as high as you might make for yourself with a restaurant," Kyla qualified.

Afton snorted. "You might be surprised. The profit margin in restaurants is very thin. I cook because I love to cook. Not because I expect it to make me rich."

"Well, as we're a small family business, the income fluctuates, but in addition to the salary that's attached to all of this, we also want to offer you an ownership stake in the company."

She stared at them. "You'd give me part ownership of the company you built?"

"Well, you'd be helping us to build it bigger," Sophie explained.

Kyla opened the satchel and pulled out some folders, sliding one to each of them. "I've put together some spreadsheets to show you our growth since we started, as well as projections for what we expect to continue as things move forward."

Afton listened to her pitch with only half an ear. They were offering her the chance to do the sort of cooking she liked, without the stress of a restaurant. As they'd said, she wouldn't be getting rich this way, but it would be a solid opportunity.

"You'd still have the time to expand the personal catering, if that's something you're interested in continuing," Kyla qualified. "And while the hours might be somewhat unusual compared to a typical eight-to-five, you'd easily be able to juggle the demands of family."

Afton lifted her gaze to Kyla's.

Her friend smiled. "You're as much or more of a mother to Freya as Dayna ever was. I dinna imagine you want to give that up any more than I want to miss time with Lily."

She didn't, and that Kyla understood that meant so much.

"It's a very generous offer." One that her heart wanted to leap at. But she'd learned not to leap before considering all the angles. "Can I have some time to think about it?"

"Of course! And if you have any questions for us, please ask," Sophie said. "We know this is rather fast, and probably there are aspects we haven't considered."

"Like the fact that I'll still need a commercial kitchen on site. I pulled off a miracle using what you had, but that wouldn't be practical as the normal course of things."

"Fair point." Kyla made a note on one of the pages in her folder.

"If I end up saying yes, I'm more than happy to put the money I intended for the restaurant renovation into the construction of my own facilities. That seems only fair."

Kyla nodded. "To a point. It would be considered a business expense, so we can accommodate that in other places. If you can put together your needs there, we can start considering where one would best fit and begin running the numbers to see what it would cost."

Sophie checked her watch. "We need to go. We've got a meeting with a prospective bride in an hour. But we'd really love to have you come on board, if that's something you're interested in."

Feeling buoyed, Afton saw them out. The moment she shut the door, she wished she could call Hamish to tell him. This felt like the perfect option. Certainly, it was a lot more appealing than the idea of a food truck. Enthused and already wanting to put together some estimates on costs, she brought her laptop to the kitchen table. Out of habit, she checked her email to find one from Chef McLeod.

Dear Afton,

I hope last night's council meeting went the way you hoped. But, if it didn't, I'd like to present another option. I've found myself with a recent vacancy on my staff at Whisky and Thyme, and I'd love to interview you for the position. Let me know if you're interested.

Iain

She sat back in her chair, stunned. A Michelin-starred chef wanted to interview *her*. It wasn't the right job for her, not the least of which because it was in Edinburgh instead of here. But to even have the opportunity to interview was incredibly flattering. She needed to think about the right way to respond with the utmost respect for the offer.

Before she could get any further, her phone began to ring. Evidently, it was going to be a day for interruptions.

Seeing Athena's name flashing across the screen, she frowned. Wasn't it some absurd o'clock in the morning in Tennessee?

"Hello?"

"Hey, girl!" Athena's familiar Southern drawl filled the silence, automatically making Afton smile.

"Are you calling to find out about the council vote?"

"Well, yes, and no. I do want to know how it

went, but mostly I'm calling because I'm in Edinburgh."

"What? Since when?"

"Got in last night. I'm here to hang with Moses and Zuri, and I wanted to know if you could come down. I know it's last minute and all, but I'd love to see you."

Everything in Afton yearned to talk her options over with her mentor. "Absolutely. It's a three-hour drive, and I need to make some arrangements for Freya this afternoon, but I'll be there." And maybe while she was in town, she could go by in person to speak to Chef McLeod. That seemed the best way to handle a rejection. "Where are you?"

Afton took down the address. "I'll see you in a few hours."

"Can't wait!"

She made another call to Charlotte to have her pick Freya up this afternoon, then took the time to scribble a quick note to Hamish rather than texting him and interrupting court. Bouncing with fresh energy, she left the note on the counter where she thought he'd see it and headed for her car.

Today was shaping up to be fantastic.

"IN THE MATTER of Anderson v. Anderson, the minor children shall remain with their mother, with the following provisions made for visitation to their father."

The pen fell from Hamish's numb fingers as Judge Wallace laid out the terms of the custody agreement. It didn't matter that both parents would have joint legal custody. Lewis's ex-wife would retain primary custody of the boys, meaning they'd be moving to Glasgow.

He'd lost the case. Again.

It didn't matter that the judge awarded a most generous visitation schedule to Lewis, including full summers. Or that it was determined that the minor children would remain in Glenlaig to finish out the school year. None of it changed the fact that Lewis would have to say goodbye to his sons.

None of it changed the fact that Hamish had failed his client.

As the judge continued reciting the terms of the divorce decree, Lewis wilted in the chair beside him, dropping his head to his hands. Only deeply entrenched professional decorum kept Hamish from doing the same. There was absolutely nothing he could say that would make this better. There was no point in explaining that courts still regularly sided with the mother unless circumstances gave a good reason to do otherwise. It was simply a shite situation all around.

The judge gave final remarks and adjourned, leaving Hamish with nothing at all to say to his client.

"I'm sorry."

It was paltry at best. But what more was there? Yes, he'd warned Lewis up-front that this would be a hard battle. But he'd also promised to do his best. And his best hadn't been good enough.

The big man looked at him, tears glimmering in his eyes, before he looked away and shoved back from the table. Hamish watched him walk over to his ex-wife. He didn't rant or rail. His big shoulders bowed with grief. For her part, Darla didn't appear to take any pleasure in his misery. She murmured low words about doing whatever she could to make sure he got to talk to the boys as often as he wanted and see them as often as could be managed.

Hamish understood that he'd been dismissed. There was nothing more to say, so he gathered up his papers, placing them neatly back inside his briefcase, before striding out of the room and the building.

A cold rain had begun to fall sometime since this morning. Not quite cold enough for snow, the falling slush hit his head, face, and shoulders, half soaking him by the time he made it to the car park and his sedan. Unlocking it, he tossed his briefcase on the front seat and slid inside. Then he gave in and laid his head on folded arms.

Fuck.

His body felt heavy, as if the whole world pressed down upon it. His exhausted mind began going over every argument, analyzing and dissecting, wondering what more he could have done. Wondering, too, if he was cut out for family law when this was the potential outcome. He enjoyed the personal when it was something happy. An adoption. The planning of an estate. But this... This left him utterly gutted.

Nothing in his previous career in corporate law had prepared him for this. Because he'd never failed there. But he'd been failing left and right since he'd made this big change and come home. Disappointing so many people in so many ways.

After a few minutes, the chill penetrated to his bones, and he roused himself enough to start the car and crank the heater. Then he called Marsaili.

"Cancel anything I have on my schedule for the rest of the day and the first half of next week."

A beat of weighted silence rang. "All of it?"

There wasn't a chance in hell he'd have his head screwed on straight to handle anything by then. "All of it." This wasn't a defeat he'd easily bounce back from. Wasn't a case of getting back up on the proverbial horse. He needed to do some serious thinking about what the right course really was for him and his family. Because he wasn't convinced this was it.

"Consider it done."

Aching on every level, Hamish drove home. He needed Afton. Was desperate to feel her arms around him, to have that calm she seemed to carry soak into him so he could breathe again. They needed to talk about the future beyond the rose-colored view, where everything was easy simply because they cared. But maybe that bit could wait a little, until he'd had a little comfort, felt a little less bruised.

But when he got to the farmhouse, Afton's car wasn't there. It wasn't so late that she'd have left to get Freya. Perhaps she'd gone into the village to the market or stopped by Village Blume with more dishes for her personal catering clients. Praying she'd be home soon, he stepped inside and went directly upstairs, stripping off the wet suit as he went. Leaving it in an uncharacteristic pile on the floor, he switched on the shower, waiting for the spray to warm before he stepped beneath it, letting the water beat his skin, warming him. And also battering him as he couldn't quite do himself.

The house remained quiet when he finally stepped out and dried off. He dressed again, for comfort this time, and went downstairs. There he found the folded note on the counter with Afton's neat, looping handwriting.

Hamish,

I had to go to Edinburgh for the day. Charlotte's got Freya and will bring her home in time for dinner. I'll probably be home late, so there's a meal in the fridge with instructions on a post-it. You only need to warm it up. Hope court went well today.

Afton

Disappointment sliced through him, knowing he wouldn't be getting anything he wanted today.

Edinburgh. Why the hell had she gone all the way to Edinburgh? It wasn't like her to make an impulsive trip like this without letting him know.

Her laptop sat open on the kitchen table. Realizing the screen hadn't gone dark, he strode over. She really needed to turn on a screen saver so that the screen didn't burn in. As he reached to shut the lid, he saw her email program open, his eyes snagging on Iain McLeod's name. He knew she'd been corresponding with the chef about plans for the restaurant and figured this was more of that. But then he caught sight of "interview" in the text.

Hamish hesitated, knowing he shouldn't invade her privacy but also unable to do anything but read.

The man had asked her for an interview.

Checking the date, he realized this had come in this morning.

And Afton had immediately driven to Edinburgh.

Hamish sank into the chair as realization sank in. This was his nightmare. He'd failed her, and exactly what he'd been afraid of was coming to pass. He'd promised her she wouldn't have to give up her dream to be with him, and the very day after the door closed here in Glenlaig, she'd jumped at an opportunity three hours away. And opportunity that would, unquestionably, be a significant feather in her professional cap.

Apparently, she was done wasting time on him and trying to make this small town life work.

Because no matter how much he'd done, he wasn't enough. Exactly as he'd known from the beginning. He'd failed one too many times, and his time had run out.

TWENTY-ONE

Afton stepped through the doors of Délicieux in Edinburgh and was pretty sure she'd fallen straight into heaven. The intoxicating scents of butter, sugar, and yeast in all their varied forms assaulted her senses and made her mouth water. Athena had told her about Zuri Patil's award-winning patisserie during their months of training together, but Afton had never been here. Glossy pastries and gorgeous cakes were artfully arranged in glass cases. Open shelving on the back wall housed beautiful baskets full of picture-perfect boules and loaves. Bistro tables were scattered around the perimeter of the front, and every single one was filled, but none of them by Athena.

"Welcome to Délicieux. What can I get you

today?" The smartly dressed woman in black-frame glasses smiled at her from a wheelchair behind the counter.

Afton returned the smile. "How many people answer that question with 'One of everything'?"

The woman's smile broadened into a full-on grin. "At least fifty percent. Sadly, no one's yet taken us up on it."

"More's the pity. I'm here looking for a friend. Athena Reynolds? I'm supposed to meet her here."

"Oh! You must be Afton. I'm Antonia Hawthorne. She's just in the back with Zuri." Antonia jerked her head. "Come on through to the kitchen."

Afton circled around the counter and followed Antonia through a swinging door into the bright kitchen, made sunny by the butter yellow walls and white cabinets amid all the expected stainless steel.

Athena immediately slid off a stool, beaming. "You're here!"

"I am." Afton met her in the middle for a tight hug. "God, it's good to see you."

"You too!" Athena held her at arm's length and squinted, taking her in. "You look good. Happy."

"I am." It meant so much that she could say it. That she could mean it.

"I want you to tell me all about it. But first, let me introduce a couple more of my besties to you."

Athena gestured to a petite Indian woman in a chef's jacket, her hair pulled into a tight bun that didn't quite manage to contain the riot of black curls. "This is Chef Zuri Patil, one of my classmates from *Le Cordon Bleu*. Délicieux is her baby."

"My creation, but shared with Moses." Zuri extended a palm. "It's lovely to meet you, Afton. I've heard many wonderful things about you."

Afton shook her hand. "Same. Literally everything out there looks like it's to die for."

"Oh, it is." Athena moved over to a burly black man with the kindest eyes Afton had ever seen. "And this big teddy bear is Moses Lindsey, my former pastry chef from Olympus and officially one of my ride-or-dies."

"Pleasure to finally meet the woman who talked this one into taking on a full apprentice." Moses's Southern drawl flowed over her, rich and warm, like melted caramel, and Afton liked him immediately.

"Athena told me you'd moved here to be with Zuri. How are you liking Scotland compared to home?"

"Little bit of culture shock here and there, but every bit is worth it to be here with her." He wrapped an arm around Zuri's shoulders and tugged her in.

The contented way she snuggled against him and the affection in her eyes spoke volumes about how happy they were together. The sight made Afton sigh in appreciation. It was so wonderful to see people meant to be together.

"I get the feeling that Ari's delighted with this outcome."

Athena laughed. "Oh, you know it. And of course, she takes full credit for matchmaking, even though it was totally Zuri's idea to surprise him on *The Misfit Kitchen*."

"I suppose she'll take credit for me and Hamish next, since she's the one who told me Connor was getting married?"

"As soon as she knows the full details, I'm sure she will. So, sit and tell me everything."

"I'll put on the kettle for some tea," Zuri said.

"And pick us out something delicious to go with it," Athena added.

Afton took the seat offered.

"So, what's the update? How've you been? What happened with the council meeting?"

The council meeting. Right. So much had happened today it wasn't uppermost in her mind anymore, but she'd been emailing back and forth with Athena about the restaurant proposal, so of course that would be the first thing she'd want to know about. "The rezoning didn't pass."

Sympathy flashed over her friend's features. "Oh, I'm sorry."

"You know? I'm not. I dinna think I want to open a restaurant after all."

"Really? So what do you want to do?"

"Well, I actually had another job opportunity fall into my lap this morning."

Over tea and a magnificent mille feuille, Afton explained the offer from Kyla and Sophie. She'd had the long drive to think over the details, and she was even more excited than she had been initially. When she'd finished, Athena leaned back.

"Well, that would be my own personal hell, but if that's your jam, go for it. Are you going to take it?"

"I mean, we need to hammer out some details and make sure all of this is actually going to work for everybody from a numbers standpoint, but aye, I think I am. Because it lets me do the kind of cooking I like, and it gives me the flexibility for family. That's something I'm finding is a lot more important to me than I realized."

"So, I gather things with Hamish are going well?"

"Everything with Hamish is going great. There was a bit of a... *thing* with his ex wife when she found out I'd moved in. That went over like a lead balloon. But all the dust seems to have settled from that." At least, the issue hadn't come up again in the weeks since. "Other than that, things are good." She thought about Hamish's misery the past couple of weeks. He had some things to work through regarding his job, but when she got home, she could reassure him that she, at least, was taken care of. That ought to be a load off his brain.

"Coming back to Scotland was the right move." It wasn't a question.

"Aye, it seems it was. So thank you to you and Ari for pushing me into it."

"Anytime. Of course, you *will* come back to Tennessee to visit, right?"

"Absolutely." She wanted to bring Hamish and Freya to meet the rest of her Tennessee family. The idea of Rebecca immediately adopting Freya as another grandchild—and she totally would—made Afton feel all gooey inside.

They talked for another hour, with Athena catching her up on all the news from back Stateside. Athena's boys, Dylan and Jesse, were growing like weeds. Her husband, Logan, was in the middle of spring planting. Her sister Kennedy was expecting another baby, which the family was ecstatic about. And the unshakably romantic Ari had finally been asked out by Cullen Walker, the guy she'd been crushing on for well over a year.

"We are, of course, giving her all the shit about it since she decided to interfere in all *our* love lives."

"I hope you didn't actually say love lives in front of Ari's father." Flynn would likely have an apoplexy at the idea of his teenage daughter having one.

"Oh, we're letting Pru handle Flynn's delicate sensibilities, and I'm making sure Ari's prepared for... whatever."

Afton snorted. "The girl is finally reaping what she's sown."

"Oh, in a big way."

"I hope it works out well for her."

Athena set her mug and plate aside. "I think it will. He looks at her like she hung the moon. I can't imagine finding that at her age, but it happens. Kennedy and Xander did. I just hope Cullen doesn't somehow manage to fuck it up."

Moses growled a little. "If he does, and Tiny needs me, I can totally fly back."

"Down, big guy. She's already got four overprotective men in her life, who we will have to talk down from tearing him apart if he breaks her heart. Plus me."

He flashed a grin. "Is Logan prepared to take away your knives?"

"It was *one* time, and Jayson totally deserved it."

"Speaking of knives... indirectly. Are you planning to see Iain McLeod while you're here?" Afton asked.

"I am, actually. Supposed to pop over and see him later."

"I need to speak to him. He offered me an interview, which I'm very flattered by, but I'm not going to take because, obviously, I'm not moving to Edinburgh. But I wanted to thank him in person for the opportunity."

Athena rose. "Well, there's no time like the present. We'll catch him before things get nuts preparing for service."

DARK AND DINNERTIME had long since come and gone. Hamish prowled the empty house, a glass of whisky in his hand as he waited for Afton. He'd had hours alone to stew, vacillating from grief to rage to misery. Freya had ultimately gone to Aileen's for a sleepover after school, so he hadn't had to put on any masks for her benefit. Which was good, because he didn't think he had sufficient acting chops to pull it off. Everything was falling apart, and he didn't have it in him yet to find a way to make it okay for her.

If what he feared was true, then nothing he could do or say would make up for the betrayal. Hamish didn't think he could ever forgive Afton for breaking his daughter's heart. It was what he'd been afraid of all along. That she'd become an integral part of their lives, only to disappear in the end, when her dream took her elsewhere. Somewhere deep down, he'd known from the beginning that this would be the outcome for them. But he'd deluded himself they stood a shot. That she wanted the package deal he was. That she truly loved this life they'd been building.

But the fact that she was looking for jobs elsewhere, a mere day after the council defeat? What did that say about her intentions of sticking around? Maybe she'd been looking all along, and he just hadn't been aware. He'd thought they were on the same page. But wasn't that always his failure? Believing he knew where his partner stood and being blindsided when he found out he was wrong? Because he wasn't enough. How long before Freya began to blame him for losing all the important women in her life? How long before she decided her mother was a better bet and left him to move back to Edinburgh? Then where would he be? Alone, rattling around this big, empty house that was full of memories of them both?

As headlights finally flashed through the windows, he rose to pour himself another whisky. A rare indulgence as a single parent, since he was always on duty. But Aileen's parents would take care of Freya tonight, and he needed a hit of liquid courage to get through what was bound to be a horrific conversation.

Hamish could feel her boundless energy as she came into the room, even before he turned. And he knew.

"I'm sorry I'm so late. We got to talking and lost track of time."

"You got the job."

Confusion and surprise flickered over her face. "How did you even—? Doesn't matter. Aye, I did. I'm excited! We've still got a lot of details to work out about the start date and all that, but it's going to be amazing. I couldn't wait to get home to tell you about it."

She was radiant, fairly glowing with enthusiasm for this opportunity. She truly wanted this. Which meant, in the end, she didn't want him. Didn't want them. Because there wasn't a trace of conflict or grief that taking the job meant leaving everything she'd built here.

Maybe bailing on the marriage pact had taught her that leaving wasn't a hard thing anymore. And what had she built, after all? Everything she'd done had been temporary. A stop-gap. Any efforts toward something more permanent had been rebuffed under the guise of caution. Wait and see. Not getting ahead of themselves. So there'd been no roots. Not really. Not from her.

That was all just another of his self-delusions.

Heartbroken and feeling a little bit mean with

it, he sipped at his drink and asked the question that had been circling his brain for the past hour or two. "What is it about me that makes the women in my life think that I should come dead last?"

Afton flinched as if he'd struck her, all the joy fading. "What?"

"With Dayna, it was always her parents or social expectations. Appearances. Connections. All that bullshite. And with you, it's going to be the career. Just like I knew it would be."

She stared at him, dark eyes alarmed. "Hamish, what are you talking about?"

He drained the last of the glass and slapped it down on the counter. "Did you even think about me and Freya when you took the job with McLeod?"

Her mouth opened in shock. Because he was daring to call her out on this? Well, he was tired of playing nice.

She took a step toward him, her brows drawn together. "I *am* putting you and Freya first."

"Oh? And how's that going to work from Edinburgh? How's that going to be any better than what she has going with her mother now?"

Hamish saw the moment the blow landed.

Afton went ramrod straight, pulling that dignity she'd been born into around her like a cloak. But her eyes were stormy, furious. He felt a vicious satisfaction at that because he knew her temper was slow to rouse, and at least she was finally giving some reaction.

"Do you seriously think, after everything we've been through, that I would up and take a job three hours away with no care or thought of either of you? Is that *really* what you think of me?"

He waved a careless hand. "You just said you took the job. What else am I supposed to think?"

Her cheeks had gone ashen, but those eyes of hers were molten with fury. "Well, I guess you and I dinna know each other nearly as well as we thought."

She picked up the purse she'd set down, and he felt fresh flickers of fear.

"Where are you going?"

"I'm just hastening along the inevitable. I'm not going to stand here and fight with you where Freya can overhear."

"She's not home. Spending the night at Aileen's."

"Good. Then at least she's not here to bear witness to this. I'll be by tomorrow to start packing my things."

She strode out, head held high. Hamish didn't go after her. Not when he heard the door open. Not when it slammed again. Not when he saw the flash of her headlights backing away from the house.

Leaving him.

He sank into a chair, his whole body aching and wretched because she'd just confirmed everything he'd been afraid of and wallowing in for hours. And he was left alone in his very empty house that reminded him of her at every turn, wondering what the bloody hell he was going to tell his daughter.

TWENTY-TWO

Afton drove away, blinded by the tears she'd managed to hold on to until she got into the car. She had no idea where she was going or what she was doing. She knew only that she couldn't stay there with him. Not after the way he'd looked at her. The accusations he'd thrown at her with absolutely no proof. After spending the day flying so high that everything was going perfectly, she hadn't imagined anything could have brought her so much pain. The leading edge of it was dulled a little by fury. She knew that wouldn't last, but for the moment, she embraced it.

How *dare* he believe any of this of her? How dare he not give her the chance to speak? He hadn't even asked a single question. Hadn't all they'd been to each other granted her the benefit of the doubt? How could he automatically assume the worst of her and class her with Dayna, of all people? And based on what information? The email? It was the only way she could fathom him even knowing about the interview with Iain. In which case, what the hell had he been doing on her computer? Checking up on her? Invading her privacy?

She could have corrected him in the moment. Could have thrown all his assumptions back in his face to show him exactly how wrong he was. But if he was willing to believe this of her, did she really want to be with him after all? If he could think this, did he really love her at all? He hadn't said the words. She'd let herself believe she felt them in his actions, in his touch. But maybe she'd been wrong. Because if you loved someone, you didn't attack them without cause. And he'd clearly been spoiling for a fight the moment she stepped into the room. She hadn't seen it at first, being too wrapped up in her own joy. But he'd made up his mind and as-signed himself as judge, jury, and executioner.

How fucking *dare* he?

And now here she was, driving around in the middle of the damned night with nowhere to go and not even the basics with her, as she hadn't been planning to leave. It wasn't as if she could find a hotel for the night. And it was too damned late to bother anyone. All her friends would be asleep by now, and she didn't want to rouse them. Because that would mean explaining why she'd darkened their doorstep at this ungodly hour. Afton didn't think she could explain what she didn't understand herself, and she didn't relish falling on any of them in another bout of hysterical tears.

Instinct had her pointing toward home. Her real home. The one that wasn't hers anymore. The stables would be open. She could do what she'd always done when she was upset and go to her place. It was far enough from the manor house that, hopefully, the car wouldn't disturb Kyla and Raleigh. Maybe she'd luck out and that chest of blankets would still be in the hayloft. She could spend some time with the horses and bed down up there for the night. It wouldn't precisely be toasty and comfortable, but she wouldn't freeze, and maybe by morning she'd have found her footing again.

Before she crested the final hill, Afton switched off her headlights, navigating by the light of the gibbous moon. She parked at the far end of the stone structure, quietly shutting the car door and slipping into the relative warmth of the stable. The automatic lights flickered on as she moved down the aisle, breathing in the comforting scents of horses and hay and leather. Multiple horses roused, snorting or whickering. Several stuck their noses over stall doors to see what was going on. She paused to offer pets and scratches and felt the anger leech out, leaving nothing but grief and a pulsating ache in her chest.

A fresh bout of tears streaked her cheeks as she approached Titania's stall. The mare wasn't playing coy tonight and didn't balk when Afton reached for her. The long nose bumped against her shoulder in a question. That, more than anything else, let Afton know that Titania still considered her one of her people.

"It's been a bad night, girl. A terrible night at the end of a wonderful day."

Titania stretched her neck further, using her head to pull Afton closer.

With a little huff that would've been laughter under other circumstances, Afton reached up to scratch her ears. "You dinna have to tell me twice." She unlocked the stall and slipped inside, locking it behind her.

The mare moved into her, hooking her head over Afton's shoulder again in what counted as a hug. Afton wrapped her arms around Titania's neck, pressing her cheek against that long curve of warm muscle.

"I dinna know what happened. How can

Hamish believe this of me, when I've bent over backwards and done everything possible for him and Freya to make their lives better? I didn't even consider taking the interview for the job in Edinburgh he thinks I accepted. I didn't want it. I dinna know if I'd have wanted it if Hamish hadn't ever been in the picture. I love being home in Glenlaig, even if it's not here."

Titania shifted her bulk to lean against Afton. That just made Afton cry harder.

"It hurts so bloody bad. There's a part of me that canna believe what just happened. *My* Hamish attacked me. I never would have believed him capable of anything like that. He's always been a man who asks questions to get answers. He listens when people speak. And yet he'd already decided, already made an assumption about me and what I'd done based on... what? An email? The fact that I'd gone to Edinburgh today without telling him in advance? He didn't call, didn't text. Granted, Neither did I, but I knew he was in court today, and I didn't want to interrupt. I was going to tell him everything when I got home. But I didn't get the chance because he just laid into me."

Titania snuffled her hair.

"I know I have to tell him he's wrong at some point. He's made an arse of himself, no question. But I dinna know if I can forgive the fact that at the first real challenge or problem, he caved and turned on me. I dinna know if I can be with him after that."

The mare snorted as if in agreement.

"I'm so tired, girl." The weariness reached down deep into her bones. Time to find herself a makeshift bed for the night. She stepped back, stroking Titania's neck and pressing her brow to the horse's. "I'm going on up to the hayloft. Thank you for listening."

Titania lifted her mouth and brushed it against Afton's cheek in a wuffling kiss.

Afton kissed her velvety nose. "Goodnight."

Slipping out of the stall, she made her way to the ladder leading up to the hayloft and climbed. As she'd hoped, the chest of blankets was still against the wall, exactly where she'd left it. The blankets inside were dusty, but they'd do. She pulled them out, making a nest in the hay, then using the last of them to wrap herself as best she could. It was still chilly, but it wasn't as if she really expected to sleep tonight, anyway.

Exhaustion got the better of her, though, because she bolted upright when a light shone over her face.

"Afton?" The light immediately shifted. "Honey, what the hell are you doing sleeping in my barn?"

HAMISH HADN'T SLEPT. His house and bed felt too big and empty, and his heart hurt too damned bad. Whichever way he spun this, his daughter was going to be crushed. And he just... didn't know how to handle that because he was crushed, too. Afton had walked away from him. When things got tough, she'd run. Just like she had before. Not to the other side of the world. At least, he hoped not. But Edinburgh might as well be another country for all it meant she wouldn't be a part of his life or Freya's. God knew, Dayna wasn't about to cede any of her time with Freya to the likes of Afton.

Which meant... what?

Maybe coming home had been a mistake. Maybe Dayna had been right that he looked at life here through rose-colored glasses. Because everything had been harder since he'd moved back. He'd wanted to give his daughter a chance to thrive and himself a chance to heal. And he thought they'd managed that. At least, since Afton came back into their lives. And now she'd be leaving again. Sooner rather than later, if her declaration last night was to be believed.

That was probably on him. He could've been

less antagonistic. That streak of mean reminded him far too much of how things had been with Dayna in the end, and he hated that. That wasn't the sort of man he wanted to be. Wasn't the example he wanted to set for his child. But how could he sit there and listen to her tell him with such joy about choosing her dream over them? And why the hell was life so fucking unfair that they couldn't find a way to have both? Why couldn't she have waited so they could find a solution together?

Because she's lost faith that you can do that for her. You couldn't even deliver on one basic promise to convince the council to rezone, and that should have been a dead cert.

His head was pounding when he stumbled downstairs. He needed to see to the bloody goats since neither Freya nor Afton was here, but they could wait until he'd had coffee. It wasn't until he spotted the empty carafe that he realized he'd instinctively expected Afton to do the night before setup. That was one of the million small things she'd taken off his plate that made his world run smoother. Something he'd taken for granted when he'd been determined not to take her for granted. Had that been part of what ultimately drove her to want to leave? The realization did nothing to improve his already foul mood.

He fumbled his way through measuring grounds and adding water, setting the whole thing to brew, then stood glaring at the pot as it filled, as if that would speed up the process. Realizing he might as well deal with the goats, he shoved his feet into some boots and trudged out to the barn. The temperatures were warmer today, and the forecast wasn't for rain, so he elected to let the lot of them out to forage. The fences had been shorn up and extended high enough that they ought to keep the herd inside.

"Go on. Go eat." He opened their pens and waved the lot of them out.

With bleating excitement, most of the goats bolted for the door. Save for Prue, who gave him a baleful glare and promptly bashed him in the leg with her head.

"Ow! What the bloody hell was that for?"

She screamed at him, as if to call him out for sending her preferred caretaker away, then sauntered after her brethren.

Everyone was pissed at him, it seemed.

"Take a number," he muttered and plodded back to the house, where the coffee was finally ready.

He took his first cup to the kitchen table and sipped, scalding his tongue. Even that bare taste had him grimacing. Of course, Afton's coffee was better. But caffeine was caffeine. Once it had cooled enough, he downed a couple of painkillers with it and sat, waiting for the throbbing to ebb enough that he could think again.

The sound of the door opening had him jerking to his feet. But it wasn't Afton. Instead, Connor strode into the room.

"I come bearing baked goods. Angus made a fresh batch of oatcakes this morning and decided to share." His cheerful friend set a bag on the counter, then took a good look at him. "You look terrible. Celebrate too much last night?"

Hamish squinted at him, thinking that smile hurt almost as much as the sun. "What are you talking about?"

"You ought to be thrilled."

"About what?"

Connor arched a quizzical brow. "About Afton taking the job."

Hamish fought not to grind his teeth together. "Why the fuck would I be thrilled about her taking the job and leaving me?"

Connor angled his head. "What the fuck are you on about? Why would she leave you when she took the job to stay with you and Freya?"

That made absolutely no sense. He rubbed at his aching head. "What are *you* on about?"

His friend was staring at him as if he were seriously hungover. And yeah, he was. But that wasn't clearing up what Connor was saying.

"Afton is going to be the new full-time, in-house caterer for Ardinmuir Event Planning. She accepted the job yesterday."

Hamish dropped his hand and stared. "What?"

"Didn't she tell you?" Connor glanced around, as if just realizing she wasn't here. "Where is she, anyway?"

"I dinna know."

Connor lost the cheer he'd arrived with. "Didn't she come home last night?"

"She did. Briefly. But she didn't tell me that. I thought she took a job in Edinburgh with that Michelin-starred chef we met." He began playing what he remembered of the conversation back in his head, remembering the look of hurt and betrayal on her face. Because he'd assumed the worst, based on insufficient information. "Shite. Why didn't she say anything?"

"I dinna ken. What did you say to her?" Connor stepped closer, his shoulders bowing, his expression tightening in a big brother sort of way. "Why would you think she took a job in Edinburgh?"

"Because she got an interview with Iain McLeod, and she went to Edinburgh yesterday."

The door slammed again, and Hamish jerked

toward the front of the house, wanting to apologize immediately, admit he was an idiot.

But the quick squeal let him know it was Freya. She stepped into the kitchen. "Hey Uncle Connor. Hey Da." She was flipping through a book in her hands.

"What's that there?"

With a happy bounce, she opened the cover. "It's one of Athena Reynolds' cookbooks. Afton got an autograph for me yesterday."

Hamish blinked. "By Athena Reynolds?"

"Duh. Aye, by Athena Reynolds. She's in Scotland for a visit and asked Afton to come down to see her in Edinburgh yesterday."

"How did you know that? Have you seen her?"

Freya frowned. "No, she texted me that it was waiting for me in the front hall."

She hadn't texted Hamish. Then again, she didn't habitually text him on days he was in court because she didn't want to disturb him. And when she'd gotten home last night, she'd said she couldn't wait to tell him about her day.

Oh, fuck.

He'd accused her of the worst possible thing. He hadn't asked a single question and had convicted her in his opinion, hurting her so badly that she hadn't even defended herself with the truth. She'd just left.

Hamish felt all the blood drain from his face.

Connor was glaring justifiable daggers at him.

As the full breadth of how badly he'd fucked things up began to sink in, his daughter asked, "Where is Afton?"

Because he couldn't say anything else, he scrubbed a hand over his stubbled cheek. "I dinna know. We had a fight."

Freya's face went hard. "What did you do?"

Because, of course, even his twelve-year-old was aware that this was all his fault, even though she didn't even know what was going on. Certainly guilt was written all over his own face.

"I did something I shouldn't have. I made assumptions without sufficient evidence. I know better. I said some things that upset her, and she left."

His daughter went sheet white.

"For the night," he quickly amended. "She just needed to cool off. She's supposed to be back later today." He didn't add that she'd planned to come back and pack. He had to hope beyond hope he could find her before then, so he could apologize and grovel his way out of this to stop her from leaving.

Freya was breathing hard, her eyes suspiciously shiny as she backpedaled. "How could you?"

"I—" But before Hamish could figure out anything to say, she'd whirled and run from the room, pounding upstairs. A minute later, her bedroom door slammed hard enough to rattle the house.

An icepick of pain jabbed through his skull. He was way too hungover to deal with this. Sinking into the nearest chair, he dropped his head into his hands.

"Well, you fucked up."

"I am aware."

"What are you going to do about it?"

"I have to find her first." She clearly hadn't gone to Ardinmuir or Connor wouldn't be here.

"Might I suggest you do something radical and pick up a phone?"

"I dinna think she's going to talk to me or answer after the things I said."

"Then start with a text. Admit you were wrong and say you want the opportunity to apologize. Ask her not to go. You get the gist. Talk to her and actually listen this time."

"Aye." He'd do all of that. God, he hoped she'd give him another chance to make up for this.

"For what it's worth, I dinna think she'd have gone far. Most likely to Malcolm and Charlotte or to Kyla and Raleigh. Depending on what she said, you might have to get past some gatekeepers to talk to her, but I dinna believe she'd up and leave town without resolving things. Marriage pact aside, Afton's not a runner. She's never been a coward. If she left last night, it was because she was hurt."

That was definitely on him. He'd fix it. He had to find some way to make this okay again. "I need to talk to Freya first. Do you think you could stick around and keep her company, while I go hunt Afton down to apologize?"

"Sure. I can do that."

"Thanks. Let me go say my piece to her."

Hamish climbed the stairs slowly, with no idea what to say. No parent wanted to admit to their weaknesses in front of their children. But owning mistakes was a lesson they all needed to learn, and he'd made a huge one.

He knocked on Freya's closed door. "Freya, love. I want to talk to you."

There was no answer.

Pressing an ear to the door, he listened for sounds of weeping, trying to gauge if he was in for an angry or upset tween. But he heard nothing. With one more knock, he pushed the door open.

She wasn't on her bed. Wasn't curled in the reading chair in the corner. The bathroom door hung open.

"What the...?"

A flash of motion pulled his attention to the window. It was open, the curtains billowing in the breeze.

He bolted across the room, sticking his head out the window. "Freya!"

But there was no sign of her below and no answer to his call.

His daughter was gone.

TWENTY-THREE

"I canna believe that Hamish would say any of those things." Kyla frowned over her tea. "That's just not like him."

"That's more or less the conclusion I came to sometime around three in the morning." Afton had played that interaction back in her mind over and over again. He'd been in a dark place before she ever got there. She'd attributed that to the assumptions he'd made, believing that she was leaving him and Freya. But something else must have happened. Because, no, lashing out at her as if she was another person who'd hurt him *wasn't* like him.

"He had court yesterday. Maybe the case went badly. Or maybe Dayna did something. He's been off ever since she confronted him about me moving in. I dinna know."

"I absolutely understand why you walked out last night and didn't correct his assumption. That would have made me livid, too. But before you do something drastic and end things, I think he deserves to know the truth. So he knows how badly he screwed up. Speaking of which, under the circumstances, do you still want the job?" Kyla's face was carefully neutral as she asked, which Afton appreciated.

"Aye. Even if he doesn't pull his head out of his arse, I still want the job. It's the kind of cooking I want to do, and this is where I want to be."

"Okay. Well, then perhaps you want to go try to fix this?"

Afton winced. "I think I might need another cuppa for fortification."

Kyla grinned. "It won't hurt him to stew just a little bit longer. Here, I'll pour us more."

She took their mugs to the counter and the waiting teapot of strong Scottish breakfast tea.

Afton's phone dinged with a text. Spotting Hamish's name on the screen, she snatched it up, expecting an olive branch or a request to talk. But what she saw had the blood draining out of her head.

Hamish: **Freya is missing.**

"Oh, my God."

Kyla swung toward her. "What?"

But Afton was already dialing. He picked up almost at once. "What happened?"

Hamish sucked in a breath. "She came home and found out I'd upset you—I'm sorry about that. Connor's here. He told me about the job. The real job."

So he finally knew the truth. And in this moment, it didn't matter a damn. "We'll talk about it later. What happened with Freya?"

"She was upset that I screwed up and stormed off to her room. Connor was going to stay with her while I came to find you, but I went to talk to her before I left, and she was gone. Snuck out her bedroom window and climbed down the trellis. We've looked everywhere. She's not in the barn, not with the goats. I don't know where she's gone."

Afton could hear the strain in his voice as he tried to hold it together. "Okay. It's going to be okay. She can't have gone far. How long has she been gone?"

"I don't... half an hour? Forty-five minutes? Feels like a lifetime."

"Have you called anyone else? Did you check with Aileen or Esme's parents? Have them ask the girls if they've heard from her?"

"That's a good idea."

"Do you have their numbers?"

"I... think so?"

"I'll text them to you. Call and check in with them. I'll call Malcolm and Charlotte and let Kyla and Raleigh know. I'm closer."

"You're at Lochmara?"

"Aye. I'll let them know, and we'll all head your way."

"Okay."

The moment she hung up, she met Kyla's wide, worried gaze. "Freya's missing?"

"Run off, most likely. Gone less than an hour. Where's Raleigh?"

"This time of day, out with the stock. I'll radio him."

"I'll call Malcolm." She paced away and hit his contact in her phone. It rang a few times before he picked up.

"Afton."

"Drop whatever you're doing. Freya's missing. We need all the warm bodies we can get to help search for her." She gave him the brief summary and heard him shouting for Charlotte and Gavin.

"We'll be along as soon as we find Gavin."

That gave Afton pause. "He's not there?"

"No. He was out doing chores earlier, but he's not out there now."

It might have been a coincidence, but... "Malcolm, have you taught Gavin to drive?"

"Aye, the same as I did you at that age. He needs to be able to get around the place for chores and if anything happens."

"Are any of the farm vehicles gone?"

"Hang on, I'll check."

She paced the kitchen as she waited.

"Aye, it looks like the UTV is gone."

"Okay, head on over to join Hamish at his place. I'm going to check something first, then I'll be along shortly."

Kyla was on the radio with Raleigh. Afton didn't interrupt, instead shoving her phone into her pocket and stepping outside. She might be wrong, but just in case, she had to check. If Freya was trying to truly leave, the only non-adult she knew who might be able to drive was Gavin. They were friends. If she'd contacted him for a ride... where would she ask him to take her? To find Afton, presumably. Either to try to fix what her father broke, or to reassure herself that Afton wasn't leaving. And she knew that when Afton was upset, she'd come here. To the stables.

Afton burst into a sprint, heading for the familiar stone building she'd retreated to just last night.

Please let me be right. Please let me be right.

Afton slipped inside, noting the classical music Raleigh had pumping through the speakers. It meant she couldn't hear anything over the horses and the music, and no one else would be able to hear her. She made a beeline for the ladder to the hayloft. Quick as a cat, she climbed up to peer into the darkened space.

And there Freya was, curled up on the pallet she'd made for herself last night, crying.

Relief made her limbs weak, but she shoved the rest of the way into the loft. "Hey, sweet girl."

Freya's head snapped up, and she flung herself straight into Afton's arms. "Dinna go! I know Da screwed up, and he hurt you, but he's sorry, and please give him a chance to explain and make it up to you and to apologize. Please dinna go!"

Afton's heart cracked right in two that Freya was so terrified of losing this family they'd built. She didn't know where she stood with Hamish, but now that she was calmer, she recognized that something else was driving his reaction. He knew he'd fucked up. Knew that they'd have more to talk about. She wasn't willing to throw away what they'd found just because he messed up. She wanted to know what was underneath that reaction. They'd have to find a way forward, because she wasn't ready to give up on them.

She squeezed the girl tighter. "Hey now. Hey. I'm right here. I'm not going anywhere."

"But the two of you fought, and you left."

"I needed the chance to cool off. Sometimes grownups fight. It doesn't always mean we're going to split up."

"I dinna know what he did, but it must have been bad."

Afton snorted a little. "It wasn't good. And he and I do still need to talk about all those things. But sweetheart—" She pulled back far enough to look into that face, into those eyes that were so much like her father's. "—No matter what happens between me and your da, you're never going to lose me. That's a promise. I dinna care what any kind of law or blood says. You're mine, and you always will be."

Freya sniffed. "Really?"

Afton gently wiped at the tears still streaming down her cheeks. "Really."

Freya hugged her tight again, and Afton held on for all she was worth, stroking that silky dark hair.

"Not that this isn't a lovely moment, Cricket, but we need to let your father know that you're okay. He's beside himself."

The girl winced. "Okay. He's probably going to be pretty mad."

"He'll be so relieved you're okay, he'll get over it. And we'll talk about the rest."

"What if he grounds me?"

"I promise to advocate on your behalf. *If* you promise never to do anything like this ever again."

"Cross my heart."

"Okay then." With one hand, Afton pulled her phone back out and sent the text.

Afton: **I've got her. She's okay. I'm bringing her home.**

HAMISH RUSHED OUT of the house the moment Afton's car turned into the drive. He was waiting when Freya's door opened and she stepped out, not quite meeting his eyes. He didn't give a damn. He just pulled her in, holding her tight. "I'm so glad you're okay."

After a moment, her arms came around him in a hug. "I'm sorry for worrying you." She pulled back to look up at him with sober eyes. "I was trying to fix what you broke."

Well, didn't that just stab him right in the heart? Throat tight, he swallowed. "Well, while I appreciate the thought, it's on me to do that." He lifted his gaze to Afton, who'd slid out of the car.

There was a familiar reserve around her that he hated. But he deserved that. He was the one who'd made her feel unsafe, and he didn't know how he was going to make up for that. He only knew he had to try.

Connor joined them from the house. "You two need to talk, so I'm gonna take the juvenile delinquent, and we're going to hang out with Sophie and Angus."

Freya bolted for his 4x4.

"Just let us know when to bring her back, aye?"

Without waiting for confirmation, Connor made his own getaway, slipping into the driver's seat and disappearing with Freya, leaving Hamish alone with the woman whose heart he'd trampled all over.

"Thank you for bringing her home. For finding her. Where was she?"

"In the hayloft at the stables at Lochmara."

He blinked. "Your old hiding spot?"

Afton inclined her head. "She texted Gavin. He came to get her."

"He can *drive?*"

"He lives on a farm. Of course he can drive. So could I at that age. That's why it occurred to me, when they couldn't find Gavin to help search, that maybe she'd texted him to ask for a lift."

"How would she even know to go there?"

"Because I showed her myself the day that Dayna was here. She was upset, and she was coming to find me. Which was actually pretty solid thinking on her part, because that's exactly where I would have been if Raleigh hadn't found me last night."

"You were going to sleep in the barn?"

She shrugged. "It wouldn't have been the first time. It was late. I didn't want to bother anybody, and I didn't really want to explain myself." Both arms wrapped over her middle in a self-protective gesture he recognized.

Hamish hated himself a little more for making her feel uncomfortable. "Can we go inside and really talk?"

"I think we should." Her even tone didn't give anything away.

He deserved that.

Gesturing her ahead of him, he followed her inside. Of course, she went to the kitchen. It was where she always felt most in control, most comfortable. Though she didn't move to make anything. Maybe she didn't plan to be here long enough for that.

"So, Connor told you."

"And Freya—about why you actually went to Edinburgh yesterday."

Afton arched one pale brow, waiting.

"There is no amount of I'm sorry, or apology, that can make up for the things that I said to you yesterday. For the fact that I didn't even ask for your side of the story. I was in a very dark headspace. I made unforgivable assumptions, and I took all of that out on you without verifying the facts. I own all of that. I own your right to be mortally upset and want to walk away from me. But I am begging you to give me another chance to make it up to you."

When she didn't immediately respond, he began to sweat.

"What I'll give you is a chance to tell me what's really going on. What happened?"

"I lost the custody case."

Her expression instantly softened. "Oh, Hamish, I'm so sorry. I know how important that was to you."

"It would have hit me hard no matter what, but it hit me worse because Dayna has been threatening to take me back to court over custody of Freya."

Her mouth fell open. "Why didn't you tell me? I told you I'd move out. I would do anything to make sure Freya was okay."

"I didn't want you to move out. I didn't want anything to have to change because of her. Because we've done enough changing of our lives because of her. But I've just been waiting for the other shoe to drop ever since. It's left me on edge, thinking about all of this shite with my divorce. It all just piled up on me, and I took it out on you. That's unforgivable, because it really wasn't about you. It's about me. It's about me not feeling worthy of you." He hadn't meant to say it. But now that it was out, he figured he might as well go for broke and spill it all. "I feel like I have done nothing but fail you at every turn, and you deserve better than that."

She stared at him, comprehension seeming to dawn. "Hamish, do you think I love you because I somehow think that you're this perfect hero?"

"You love me?" After all the uncertainty of the past twenty-four hours, hearing it gave him the first glimmer of hope.

She huffed. "Focus. Aye, I love you. This is not supposed to be a surprise. I have always loved you. And it has nothing to do with you being perfect at everything. I love you because you saw me when no one else did. You recognized my struggle when no one else did. You tried to find a way out for me. And you did. Maybe it wasn't the one that any of us wanted, but you found a way out. As hard as that was for me to do, it actually turned out well for everybody, so I canna say that I have any complaints there."

With a sigh, she stripped off her coat and began to pace. "When I came back, I had no idea what I was going to find. I just thought I was going to be closing off some loose ends so that I could truly start over somewhere. I didn't think it would be here, and I sure as hell didn't think it would be with you. And then here you were. Divorced. Finally available. Interested. Even though you apparently didn't want to be."

"No, it was never that."

Afton held up one slim hand to stay him. "You didn't think you had enough of yourself to give me, and I tried to respect that, even though I really felt like that was my call to make. I stepped in anyway, to help because you needed it. Because you were drowning. Everybody deserves someone who cares enough to step in when they're drowning. You did that for me, and I told you it was my turn to do that for you."

"You saved me. In so many ways, big and small, that I can't even articulate." So many ways he'd taken for granted.

She continued to pace, shrugging that off. "Everything just kept falling like dominoes, pushing us forward, forward, forward. Together. Then it became more. We became a family, and I cannot begin to tell you what a gift that is for me. It made me so happy because that's exactly what I wanted."

Made. Wanted. Past tense. Hamish's chest went tight, and he held in his urge to interrupt, because she clearly wasn't done yet.

"I knew you were off for some reason. What I dinna know is why you couldn't talk to me about it."

"I didn't want to burden you."

"Hamish, that's what partners do. It's not a burden. It's helping to share the load. I am not some blushing damsel."

"I know. I know. And I've been letting you carry the lion's share since you came into this."

"So what? I can handle it. I am more than willing to do that for you because I love you. Because you need that right now. When it's my turn, you'll return the favor."

Did that mean she was sticking around? That he'd have the chance to return that favor?

"You know what your problem is?"

He had a few ideas but wanted to know what her take was. "What?"

"All your life, everything has come to you too easy."

"What?" Insult began to bloom through the low-level panic.

"You were a brilliant student. You're a brilliant lawyer. Regardless of the fact that you hated it, you slipped into that upper-crust world of Dayna's, with all the social connections and politics and all of that shite. That came easy to you. Fatherhood came easy to you. You're great at it. You have always been the man everyone else could count on. Have a problem? Hamish will find the answer. You've never *really* had to struggle with real failure at anything until you got divorced. Until you had to figure out the whole single parent thing. Until you came back here and started trying to build a different life. And because that's been hard, it's made you question whether it's right at every step along the way."

She moved closer. "But, Hamish, something being hard doesn't make it the wrong thing. It makes it the thing that's worth fighting for. This family we've made, this relationship that we've built, is worth the hard, no matter what we have to face. Whether that's another court battle with your ex-wife. Whether it's you having to struggle to build this small-town law practice, or whether you ultimately decide to take some other job. All of that? That's life. The struggle doesn't matter, so long as we're in it together. And I intend to be. Our first thought at a job for me didn't work out. And that's fine. It turns out, I didn't want it. Then fate dropped the perfect answer into my lap. One that allows me to do exactly what I want to do, on the terms I want to do it, and still have plenty of time for family. Assuming you still want that. Because I do."

"You do?"

Another step closer and she laid a hand on his arm, bridging the gap between them. "Aye. I love you. I haven't said it outright before now because I didn't want to push anything. But screw that. There's no more room for misunderstanding. I love you, and I want to be with you through whatever it is life throws our way."

Hamish reached for her then, shaking as he pulled her closer, beyond grateful that this incredible woman was willing to give them another chance. "I love you, too. I should have said it every day, from the moment you came back into my life. And I'll say it every day for the rest of our lives, if only you'd be willing to spend it with me."

Feeling more than a little reckless with relief, he reached into his pocket and pulled out the ring, watching Afton's eyes go wide. "This is not at all how I wanted to do this. I dinna know how I thought it should be done. With some sort of romance or flair or something. I've been carrying it around for weeks, trying to find the right time to ask. But you're right. We're past the point where we should leave any room for confusion. So let me be one hundred percent clear. I love you, Afton. And I want to marry you. Sooner rather than later, if I have my way. If that's something you want."

The shimmer in those big brown eyes turned into tears that slid down her cheeks. "I have one condition."

"Name it." He'd do anything for this woman.

"Don't ever not give me the benefit of the doubt again. We're going to fight and have misunderstandings. And that's fine. But promise me, here and now, that you'll talk about it, instead of flying off the handle."

"I can absolutely promise that."

"Then, yes, I'll marry you. Sooner rather than later."

They both watched as he slid the ring onto her left hand. Then he drew her in and kissed her, pouring out every drop of love and apology he could muster and soaking in the taste of forgiveness.

There was nothing sweeter.

Afton sniffed back her happy tears. "Freya's going to lose her mind."

"Aye, she probably is. This might even be enough for her to forgive me. Should we call Connor to bring her home?"

Her mouth quirked as she linked her arms around his neck. "I think it can wait a while longer, aye? We've got some making up to do."

Huffing a laugh, he boosted her up and moved toward the stairs. "I do love the way you think."

"So, you see, in a complicated, Southern sort of way, that makes me Afton's brother. She's got three others back home in Tennessee, and all of us would be more than happy to kick your ass if you step out of line." Jonah Ferguson delivered this speech with his easy Southern drawl and a smile.

Oh crap.

Afton picked up the miles of skirts of her wedding dress and started on her way to intervene, but it wasn't exactly easy to navigate with a cathedral length train, even with it bustled.

Entirely unruffled, Hamish extended his hand. "Thank you for looking out for her."

The former Navy SEAL who'd adopted her as family stared Hamish down for a moment before taking the offered hand and letting his grin stretch wider. "Good answer, Colquhoun."

A little out of breath from carting thirty pounds of wedding dress in heels, Afton linked her arm through Hamish's and fixed Jonah with a mock glare. "Jonah, are you harassing my husband?" The thrill of being able to say it shot through her, leaving her so giddy it was hard to hold on to the stern expression.

"Damn straight. Seems like you got a good one, though."

"I certainly did." Beaming, she tipped her mouth up to Hamish's for a quick kiss that made her sigh before turning her attention back to her unofficial big brother. "I'm so glad you were able to come."

"Are you kidding? We wouldn't miss it, and there was no way in hell Rachel was passing up the chance to make your wedding cake." He automatically glanced toward his wife, who stood a dozen feet away, chatting with Charlotte, their son Matt propped on her hip. His chubby hands flailed toward the plate of cake Charlotte held. "Excuse me, I've gotta go rescue my wife from the imminent threat of icing."

They watched as he leapt the distance, putting himself between his son and temptation.

"You handled that well," Afton observed.

Hamish shrugged, looking resplendent in his wedding kilt and Argyle jacket. "He just cares about you. They all do. It's lovely to see."

"And here's our girl." At the sound of the familiar voice, Afton turned to find Rebecca beaming, arms open wide. Grey was right behind.

Afton moved in for a warm, maternal hug. "Thank you both for coming all this way."

Grey squeezed her next. "We wouldn't have missed this. And neither of us will complain about having a reason to regularly come back to the site of our honeymoon for a visit."

"It was such a moving ceremony," Rebecca gushed. "You grew up in a really lovely place."

"I did." Afton looked around at the gardens that had been her playground as a child, past the outbuildings, toward the hill overlooking the loch for which her ancestral estate had been named. It was all part of the perfection that here, almost two years to the day she'd run away, she said 'I do' to the man she'd always loved. The man who'd given her choice, so that, at the end of it all, she could choose him. It felt as if she'd finally come full circle.

When Hamish had asked what sort of wedding she wanted, she'd insisted on something small and family only. She'd never been lured by the flash or pomp and circumstance that had been expected as part of the pact. And, honestly, Connor and Sophie had more than taken care of that with their own wedding. When she'd asked Raleigh and Kyla if they could have the wedding here, they'd been delighted to accommodate. Today was the first time that being here didn't hurt. Maybe part of that was because she finally had those roots—between the man and daughter she loved, and the friends who'd gone out of their way to make sure she knew she was appreciated and wanted. As for Lochmara, she'd found a middle ground where the estate was still the home of her heart, where her roots and ancestry lay. While Raleigh was the official owner and steward, he knew that this would always be partly her place, and he'd welcomed her to spend as much time here as she wanted. She'd finally come to understand that he meant it. He really was that open and generous, and he'd become another of those adopted brothers.

Hamish reached out to shake Grey's hand. "I'm so grateful you were able to come, and I'm so pleased to finally get to meet Afton's Tennessee parents."

Rebecca got a little misty-eyed at that. "Oh, we certainly think of her as ours. And, of course, the rest of the family sends their regrets. Somebody had to stay home to run everything and run herd on all the grandbabies. But you know Cayla's planning a massive reception for the next time y'all are able to make it to Tennessee. And Holt's going to try to one-up Rachel's cake."

Warmed through, Afton grinned. "We will absolutely make that happen. I want Hamish and Freya both to see Eden's Ridge and meet everybody."

"We're thinking maybe the end of the summer, before she has to go back to school," Hamish explained. "But we're still negotiating terms with her mother."

They'd arrived at some sort of truce with Dayna. She wasn't taking them to court, which was more Freya's doing than anyone else's. Neither of them knew what she'd said to her mother, but Dayna had dropped the whole thing. Afton and Hamish were too grateful to press further.

"We'll be happy to see y'all whenever you can make it."

Athena wandered up, two glasses of champagne in hand, Ari by her side and Freya trailing a little after. "When's that happening? Because the inn is gonna be full up with folks who want to see you and meet your family."

"End of summer, we hope," Afton told her.

"Oh! I've always wanted to visit the States," Freya said.

Ari wrapped an arm around her shoulders. "We'll take good care of you when you do."

Afton hugged Athena. "Thank you so much for coming. And so much for cooking our gorgeous wedding meal."

Athena passed her one of the glasses and toasted. "It's a sign of how much I love and respect you, girl."

"It meant a lot."

Ari simply grinned at Hamish and Afton and mimed dusting her hands off. "Another successful match under my belt."

"Another?" Freya held up a hand. "Excuse me, I'm the one who parent-trapped them."

"And good for you—but she wouldn't have been here to parent-trap if not for me," Ari argued. "Which makes this..." She paused and began silently counting on her fingers before giving up and shrugging. "Well, more than a dozen."

Freya's eyes went wide. "That's... a lot."

With a wide, cheeky grin, Ari buffed her nails on her dress. "It's a gift."

"I feel like I need to hear all about this."

Clearly recognizing a kindred romantic, Ari linked her arms through Freya's. "Oh, honey, let me teach you my ways."

As the pair of them wandered off, Hamish murmured, "Do we need to worry about that?"

Barely able to hold in her laugh, Afton said,

"Only if they end up on the same continent for longer than a week at a time."

Athena watched her niece. "I don't know. I think Ari works fast. She could totally corrupt her in three days."

"Oh, boy," Hamish breathed.

Afton and Hamish continued their duties as bride and groom, circulating among all their guests, accepting congratulations, handing out thanks, as music continued to play and the summer sun began to finally set. She was tired, but in the best possible way. Everyone she loved was here and had contributed something to their special day.

Malcolm caught her near the edge of the dance floor, pulling her into one of his now familiar bear hugs. "Congratulations, lass."

"Thank you."

"I've been thinking a lot about your parents today and how proud and happy they'd be for you."

Throat tightening with emotion, she linked her arm through his and tipped her head to his burly shoulder. "That means a lot. That was really why I wanted to do this here. I feel closer to them. Like they're looking down on us and giving their blessing on how everything turned out."

From across the dance floor, Hamish broke away from where he'd been speaking to Ewan and

Isobel, weaving his way through the handful of people to join her again.

"Malcolm. May I steal my wife for a dance?"

With a surprisingly courtly gesture, Malcolm bowed and stepped back.

As Hamish took her hand and pulled her onto the floor, the opening bars to Etta James' "At Last" poured out of the speakers.

Afton relaxed into his arms. "I canna think of another song more appropriate to end the night on."

"Are you ready to end the night?"

One corner of her mouth quirked up. "This part of it. We've been socializing for hours."

Heat and amusement lit those beloved Celtic blue eyes. "Understood, Mrs. Colquhoun."

She sighed. "That will never get old."

"I hope not. Because I'm banking on at least fifty years of it." He pulled her closer as they swayed. "Are you happy with how today turned out?"

"I'm happy with how *life* turned out across the board. I finally got you. I finally got roots and home and family. That's all I ever wanted."

Hamish pressed his brow to hers. "I love you, Afton. And I want to spend the rest of our lives being the husband and partner you deserve, through whatever else comes our way."

She hesitated. "What about being a father again?"

He jerked back, eyes going wide. "Are you...?"

"No. But I think we should. If that's something you want. So long as you dinna think Freya will feel like she means any less to us."

"I think there's nothing that would delight her more than getting to be a big sister. And I am in full support of getting started with that plan tonight." The promise of pleasure and love thrummed through his voice.

Deliriously happy, Afton tipped her mouth close to his. "Then, Mr. Colquhoun, we'd best start making our excuses."

CIARA KEPT to one corner of the event kitchen, going over last-minute changes to the guest list and meal requests. "We've got two more vegetarians and three others who want to swap beef for fish. Can you accommodate that?"

Across the room, a very pale Afton flitted from stove to counter at a speed much slower than usual. She rubbed at her temple. "Aye, that should be fine."

Frowning, Ciara set down her clipboard. "Are you alright?"

Afton waved her away, her skin looking a mite clammy. "No, I'm fine." Then her cheeks turned almost green, and she hunched over the sink and vomited.

Megan Murtaugh, the sous chef, leapt back. "Oh, God."

Ciara closed the distance, already reaching for Afton. "Go get Hamish."

The girl gave them a wide berth before bolting from the room.

Ciara nudged Afton into a chair and retrieved a small garbage can from the office, shoving it into Afton's hands.

"I'm fine."

"You just vomited into the..." Ciara craned to look toward the sink where something had been draining. "I dinna know what was in there, but we're going to need more of it."

Afton dropped her head into her hands. "Damn it. I swear I'm not sick."

Hamish rushed into the room. Ciara backed up to allow him access to his wife.

"What's wrong, love?" He pressed the back of his hand to her clammy cheek.

"It's fine. I'm fine. I'm not sick." She lifted her gaze to his and arched a brow. "It's not catching."

The light bulb hit them both at once.

Hamish gasped, his eyes dropping to her belly. "Are you...?"

Afton offered a weak smile. "Surprise?"

He took her hands. "Really? Are you sure?"

"I haven't made it to the doctor yet, but I took the test yesterday. Unless something I ate has gone off, I think we can consider this confirmation."

Feeling like a voyeur for being here during this moment of private joy, Ciara turned away, a little choked up herself. She knew they wanted this. That they'd been trying for months. To give them a few more moments alone, she went to the fridge and found some ginger ale, pouring it into a glass. Then she returned to the kitchen and pressed it into Afton's hand.

"Congratulations to you both. We'll absolutely celebrate this later, but we still have a reception to prep for. What do we need? I'll run into the village and pick up ingredients to replace whatever it was that got ruined."

As Afton reeled off ingredients, Hamish set to cleaning the sink.

Armed with a list, Ciara drove into the village, relieved to get away for a little while so she could wrestle with all these emotions. All her people were happily engaged or married and popping out babies. And here she was, alone again. This time by choice after having ended a long-term relationship with a guy she'd thought could be it but wasn't. Ruthlessly, she shut down that train of thought. No point in dwelling on it.

Inside the market, she grabbed a trolley and began rushing through the aisles, searching out the items on her list. Woman on a mission, she whipped around to the produce section and bumped right into someone.

"Oh, I'm so sorry. I—"

"Ciara."

Triple crap. "Brodie. What are you doing here?" Her ex lived in Braemore. She wasn't supposed to have to worry about running into him here.

"Needed to pick up some of Pippa Wallace's cheese for my mum. You know how much she loves it."

"That's nice of you." She made to move around him, but he sidestepped, blocking her path.

"It's good to see you. I miss you." His hangdog, hopeful expression reminded her that letting him down gently hadn't worked out in her favor. He kept showing up, surprising her in all sorts of places, wanting to get back together.

"I'm sorry. I'm working. I can't right now." She really couldn't ever. That was the whole reason she'd broken up with him.

Hurrying around him, she gathered up the list of

ingredients and made a beeline for the checkout, calling it a win when he didn't follow her around like a lost puppy. She made polite conversation with Phillip Conlin as he rang up her purchases, and tried not to be obvious that she was scanning the store.

Maybe Brodie had finally gotten the hint and left?

"Have a good day, Ciara."

"Cheers, Phillip." She turned to grab her bags, only to find Brodie there.

"Let me help you carry these to your car."

She didn't want his help. She didn't want to be anywhere near him. All these chance encounters were starting to feel less than chance, and he was making her more than a little uneasy. But she bit back the acerbic reply.

The sooner I let him do this, the sooner I can get out of here and get back to the castle.

She grabbed up the last two bags and hurried to her car where she'd parked it on the high street, hoping the pace would keep him from attempting more conversation. She *had* to find some way to convince him that things between them were truly over.

At her car, they loaded things into the boot. She shut it and moved around toward the driver's side door. "Thank you. I really need to go. We had a kitchen emergency before today's event, and there's not a lot of time to fix it."

Brodie crowded her against the car, such that she couldn't open the door. Her heart began to thump because he was much too close in an entirely inappropriate fashion, his eyes intense on her face.

"Brodie, back up. I really need to get back to work."

"Ciara, love. I just want to see you." He reached out to touch her face, and she backed up, coming up short against the side of the vehicle.

Her brother had been a Royal Marine. She knew how to ward off an attack and unwanted advances, but the year she'd spent with this man stopped her from driving her knee into his balls. She didn't want to hurt him. She just wanted him to *go*.

Brodie was still talking, but she wasn't really listening. At the edge of frantic, she looked around to see if there was anyone she could call on for help. And half a block away, she saw a familiar face. Her relief that he was here, that he was close, had her all but sagging at the knees as she lifted an arm and called out, "Hey, Professor."

The use of the old nickname was deliberate, a callback to a time when they'd been more to each other than the cold, polite strangers they were now.

She just hoped he heard and understood what she needed him to do.

That long-legged stride closed the distance in moments, and he neatly inserted himself between her and her ex. "There you are." He tucked her against his side, like she was made to go there. Ciara was so relieved to feel the bulk of him, to know he'd put a stop to this—whatever this was—she didn't complain.

He turned an affable gaze to Brodie, who stood a couple paces back now, his chest and shoulders bowed up, his stance aggressive, which was a really foolish thing to do given that her human shield probably knew eighty-seven ways to kill a man with a piece of string and a paperclip.

"Who the hell are you?" Brodie demanded.

The arm around Ciara tightened and one big hand slid down to curve possessively around her hip. "The boyfriend."

"You're not," Brodie scoffed.

"I assure you, I am. Isn't that right, Hellcat?" In one smooth move, he shifted so they were front to front, and he gazed down at her with so much heat and possession, Ciara's breath clogged in her throat.

Then he did the worst thing possible.

He kissed her.

Ciara tried to hold out against it before her brain pointed out that giving in would back up the story they were presenting here and perhaps finally make Brodie see sense. But her brain was really just a shameless hussy who'd missed the feel of this man more than she could express. She melted into him, fisting her hands in his shirt and rising to her toes to take a deeper taste herself. She'd told herself that she'd imagined how good it had been between them, but clearly her memory was faulty. This was even better.

By the time he lifted his head, hers was spinning. She stared up into his molten brown eyes, close to him for the first time after years apart, the memories of their night together swirling through her mind. Then she remembered why she was here.

"Is he gone?"

"Aye, he walked away a few minutes ago."

Trust him to have actually had enough of his brain to notice. Damn him.

That easy affability was gone as he stared down at her. "Are you okay?"

"Yes." No. That kiss had wrecked her, and she had to get herself under control so she could go back to the castle and pretend everything was fine. She jerked away from him. "I've got to get back to work." It was the most words she'd said to him since he'd moved to Glenlaig to start the outdoor adventure company with the rest of his friends.

"Ciara." He said her name in that dark rumble that still haunted her nights.

But she ignored him and yanked open the car door, sparing him one glance. "Thank you for the rescue. This doesn't change anything. I still hate you for what you did." Better put them both back on even footing. Reestablish the status quo.

But as she drove away, her lips still tingling from his, she had to acknowledge to herself that there was a part of her that definitely didn't hate him. She just couldn't let it win.

***

Choose Your Next Romance

I KNOW, I know. Evil author is evil. Kilted Hearts is over, but our adventures in Scotland are NOT! Keep your eyes peeled for the Special Ops Scots series in 2024! You can go ahead and preorder the prequel, *One Fine Night*, which covers Ciara's backstory with her mysterious rescuer.

You can also grab the BONUS EPILOGUE for Afton and Hamish right here: https://books.book funnel.com/a-little-lagniappe/ko22rswymi

In the meantime, if you're new to my work, you'll be happy to know I love a good crossover.

Many of the secondary characters you saw in this book have their own series!

If you'd like to get to know Athena and Ari, go check out *The Misfit Inn* quartet, which begins with *When You Got A Good Thing*. Athena is number 3 in that series in *Stay A Little Longer,* and while each book is standalone and can be read out of order, it's really so much better if you read them in sequence to watch the evolution of Ari, who's in all of them.

If you'd like to get to know Rebecca and Grey, they're the final installment of the Bad Boy Bakers series, which begins with the prequel novelette, *Rescued By a Bad Boy* and the follow up novel, *Mixed Up With a Marine.* If you want to jump straight to Rebecca and Grey, you can do so in *Caught Up with the Captain.*

Happy reading!

OTHER BOOKS BY KAIT NOLAN

A complete and up-to-date list of all my books can be found at https:// kaitnolan.com.

**KILTED HEARTS
SMALL TOWN CONTEMPORARY SCOTTISH ROMANCE**

- *Jilting The Kilt* (prequel)
- *Cowboy in a Kilt* (Raleigh and Kyla)
- *Grump in a Kilt* (Malcolm and Charlotte)
- *Playboy in a Kilt* (Connor and Sophie)
- *Protector in a Kilt* (Ewan and Isobel)

- *Single Dad in a Kilt* (Hamish and Afton)
- *Kilty Pleasures* (Jason and Skye)

BAD BOY BAKERS
SMALL TOWN MILITARY ROMANCE

- *Rescued By a Bad Boy* (Brax and Mia prequel)
- *Mixed Up With a Marine* (Brax and Mia)
- *Wrapped Up with a Ranger* (Holt and Cayla)
- *Stirred Up by a SEAL* (Jonah and Rachel)
- *Hung Up on the Hacker* (Cash and Hadley)
- *Caught Up with the Captain* (Grey and Rebecca)

RESCUE MY HEART SERIES
SMALL TOWN MILITARY ROMANCE

- *Someone Like You* (Ivy and Harrison)
- *What I Like About You* (Laurel and Sebastian)

- *Bad Case of Loving You* (Paisley and Ty prequel) Included in *Made For Loving You* (Paisley and Ty)

THE MISFIT INN SERIES
SMALL TOWN FAMILY ROMANCE

- *When You Got A Good Thing* (Kennedy and Xander)
- *Til There Was You* (Misty and Denver)
- *Those Sweet Words* (Pru and Flynn)
- *Stay A Little Longer* (Athena and Logan)
- *Bring It On Home* (Maggie and Porter)
- *Come Away with Me* (Moses and Zuri)

MEN OF THE MISFIT INN
SMALL TOWN SOUTHERN ROMANCE

- *Let It Be Me* (Emerson and Caleb)
- *Our Kind of Love* (Abbey and Kyle)
- *Don't You Wanna Stay* (Deanna and Wyatt)
- *Until We Meet Again* (Samantha and Griffin prequel)
- *Come A Little Closer* (Samantha and Griffin)

- *Just Wanted You To Know* (Livia and Declan)

WISHFUL ROMANCE SERIES
SMALL TOWN SOUTHERN ROMANCE

- *Once Upon A Coffee* (Avery and Dillon)
- *To Get Me To You* (Cam and Norah)
- *Know Me Well* (Liam and Riley)
- *Be Careful, It's My Heart* (Brody and Tyler)
- *Just For This Moment* (Myles and Piper)
- *Wish I Might* (Reed and Cecily)
- *Turn My World Around* (Tucker and Corinne)
- *Dance Me A Dream* (Jace and Tara)
- *See You Again* (Trey and Sandy)
- *The Christmas Fountain* (Chad and Mary Alice)
- *You Were Meant For Me* (Mitch and Tess)
- *A Lot Like Christmas* (Ryan and Hannah)
- *Dancing Away With My Heart* (Zach and Lexi)

WISHING FOR A HERO SERIES (A WISHFUL SPINOFF SERIES)
SMALL TOWN ROMANTIC SUSPENSE

- *Make You Feel My Love* (Judd and Autumn)
- *Watch Over Me* (Nash and Rowan)
- *Can't Take My Eyes Off You* (Ethan and Miranda)
- *Burn For You* (Sean and Delaney)

MEET CUTE ROMANCE
SMALL TOWN SHORT ROMANCE

- *Once Upon A Snow Day*
- *Once Upon A New Year's Eve*
- *Once Upon An Heirloom*
- *Once Upon A Coffee*
- *Once Upon A Campfire*
- *Once Upon A Rescue*

SUMMER CAMP
CONTEMPORARY ROMANCE

- *Once Upon A Campfire*
- *Second Chance Summer*

ABOUT KAIT

Kait is a Mississippi native, who often swears like a sailor, calls everyone sugar, honey, or darlin', and can wield a bless your heart like a saber or a Snuggie, depending on requirements.

You can find more information on this *USA Today* best selling and RITA ® Award-winning author and her books on her website http://kaitnolan.com.

Do you need more small town sass and spark? Sign up for <u>her newsletter</u> to hear about new releases, book deals, and exclusive content!